the heir of
light
and
shadows

the heir of *light* and *shadows*

stella jade

M'lan Book Publishing LLC

A Note from the Author:

To every writer who came before me and every reader who turns the page, *thank you.* Stories are how we remember we're NOT alone. And this one...*this* one is for every person who ever felt like they were caught between two worlds.

You know who you are.

To my readers, if you enjoy this book, kindly leave a review on whichever avenue you purchase the book.

Get a glimpse of book two at the end of this book. *A Bond of Blood, Stone, and Fire* releases July 14, 2025.

Until the next book,
Stella Jade

Acknowledgments

This book would not exist without the unwavering love and encouragement of the people who walked beside me through every word, crazy idea, doubt, and breakthrough.

To my early readers and critique partners, your insights shaped this book into what it is. Thank you for catching the things I couldn't see, for asking the hard questions, and for loving these characters as fiercely as I do.

I want to especially thank Jack Beal/Ophelia Crow and Andrea Straub-Allen for taking *the Heir of Light and Shadows* journey with me. You both have been with me since day one and have been instrumental in making this book (and book two) come alive. I still don't know who is going to win over Brody...

To my friend and editor, Carol Harkavy, thank you for polishing my roughest pages. Your dedication to this story gave it the edge it needed.

To my friend (and fellow author) Anna Marie Hrivnak, thank you for believing in me when I sometimes forget to believe in myself.

To my family, everything I do is for you. And I love you so much.

And finally, to you, the reader, thank you for walking this path with me. Whether this is your first visit to Elgoria, or you've been with me since page one, I'm grateful.

This is only the beginning.

-Stella

Part One

chapter 1

"Can we cut the small talk, Director?" Brody said, taking his mug of coffee in one of his big, firm hands.

He didn't mean to be disrespectful, but he knew Nunez wasn't there to trade recipes. Nunez, unperturbed, kept her dark-hooded eyes fixed on Brody as she sipped coffee from Brody's *Shit just got real* mug, a keepsake from his sister's wedding. The mug was apropos of the Director of the FBI being at his home; he knew whatever she wanted was serious.

As if on cue, in her husky voice, she said, "I have a job for you."

Instinct found Brody shaking his head no before the word even came to his lips. He wasn't going back to the FBI. Not for anything. Not after...

"No," he said. "I'm out. I've been out. And the past six months have been surprisingly peaceful for me."

"Brody...relax. I'm not asking you to come back to the Bureau."

"You're not?" he asked. He leaned forward, bracing his arms on his knees, curious now to hear what request brought the Director of the FBI to his house.

"It's a special job, for me. Off the books. I can't involve the FBI or anyone official, for that matter."

"Okay," he replied. "You have my attention."

Brody hadn't known Nunez long; he had only worked for the Bureau for those two years. But what he did know about her was that she was a strict, play-by-the-rules director. Her needing him for something "off-the-books" was a deviation from her usual character. He sat back in his chair again, relaxing his broad shoulders against the back of his off-white sofa. Nunez sat tall across from him in one of his navy blue accent chairs. She kept her shiny black hair in her usual tight, low bun and wore her gray suit, and Brody wondered if she ever wore anything but.

"You know, my father was a good, honest man."

Nunez's eyes glazed over with a faraway look as she spoke.

"He always told me that having a few fiercely loyal friends was better than a lot of fair-weather ones. He kept his circle small and urged me to do the same."

Nunez paused for a sigh. She cupped her mug in both hands, not meeting Brody's eyes as she spoke.

"My father had a friend named Harold, whom I grew up knowing well. He was a quiet, stocky man. Fiercely loyal friend to my father, and my father to him. If my father ever needed anything, Harold was there. After my mother left us, there were days I thought we might not eat. But Harold took care of us, got my father back on his feet..."

She paused again before continuing.

"On his deathbed, my father asked me if I would look after Harold once he was gone. So, I did. I visited him at least once a week, brought him a hot dinner, made sure his nurses were caring for him properly. Then one day, last year, Harold asked me if I could help him with something important. He was reluctant to tell me the details, but he said he'd run out of people to trust."

Brody hadn't realized Nunez was this… human. She had a standoffish, impersonal approach to people, so her sharing these intimate details about her father and his friend was intriguing, to say the least.

"Harold Yates was an interesting man with a fascinating lineage," she continued. "He had inherited a large sum of money. We are talking about enough money to challenge even the royal family's assets. Consequently, people were looking to kill him and his family over that inheritance."

"You said *was*," Brody said, sipping his coffee again. "Harold was an interesting man. Does that mean…"

"He's dead, yes, but of natural causes, thank God."

"Why would someone want to kill Harold's family for this inheritance?"

"It's complicated," Nunez responded. "Even more than I could have imagined."

"What does Harold's inheritance have to do with why you're here?"

"I'll tell you everything in time. But I'm here because I need you to protect a member of Harold's family, his granddaughter, Lizzie. She's thirty-two. Only child. Her mother died in an accident several years ago, and she was estranged from Harold. He kept it that way on purpose to protect her. She has no idea about her inheritance or…" Nunez stopped, swallowing hard, like she was doing everything in her power not to say the rest.

She shifted in her seat and then cleared her throat.

"Brody, how comfortable are you with the uncomfortable?"

"You're talking in tongues, Director."

"There's a lot more to this case, and I need to know you would be all in, no matter what you learn."

The proposition sounded intriguing, mysterious, and maybe a little frightening—all the qualities that had drawn Brody to the FBI in the first place. But Brody was no senior special agent...he wasn't any kind of agent anymore. So he asked the question that had been burning in his mind since the moment Nunez arrived.

"Why me?"

"You were a good agent, Brody."

"Cut the shit, Director. I was a junior agent with basic skills at best. Why me?"

Nunez sighed.

"You have empathy, Brody."

She met his eyes.

"You're the kind of guy that will do the right thing. I need that. *Lizzie* needs that."

She raised her brows slightly.

"We don't see that much anymore. Everyone's either too scared or too busy helping the wrong people. And I don't know exactly what we're going to learn once we get deeper into this case. I need someone who isn't attached. And you fit the description."

"Hmm," was Brody's response as he studied Nunez's penetrating eyes. She needed someone who had nothing to lose. He'd spent so long trying to forget his past, and here it was, standing on his doorstep, disguised as an opportunity. He let out a heavy sigh as his eyes focused on a picture frame on his fireplace mantel. He and Nina grinned widely as they held each other tightly on Hemmy's yacht. Ten years down the drain. *Well, fuck Nina, and fuck Hemmy, too,* he thought. They deserved each other. Brody had already lost everything. He took a sip of his coffee—it'd cooled down but still tasted good. "I'll do it."

"Good," Nunez said. "Welcome to the shadows, Brody."

"Do I get a team?"

Nunez contemplated his request for a moment.

"Only recruit people you trust completely," she said. "They'll be filled in on an as-needed basis. And I'm going to bring a couple of my own to the team as well."

She stood up, smoothing out her suit. "As I said, I'll brief you more as you go along, but here's what you need to know for now. Lizzie is a graduate student at Rutgers University Camden. She's getting a master's degree in psychology, and we've just intercepted one of her classes and replaced it with another one. You're going to play the role of a graduate student, and on Wednesday, you'll show up at Rutgers campus, Building 133, Auditorium Two."

"What class am I taking?"

Nunez smirked as she stood from her seat.

"One I think you'll enjoy. The professor teaching the class is a trusted retired agent. He's an actual professor and has been teaching classes like this for years. I need you to be into this student thing."

"And here I thought I was done with school."

Brody's joke did not elicit a smile from Nunez. She made her way to the front door, Brody following her. As she grabbed for the door handle, she turned.

"Wednesday, before class, we'll meet to go over more. I appreciate your help with this matter, Brody, and you'll be paid well for your services."

Good. He needed the money, now that Nina was living off half of his with his best friend. He growled under his breath at the thought.

Nunez continued.

"But you should know that while I'm no longer officially your boss and you don't work for the Bureau anymore, for this job, I'm in charge. And I have three rules that you must swear to stick to."

"Okay," Brody responded.

"One, you're going to need to be all-in emotionally, but you must never get too close to Lizzie, no matter how closely you find yourself working with her."

"Don't get too close to the subject," Brody smiled. "Got it."

"Two, don't interfere unless it's necessary."

"Don't interfere unless the whole thing is going to shit. Got it."

"And lastly, and most importantly, never tell Lizzie any details about the case."

"Aye aye, Director."

"And one last thing," Nunez said, gripping the handle of the door tightly.

"You said three things…"

"This is different, Brody." Her tone became more serious while Brody braced himself for an inevitable lecture. "What happened to your uncle wasn't your fault."

Nunez looked around Brody's living room, focusing on the photo on the mantel. Her judgment seeped through her skin like smoke through a vent.

"You've let it destroy you from the inside out. But Nina's gone. Take her shit down and throw it away. It's time to let go."

chapter 2

Lizzie Degan hugged her books close to her chest with one arm as she stepped into Building 132. Out of nowhere, her graduate history of psychology class had been canceled, not just for today but for the entire semester.

The only reason she could think of was that something terrible had happened to Professor Steinberg, but she hoped that wasn't the case.

Lizzie made her way up a set of stairs, down a long, drab hallway with dull lighting, and knocked on a tall wooden door. As if she were expected, her small-statured, skinny guidance counselor, Mrs. Bloom, opened the door.

"Miss Degan, I'm glad you're here," she said. The pale-skinned counselor ushered Lizzie into her office and motioned for her to sit in a brown leather chair.

As Lizzie took a seat, she put her books and laptop bag on the floor beside her. Mrs. Bloom strode over to her desk and sat down, fixing her wide, round spectacles more securely on her face.

"As you know, Professor Steinberg had to cancel his class due to an emergency."

"I hope he's okay," Lizzie said.

"Nothing a little rest and recovery can't fix," Mrs. Bloom said with an overly enthusiastic smile. With trembling fingers, she thumbed through a hard copy of Lizzie's school records.

Given her counselor's skittish behavior, Lizzie knew the professor was not coming back, but she didn't pry any further. She simply prayed he recovered from whatever had happened.

"Still, he couldn't continue the class, and the dean felt it better that we cancel it for the semester. Now, that leaves you with two options for this semester. There's a graduate Abnormal Psychology course. They're already near midterm, so you'd have lots of make-up work, but you can take that if you wish. Or we have another option—with an adjunct professor who has been teaching a special topics elective called Inside the Killer's Mind. He's agreed to run the class from now until the end of the semester and shorten the length of work. It's an in-depth analysis of psychological disorders that cause violent acts, a crossover with our Criminal Justice master's Program." Mrs. Bloom shrugged. "The decision is up to you, Lizzie, but I recommend the latter class. I would hate for you to have to make up so much work in another class and put additional stress on yourself."

"I understand," Lizzie said. "When does this class start?"

"Wednesday. Same time. It's 3:00-4:30 p.m. on Mondays and Wednesdays, Building 133, Auditorium Two." Mrs. Bloom kept her eyes fixed on Lizzie's file and continued with a thin smile crossing her lips, "I assume that still works for you, considering it's the same days, times, and location as History of Psychology."

"Do I need any books for the Inside the Killer's Mind class?"

"Professor Dune has an unconventional way of teaching,

so I don't know for sure. But he plans to post a syllabus and course requisite by Wednesday morning."

"Okay," Lizzie shrugged. "I guess I'll take that one then."

"Very good," Mrs. Bloom said, offering a genuine smile now. "How is your other class going?"

"It's going well."

"And you still think you want to do three classes next semester?"

"No, you were right. Two is plenty. Between work and school…"

"Good choice." Mrs. Bloom paused before saying, "All right, well, you know where to find me if you have any questions, Miss Degan. I'll make sure I add you to Wednesday's class."

Gathering her things, Lizzie thanked Mrs. Bloom and then left Building 132. As she walked across campus toward her car, a voice from behind startled her, and she turned to see intense, hazel eyes glaring into hers. A tall, attractive man stood before her, and although he looked vaguely familiar, she could not quite place him.

"Are you Lizzie Degan?" he asked in a lilting accent.

"Yes," she answered in her usual, pleasant way.

The man didn't say anything else right away. He kept his eyes narrowed and studied her as if she were artwork on display in a gallery.

"Can I help you with something?" she asked, still pleasant but with a slight edge. After all, it wasn't normal for someone to call out her name and stare at her with strange facial expressions. It gave her the creeps, no matter how handsome he was. He didn't seem threatening, but she was glad to be in a public place.

"So, it's true," he replied, pursing his lips. He wore his confidence well, but Lizzie couldn't help but sense something dangerous lurking behind his entrancing gaze.

"What's true?" she asked.

"You exist."

His voice was hypnotic, deep, and smoky. She swallowed deeply.

"What do you mean by that?" she asked.

A nervous laugh involuntarily escaped her, a combination of his presence and the absurdity of his response. Someone had to be playing a prank on her. But who? She didn't know many people at school, having started her graduate program just a few weeks earlier.

Lizzie couldn't fathom what he meant by what he said, and she wondered if he was a classmate. *Do I know him? No, I don't.* He had one of those unforgettable faces with strong, sharp features, piercing eyes, and a tall, muscular physique. She would have remembered him, for sure.

"You'll find out." He paused before saying, "I'll see you soon, Lizzie."

He drawled out the last part of her name with a finality that made her shudder. She could feel his danger down to her bones, laced with a memory of something. A dream she'd had? A nightmare?

Suddenly, someone bumped into Lizzie's shoulder, and in her edgy state, she quickly turned to see who it was. A throng of undergrads had plowed by her; one guy had accidentally stumbled into her, laughing about something his friend had just said.

"I'm so sorry," he said.

"It's fine," Lizzie said.

A brief, jarring rush of vertigo overcame her, as if the ground had shifted a few degrees off center. For a moment, Lizzie felt a spiraling sensation in her chest that left her unsteady on her feet. She blinked hard, trying to regain her balance. And just like that, it was gone. *Probably nothing,* she told herself. *Likely stress.*

She quickly turned back to face the strange man who

stood before her.

But he was gone.

In the seconds she had turned to see who bumped into her, the man had fled the scene, and Lizzie was left to unpack what had just happened. She couldn't make sense of it.

Her fingers fumbled over buttons on her phone as she dialed her boyfriend, Miles. When he didn't answer, Lizzie hurried through the campus parking lot to her car, looking over her shoulder more than once. All the while, a knot tightened in her gut, and only when she was safely in her car with the doors locked did she breathe a sigh of relief.

A warning light blinked on her dashboard, some icon that Lizzie could tell wasn't good. But there was no way she was sticking around campus to find out what it was, not after what had just happened. She would have Miles check her car when he got home from work later.

As Lizzie drove, her thoughts focused on the stranger. *Who was he?* His alluring voice echoed in her mind. "So, it's true. You exist." He knew her name, her full name. And what did he mean when he said, "You'll find out...I'll see you soon"?

For a brief moment, she swore she felt the man watching her again, even though she was far from campus.

He was long gone, but something unseen still lingered. A shiver ran down her spine, and Lizzie gripped her steering wheel tightly.

Something bad was coming.

She could feel it.

chapter 3

ime to take out the trash.

Nunez had been right. It was time for Brody to clean up his life—purge his mind, surroundings, and life of everything that happened in the past two years. He wasn't going to touch his uncle's death. That tragedy still weighed heavily on him, and it was easier for him to shove it far away from his mind and focus on work instead. But his wife leaving him for his so-called best friend? Could he begin to let that go, even though he still felt as though they'd pinned him to one of those spinning spike boards and each took turns throwing knives into his chest?

He dumped the photo of Nina and himself into a waste basket and immediately took a sip of beer. This was his sixth beer tonight. He didn't drink often anymore, had drunk enough during those months when she first left, but he needed the crutch to let go of the gut-wrenching pain that had tortured him for a year and a half.

Not that he had been sitting around pining for Nina. He'd invited more women into his bed in six months than he cared to admit. For a while, the excitement, fun, and sex kept him satisfied and moved Nina away from the forefront of his mind. But eventually, the whole process made him feel lonely again. When Brody was younger, he had loved being in lust, but now, at thirty-four, he wanted to be in love. He had been happy in his marriage, content to stay with Nina until they were old and gray. Nina was happy, too, wasn't she?

A text message popped up on Brody's phone, distracting him from thoughts of Nina.

Lilly: *You free tonight?*

Brody: *Sorry, busy.*

Lilly: *With what? I could COME help you…I'll bring those panties you like.*

Brody: *Can't tonight. Maybe another night.*

Lilly: *Okay. Fine. I get it.*

Brody: *It's not like that…*

Brody wasn't into Lilly, except for their inconspicuous meetings at his place. Lilly wasn't single, but her boyfriend strayed often, and being with Brody was her way of getting revenge. He took another swig of beer and put more of Nina's things in the trash. She hadn't come back for them, and the divorce had been finalized six months ago.

Mips, Brody's calico, jumped up on the top of the sofa and purred, patiently waiting for a pet from Brody. He stroked the fur between her ears, and she purred louder.

Despite all that had gone on, Brody meant it when he told Nunez the last six months had been surprisingly peaceful. He'd focused on work as head of security at a local security company; he'd taken in an old discarded German Shepherd named Kado from the kill shelter who was blind in one eye; and then he rescued a kitten from a dumpster and named her Mips (Moderately Impish, Perfectly Sweet)—his niece had come up with the name. Kado had almost killed Mips within the first week, and it took some time for the two to get used to each other. But eventually, Mips grew on that old Shepherd, who soon began to deteriorate from old age. By the time Kado passed over the Rainbow Bridge, he had become best friends with Mips, and Brody felt comfort in knowing the dog had lived out his last months happy and safe. Now it was just Brody and Mips, but he could tell the cat wanted a companion.

"Someday," he said to her, petting her again on the head, "I'll get you a golden retriever. Would you like that?" Mips just stared at him.

Brody picked up the last framed picture on his side table. It was of him and Nina at their wedding, both with radiant smiles on their young faces. They were happy. He knew they were. But Nina had betrayed his trust, acted like the last ten years meant nothing. What killed him most was the quiet truth he couldn't ignore: it wasn't the cheating that broke them. It was the drinking. The yelling. The void inside him that he wouldn't let her touch.

He was the one who had destroyed his marriage.

Hemmy was the safe place Nina found as Brody navigated the darkest part of his soul. She needed security from Brody, and he couldn't give it to her. So, Hemmy did. Nina had tried to get Brody the help he needed, but he had been too stuck in his trauma to realize Nina could only take so much. He pushed the memories away from his mind. It was all over now. That was his past, and he had worked hard to reinvent himself.

In one of those annoying retrospective insights, he realized he was thankful Hemmy took care of Nina the way he did, so she wasn't alone, wasn't afraid.

But still, *fuck Hemmy, and fuck Nina.*

He took the photo and threw it in the waste basket. Finally, she was gone for good. And maybe peace was overrated. He pulled out his phone and sent a text to Lilly.

Brody: *Turns out I am free tonight. Come over. Bring the panties.*

chapter 4

Lizzie had arrived home, still feeling unsettled from her encounter with the guy on campus. Miles had observed her knitted brows and clenched jaw and immediately pulled her into his arms, demanding to know what happened.

"What did he look like?" Miles asked, his possessive grip tightening.

"Tall, dark hair."

"How dark?" he asked. "Like mine?"

"Lighter than yours," she said. "A medium brown. And his eyes were hazel."

A low guttural grumble erupted from Miles.

Miles' hair was as blue-black as a midnight sky. His eyes were bright green, like sunlight on deep forest leaves. Those eyes had once made her feel safe, and given her past, she desperately needed that. But lately, they reflected a haunting, frightening melody.

The unease hadn't started today. Three days ago, she'd come home to Miles shouting into his phone. Not angry, but threatening, like he meant every word.

"One more stunt like that, and he'll be in pieces in the

back of my fucking trunk! You hear me?" Miles had yelled, and Lizzie had frozen in the doorway.

He hadn't heard her enter, so she backed out quietly and reopened the door louder, pretending she'd just arrived. He'd hung up fast. Smiled when he saw her. And that was it. Lizzie never brought it up.

"You're not going to school without me anymore," he said, bringing her back to the present.

"The encounter was strange, but don't you think you're overreacting?" Lizzie replied. Yes, the guy had been a little off-putting, but the school was a public place. She didn't need a bodyguard for one little encounter.

"Do you have any idea why he was there?"

"No," Lizzie answered. "And I have no idea why he would care if I existed or not. For all I know, this could have something to do with my dad." Lizzie's mention of her father caught in her throat. "Miles, do you think this could have something to do with him?"

Miles shrugged. "It's possible. Have you heard anything from him?"

"No," Lizzie lied. She hated asking Miles about him, but she needed to talk to someone. No one wanted to talk about her father—not her stepdad, not her best friend Misty, and not Miles. Those were the only people she trusted, and they refused to listen. She couldn't tell Miles her dad had emailed her, and with a warning, nonetheless. He would be furious, arguing how terrible her father was and how she shouldn't answer him. Not that her dad would answer her—she had replied to his email and heard absolutely nothing back. She'd called his cell phone seven times. No answer. He'd done this to her before, hadn't answered for a few months because he was on some "job." But he had never sent her a warning and then went MIA.

"Just the thought of this guy messing with you, stalking

you, makes me angry," Miles said, still ranting about the campus encounter.

"It might not be that serious," Lizzie said, trying to ease the tension, but in her heart, she knew whatever the man's intentions were, they weren't good.

"You're sure that's all that happened?" Miles asked, searching her eyes with his.

"Yes," Lizzie said. "But the 'check engine' light is on in my car."

"I'll take a look. If I need to take it to the shop, then you'll have to let me drive you to work and school, at least for a couple of days," he sighed.

"Yeah, okay," she replied.

Her fear spoke louder than her peace, and given the circumstances, maybe it was better that Miles drove her. What if that man showed up at her work? What if he showed up on campus again? The idea that Miles would be there comforted her a little as she felt the trapped tension inside her loosen its grip.

"Your stepdad dropped off a letter for you today," Miles said in his low, rugged voice, changing the subject.

"Who's it from?"

Miles didn't have to say anything more. Keeping Lizzie still locked in his left arm, he used his right arm to reach over to the side table. She caught his irresistible, familiar scent of oud wood and dark leather, a scent that grounded her in the safety she craved.

Miles handed her a letter, and she felt her breath slow. She didn't need to open it. The name on the envelope, *William Harold Yates*, was enough.

Her grandfather.

"Are you going to open it?" Miles asked.

Lizzie held the envelope in her hands, turning it over to the front where her name had been written in his handwriting.

Her stepfather, Dan, had told her Harold had died. Knowing Lizzie wanted nothing to do with her grandfather, Dan offered to help clean out Harold's home. *He must have found the unsent letter there*, she thought. She blocked it out of her mind. She had no tears for a man who had abandoned first his daughter and then his granddaughter.

"No," Lizzie said, tossing the letter back onto the side table. "Not today, at least."

"Okay, but you should open it, Lizzie. Your grandfather is dead, but you never know. The apology you're looking for may be in that letter."

"I'm not looking for an apology."

Lizzie pulled away slightly from Miles, but his grasp was strong, and he drew her closer to him.

"I think you are," Miles said. "And I think your grandfather probably saw the error of his ways as so many people do when they get to that age."

"Well, an apology isn't going to fix all the years he hurt my mother or all the years he hurt me. I'm just not ready to read what he has to say."

And I probably never will be, Lizzie wanted to add. She had no intentions of forgiving that man, no matter what he said in that letter.

"Fair enough," Miles said, planting a kiss on Lizzie's nose. "Well, when you're ready, I'm here."

"Thank you."

"I missed you, baby," Miles said, nuzzling his lips into Lizzie's neck.

"I wasn't gone very long," Lizzie said, her voice light. Today's events had been too much, and she wasn't in the mood for sex.

"It was too long for me." Miles studied her face for a few moments before adding, "Look, I know I'm being overprotective, but if anything ever happened to you..."

He paused, his gaze steady. "I need you, Lizzie. More than I probably should."

Lizzie nodded, allowing herself to settle into Miles' arms, not because the fear was gone, but because it was easier than fighting it.

"So..." His fingers traced along Lizzie's inner thigh, pausing beside the spot that would unravel her. "Why don't we let the shitty events of today go. Take a bubble bath. You and me."

Then he leaned in, his voice husky.

"And then... you'll let me show you how much I need you."

His voice still sent titillating shivers down her spine. But she couldn't deny that lately, the distance had grown slowly, like a hairline crack in ice just waiting to split open.

chapter 5

Brody heard the click of Nunez's heels across the warehouse floor before he saw her. She'd rented a small warehouse in Pennsauken, New Jersey, about ten minutes from the Rutgers campus and twenty minutes from Brody's house. She'd set up a table and gray folding chairs for the meeting. After his conversation on Monday with Nunez, Brody called the three people he trusted most to help him with this job. They'd all agreed to do it because Nunez had a good reputation, and people trusted her easily, even Brody. But he couldn't help but feel a twinge of pain pierce through his mind. If this had happened three years ago, Brody would have called his best friend Hemmy Giordano. Now, he would never call Hemmy again, not even if his life depended on it.

"Good afternoon," Nunez said.

It was one in the afternoon, and after his meeting, Brody planned to head to campus to enjoy his first day of school as a graduate student. Even though it was all pretend, he still felt nervous, not so much because of school, but because once the lies began, he had to keep up with them. Lying to Lizzie was part of the job, but lying to his mother, sister, niece, and nephew? It felt wrong. Especially since Nunez had indicated that this job was dangerous.

Shay Tierra and her husband, Dale, were two of the best people Brody knew. Dale worked with computer systems as a top cyber-security specialist for the government; he could hack into any computer system or program in the world. He was useful in stopping attacks from other hackers who were just as good in a race-against-time profession. He also had access to lots of cool tech that could aid in this operation. For instance, nearly invisible, gel-based earpieces that used targeted sonic vibrations to transmit sound directly through the inner ear.

Shay, on the other hand, had been a detective at the Cherry Hill Police Department for years. She was honest, smarter than most women he knew, and with her blackbelt in Jiu Jitsu, she could kick most people's asses too. He'd known Shay for over half of his life; she'd been his next-door neighbor for years.

Brody officially introduced Shay and Dale to Nunez, which was an obligatory introduction, as Nunez had vetted them first and had a good knowledge of their backgrounds before they arrived.

She then turned to the fourth member of the team.

"Punk…" Nunez said. "You're looking…"

"Old…" Punk replied in his gruff voice. "You can say it, Nunez."

She motioned to the scruff on his chin.

"I was going to say different, with the beard."

"And the missing hair," Brody added.

Punk shook his head. Special agent William Punkstone had been Brody's uncle's best friend—a truly loyal comrade who was like family. He had retired from the Bureau just as Brody had arrived, and he knew Nunez well. Punk had helped Brody as best he could after his uncle's death. Besides

Nina, he was the only one who had even tried.

"Everyone, listen up," Nunez said.

Nunez projected a presentation from her laptop onto a white screen behind where they sat. As the words appeared on the screen, Nunez began to explain important details about the case.

"I'm certain most of you have heard of the Bakers."

Who hadn't, Brody thought? They were the largest mafia family on the East Coast to date. The Bakers had their hands in everything, everywhere. Crooked cops and agents were on the Bakers' payroll, and the family's connections even spanned across the sea.

"Harold's family's money is old," Nunez said, "and the Bakers have a long history with them. It goes back to a soured friendship between the late movie director, Richard Baker, and Harold's father, Paul Watson." She took a sip of water and changed the slide. "The Bakers spent years chasing the Watson inheritance. But they hit a dead end when Harold's family vanished."

"Vanished?" Brody said, sharpening his gaze.

"Yes. Harold's parents changed his name when he was a baby to protect him. He spent his life in the shadows, hiding from the mob family who sought him. But when he died, the Bakers finally learned who he really was."

"How?" Shay asked, leaning forward in her seat.

"I was told Harold's lawyer died of a mysterious illness." Nunez raised her brows. "My take? The Bakers had a growing suspicion about Harold, who was then on his deathbed. So, they took out the lawyer. Then, Harold's will landed in the hands of someone else at the firm, someone already on the Baker payroll. And the rest is history."

"Is there anyone who doesn't work for them?" Shay said, rolling her eyes. She sat back in her seat and folded her arms.

Brody understood Shay's frustration. He hated the power

the Bakers had—hated that no one would stand up to them because no one knew who to trust. "They had the inheritance in their hands," Brody said. "So, what happened?"

"The lawyer at the firm alerted them about the last heir. And they went on a bloodthirsty pursuit. For a while, I was able to intervene. Harold had appointed me in charge of keeping important information secret. But recently, the Bakers learned about his granddaughter. They know who she is now, and they're after Lizzie. That's one of the reasons *you're* going to keep her safe."

"And the other reason?" Brody asked.

Nunez's eyes darkened. "We'll talk about that later." She shifted the subject. "One of my agents, Jaycen Juarez, the only active agent involved, is undercover. He's been giving us good intel on what the Bakers are planning."

"Would it be easier if we told Lizzie everything?" Brody asked. "She'd probably cooperate. We could move her to safety easily. Why the whole undercover gig?"

Nunez's lip curled up as she changed the slide. A picture of a dark-haired male in his thirties with dark knitted eyebrows filled the screen. Immediately, Brody didn't like him.

"This is Miles Corrigan. Lizzie's boyfriend."

"Looks like a nice guy," Dale said.

"The Bakers had narrowed Harold's heir down to a few people. Lizzie was the first one on their list. Miles' job was to confirm or deny Lizzie as the heir, and if confirmed... kill her. But after spending some time with her, he fell in love."

"Classic, I'm supposed to kill you, but I fell in love instead," Dale joked.

Brody couldn't help but let out a soft chuckle. Meanwhile, Nunez stayed stone-faced.

"According to Juarez," Nunez continued, "Miles kept stalling, saying he needed more time with Lizzie before confirming or denying her identity. But when Lizzie's grandfather died, the Bakers were able to confirm who she was. By this point, Miles had been in a relationship with Lizzie for five months."

"So the hitman has become the protector," Punk said.

"Miles is anything but," Nunez replied. "He's a cold-blooded killer. Yes, he has been doing everything he can to keep the Bakers from Lizzie, but he's losing his control. They know who she is. It's only a matter of time before he makes the wrong move, and they get what they want."

"Why not just tell him we can help?" Shay asked. "Couldn't we make him an ally? Maybe his priorities have changed."

"Miles is a wild card. Juarez says his temper is blue-hot and that he's extremely possessive of Lizzie. I'm afraid that if he thinks anyone is trying to take her away from him, he'll kidnap her out of some crazed possessive passion. Then we won't be able to help her. I don't want to take the chance. That's why Lizzie can't know who she really is. I don't want Miles screwing any of this up."

"Why don't they just kill Miles?" Punk asked. "Problem solved."

That was his personality. To the point.

"Miles' family is tied closely to the Bakers, enough that they'd rather reprimand him than kill him. At least according to Juarez. But I can't say the same for Lizzie. If they get the chance, they'll take her out."

"So, what's our plan then?" Brody asked.

"Hold up," Shay interrupted. "Couldn't Miles still do something rash, whether Lizzie learns about all of this on her own or we tell her? If she figures out the Bakers are after her, unless she's an award winning actress, she'd show some distress, and Miles is going to know."

"And if the Bakers know who Lizzie is now, aren't we racing against a clock anyway?" Punk added. "They'll get too close, and Miles will make some kind of move."

"I've thought about all of this," Nunez said. "The pressure is on for Miles right now. The Bakers are after Lizzie in full force, and that's why Brody's main job is to protect her. I need Lizzie to trust you," Nunez continued, speaking directly to Brody now. "I need her to trust you with her life and want to turn to you for help instead of her boyfriend."

"Shouldn't be a problem for Brody," Shay said. "We all know how he is with the ladies."

Brody scratched the side of his head and widened his eyes at Dale as if to acknowledge his past.

"I would be lying if I said I wasn't banking on those good looks to help in some way," Nunez said.

"Kind of feel like I'm being used here," Brody said. "Just unclear though about the not getting emotionally close to her part. You want her to like me, but not too much."

"I want her to feel safe with you and unsafe with her boyfriend. And I happen to know it's something that won't take much effort on your part. It's one of the reasons why I chose you."

"Also, am I supposed to be competing with the hitman, or…"

Brody couldn't help but make light of the subject. He understood the gravity of the situation regarding the Bakers, but what Nunez was describing sounded less like a tactical mission and more like stealing a woman from another man. That was already dangerous, and considering Miles was a hitman made it more so. He just wanted to know *exactly* what he was getting himself into.

"I know it sounds silly," Nunez said. "But if you'll just trust me, I think this plan can work."

"And if everything goes south?"

"Then we abort the mission. We can only do what we can do. If we can't protect Lizzie, at least we can say we tried."

A moment of silence passed before Nunez continued.

"I would rather you all be safe and let the chips fall where they may than put your families in danger. At some point, if it all goes badly, I'll pull the plug."

Nunez checked her watch.

"But for now, we need to wrap this up. We'll meet again on Friday. Brody, I want to see you back here at 5 p.m. Now get to class. I won't have you late on your first day. Everyone is dismissed."

As the others filed out of the room, Brody stayed back for a minute, studying the still of Miles on the screen.

If he was going to do this, there was no way the Bakers were going to touch Lizzie. Not ever.

chapter 6

Professor Dune took a seat on the edge of a desk fixed on the auditorium's stage; his hands folded over one another. Adjusting his black-rimmed glasses, he said, "This course is untraditional, but if you follow the syllabus and my rules, you'll walk away with something valuable. Got it?"

He paused, darting his eyes around at his students, who nodded at his words.

"Good," he continued. "Let's talk about your first, and only, assignment for the next six weeks."

Excitement rippled through the class.

"All right, all right. Settle down. Don't celebrate yet," Dune said. "This won't be easy. I've compiled fifteen real-world murder cases, each bizarre, messy, and psychologically complex. Not your average whodunnits."

He began to pace the small stage.

"Some of these cases are mysteries. For some, the facts just don't add up. You'll receive a case and be assigned a partner with whom you will work for the entire course.

"Over the next few weeks, your task is to compile as much information about your case as possible. The library and the internet have a lot of resources that will help you. You and your partner are responsible for conducting all of this research. After the first couple of weeks, you'll review both the materials I've provided and your own findings. Then, you'll integrate everything you've learned, including what we cover in class, into your final presentation, which is due two weeks before the final exam."

Professor Dune looked around the room.

"Questions?" When no one responded, he said, "All right then. Let me assign your partners and your cases. You're free to leave as soon as I do."

As Professor Dune called people up in groups of two, Lizzie scrolled through social media on her phone. That led her to check her emails—nothing new from her dad. And no phone call either.

"Lizzie Degan, Brody Woods," Professor Dune called. Lizzie clicked her phone screen shut, gathered her books, stood, and headed toward the front of the auditorium. Already, this class was shaping up to be better than her other class. More interesting, at least. As Lizzie reached Professor Dune, her partner appeared next to her. He was tall, broad-shouldered, with thick, tousled chestnut brown hair that was short and tapered on the sides, the top swept back in a smooth volumunous sweep. He had a sharp angular jawline with a hint of stubble, which gave him a slightly rugged appearance. He stared at Lizzie and gave her a nod, his bright cerulean eyes glistening even in the dim auditorium.

"You two have a unique case," Dune said. He held the case file in his hands. "Who wants to hold on to it?" When neither Lizzie nor her partner, Woods, answered, the professor handed it to Lizzie. "I urge you two to visit the inn associated with this case. It's a few hours' drive, but you'll find it rich with history and mystery."

"Thanks," Lizzie said, cutting a glance in her partner's

direction. He returned her gaze with a quick rise of his brows and a light smile.

Lizzie turned to leave. This Woods guy made her nervous enough that she didn't know what to say to him. Maybe she didn't need to say anything for now. She didn't want to fumble over words and sound like an idiot.

"Mr. Woods, would you stay for a second?" the professor asked, giving Lizzie the out she desperately needed. As she stepped outside of Building 133, she took in the fiery oranges and pinks that painted the setting sun of an October sky. A faint smell of bonfire, one of her favorite smells, filled her nose. The fall chill sent a shiver down her body. Immediately, she sent a text message to Miles, who had taken her car to the shop on Tuesday morning and insisted he drive her to school.

Lizzie: *Are you here?*

He responded immediately.

Miles: *Leaving now. Be there soon, baby.*

Lizzie: *Okay. I'll go to the library for a little. I can get started on my class project. It's wild.*

Miles: *See you in a few.*

"Lizzie?" a male voice interrupted, and Lizzie turned to see her partner. She felt a tingling well in her upper chest, a nervous excitement that she wished would go away. But she wasn't sure if it was because of him or remnants of nerves from the last person who stopped her on campus.

"Uh, hi." Her voice came out soft, almost gentle.

"I'm Brody."

"Hi," she said again. *Really?* she thought. *That's all you've got?* Social awkwardness had been her constant companion since the pandemic, and she wondered if she would ever grow out of it.

"I thought you might want to take my number so we can work on this project," he said.

"Oh, yeah. Sure," Lizzie said, fumbling for her phone. She entered Brody's number, and then, thinking Miles was probably close, she said, "Thanks. I guess I'll see you on Monday, then?"

"Yeah, we can figure out a plan then."

Their eyes locked on each other longer than they should have, and a slow flutter stirred in Lizzie's stomach.

"Okay, then." Brody went to leave but turned back to face Lizzie. "You should know you're not the only old student in this class," he said.

"Um," was the only sound that escaped her. He thought she was old.

"I don't mean you're old," he retracted his statement quickly. "I mean older, like not younger. What I mean is, you're not in your twenties. I'm going to stop talking now."

It wasn't a big deal. Lots of graduate students studied in their thirties, but for some reason, Lizzie could tell she was the oldest in her class, and she was only thirty-two.

"Oh, yeah. Well, sometimes life…gets in the way."

"No, what I mean is. I'm also older. Like older than you, even, I'm sure. It's probably the reason Dune put us together for this project. He wanted the old people to work together. A senior project, if you will."

Lizzie couldn't help but smile. Brody was funny and awkward. She liked that he had a sense of humor, and she felt a little more at ease with him then.

"Well, it's nice to know I'm not the only senior citizen in the class, Brody."

Her phone buzzed, and she looked to see it was Miles.

Miles: *Here.*

His text was short, devoid of any kindness, which meant Miles was angry. No doubt he was observing her from afar somewhere. Furious with her for talking to another guy.

"I have to go," Lizzie said. "Is it okay if I take the file?"

"Sure," Brody said. "Hey, are you around Friday at 11 a.m.? I'm doing some work at the library here and thought we could meet up and work on this together." He paused and then added, "So we're prepared for Monday."

"I should be able to," Lizzie said.

"You have my number. Just let me know either way."

"Oh," Lizzie said, "but you should let me know if it interferes with your senior citizen bingo class. You know, your Friday festivities."

"Hmm," he laughed. "I deserve that. One hundred percent."

He gave another one of those lingering stares that made her uncomfortable, but in a heart-skip-a-beat way.

"It was nice meeting you, Brody," Lizzie said.

"Same here." Brody smiled. "See you on Friday, Lizzie."

"See you then," Lizzie said. With that, she turned to face the street, where she saw Miles leaning against the car, glaring at her. She hated the feeling in that moment. The accusation. It made her feel like a teenager who'd stayed out too long past curfew.

chapter 7

You're not the only old student? REALLY?

Brody hadn't expected Lizzie to be so…pretty. He hadn't expected anything really, just thought she was some thirty-something with a strange family history. It wasn't that he couldn't control himself around a pretty woman—he could. But he felt something stir within him the moment his eyes met hers, and he didn't like that. His breath had caught in his throat; his words barely escaped his lips. And then he completely insulted her. Awesome.

A senior project? He couldn't think of anything better to say.

The embarrassment was overwhelming. He had never in his life responded so poorly to a person, much less a woman.

He was tasked with the job of protecting her, but he also felt a desire to. Why? He hardly knew her. Maybe it was the doe-eyes or the pain that he saw lingering just behind them. Maybe that pain reminded him of his own. Whatever it was, Brody was drawn to her. *Maybe that was why Miles fell so easily in love with her,* Brody thought. Some women were just easy to love. Or maybe the connection Brody felt to her was something deeper.

When he reached the warehouse to discuss his initial meeting with Lizzie, he decided to leave out the immediate attraction part. *The meeting was fine. Lizzie didn't suspect anything. She seemed like a normal graduate student just doing her work. I'll see her on Friday.* That's what he would say and nothing else.

Nunez had her arms crossed as she gazed at the projector. She had a large image posted on the screen of an attractive hotel. When she saw Brody, she turned.

"Well?"

"It went fine," Brody answered. Short. Sweet. Not too much detail.

"Good," Nunez replied.

Brody plopped into one of the gray folding chairs. Nunez took a seat across from Brody, rolling her shoulders back and stretching her neck. *Had she even left the warehouse today*, he wondered?

"Now, there are a couple of complications surrounding Lizzie that I would like to discuss."

She grew quiet, frowned, and started to speak before closing her mouth again. Brody had never seen her like this, as if what she was about to say was life or death.

"Your job is not only to act as a protection detail for a woman in need. Harold left behind more than an inheritance. Something far older, and more dangerous." She paused once more before continuing. "A pendant."

"What's so dangerous about an old pendant?"

Brody opened a bag of peanuts he'd bought from the campus vending machine. He popped one of the peanuts into his mouth. Nunez shifted in her seat and then cleared her throat.

"I have reason to believe this relic has connections to

something… unlike anything I've ever seen or heard of." She paused before saying, "It might even teeter on the spectrum of supernatural."

"Supernatural as in… ghosts, that kind of thing?"

Brody didn't believe in ghosts, and he wasn't about to start because of a tall tale.

Nunez grunted. "If only. I'm talking about something more powerful, an ancient realm, and that artifact might be a key to opening it. But even I can't tell you what would be behind that door."

Now Brody cleared his throat and ran his hands over the stubble of his chin. Had the Director lost her damn mind?

"Let me get this straight. You believe some pendant might open a doorway to a fantasy world with dragons and beasts." It was the first thing he could think of. "Why do you even think that?"

"Because Harold told me what he knew about the pendant's power before he died, and he said it must be protected at all costs."

"Up until this point, I've been trusting you blindly, Director. But I'm sure you can see why I might be a little apprehensive now. Could Harold have been senile?"

"He may have been old," Nunez defended, "but the man had his wits about him. And he showed me the scrolls that went with the relic. Not that I understood anything, but…"

"But you don't know if the story behind the pendant is real."

"I don't," she said. "Not for certain."

"What made Harold believe it was real?"

"He didn't go into specifics, but he knew something I didn't. He said he spent years decoding the scrolls, traveled to several countries, and traced the origins back to ancient Scotland. He was sure all of it was real, Brody. And I believe him."

"So, destroy the pendant and be done with it," Brody said. He couldn't believe how blunt he was being. His dynamic with the Director had changed for sure. But since he had nothing to lose, he didn't mind being direct, especially with a situation as crazy as this one.

"I can't."

"Why not?"

"Because Harold believed the relic was meant for Lizzie."

"How?"

She shrugged.

"Where is this artifact now?" Brody asked.

"Damned if I know. But I have an idea of where it might be, and I believe Lizzie can get us to it."

Brody leaned his elbows on the fold-out table and crossed his hands.

"Director, I have to know. Are you doing this to protect Lizzie or to obtain the artifact?"

Brody wasn't stupid. He knew that off-the-books special operations were bound to be much more than about a rescue.

"Your job is to protect Lizzie. The Bakers want to eliminate the last heir. And they'll do it at any cost. But we won't let that happen for her sake as much as ours. We cannot let a relic that might open a portal to another world find its way into the wrong hands. And if Lizzie can somehow help us find it or even use it, then we need her alive and well. From what Harold and I could decipher from the relic's scroll, the portal can only be opened by someone who is a pureblood."

"Pureblood?"

"Harold said a pureblood is called an Elven-Fae. There's a prophecy that a woman will open the portal on her sixteenth birthday. If all of this is real, Brody, I don't think Lizzie could open the portal even if she wanted to. At best, she's a half-blood, and she's well over sixteen. But I know better than to think there's only one way to do something, and if the Bakers got wind of this, who knows what they'd do to open that portal."

"Suppose the Bakers did find out about the pendant," Brody said. "The chances of them knowing what it is, what to do with it, would be slim, no?"

"Maybe, but I'm not willing to hand over any more power to them. If there's even a chance they could figure out anything about it, I don't want to take it." Observing Brody's grimace, she said, "Trust me. I was as skeptical about all of this as you are now. You should know that I struggled to accept what Harold said for some time before deciding to act."

Brody pointed to the picture of the inn on the screen.

"What does all this have to do with the inn?"

"I think that's where the pendant is. According to Harold's last words. And we must get Lizzie there to find out."

Brody couldn't believe what he was hearing, but after the past couple of years, nothing much surprised him anymore. Still, he wasn't sold on this story. Not yet, anyway.

"There is one more thing I meant to tell you."

Brody couldn't imagine what Nunez was about to say next; he braced himself for her to say she was a fairy herself.

"Lizzie's father is Chuck Degan."

Brody coughed, the tiny remnants of a peanut getting stuck in his throat. Chuck Degan, assassin? Chuck Degan the CIAs 'bitch boy,' as they called him these days. Chuck Degan had been on permanent house arrest ever since the CIA retired him. They'd given him the "fall in line or die" speech, and Chuck fell in line, even though Brody was sure the man could take them all out if he wanted.

"Does Chuck know about all this?" Brody asked. "About Harold? The inheritance? The pendant?"

"I don't believe so. Harold never told anyone, not even his wife. He only told me because he was about to die."

"Shouldn't we involve Chuck?" Brody said. "To protect his daughter? Surely with his skills, he'd be the most fit."

"Firstly, no. I'm not crossing the CIA on the Chuck Degan issue. Secondly, she has a strained relationship with him, and I don't know if she knows what he's done."

"Anything else I need to know, Director?"

"For now, that's all."

Protecting a woman, not so hard. Protecting Chuck Degan's daughter, who may be the key to opening a portal to some far-off world? It all sounded like a crazy plot for a novel.

"I want you right by Lizzie's side when she uncovers what's hidden at the Speakeasy Inn."

"What am I supposed to do? Ask Lizzie to go on a weekend getaway with me to the inn to do some schoolwork?"

"I've been thinking about the best way to get both of you there and not make it look like a dogshit coincidence. I don't have many options. There's a wedding scheduled for Halloween weekend there. I thought maybe we could insert ourselves into that. Plenty of people dressed up in costume. Unsuspecting patrons."

"What's your plan?" Brody asked. Nunez pursed her lips, and Brody seemed to read her mind. "You're going to ask the bride and groom if we can hijack their wedding."

"People are most agreeable when money is involved," Nunez said. "I'm going to offer to pay for their wedding reception if they would be willing to add an extra table, Brody. We won't be in their way."

"What are you going to say?"

"That we're undercover agents protecting a very important target in the area and that they're doing a great service for their country; and after I flash my badge, I'll say, we would like to have some fun while we're in town."

"You think they'll go for this?"

"As I said, I don't have many options."

"And even though this isn't official, you're still willing to flash your badge?"

"I think this whole situation is important enough for me to take my chances."

"Why can't we just tell Lizzie?" Brody asked. "Don't you think it would be better for everyone? For her? For me? When she finds out we've been lying to her…"

"She's just a target, Brody. Remember my rules. No deep emotional connections."

"Award-winning performance. I got it. It just feels wrong."

"I trust that you'll keep it professional," Nunez said, eyeing him. "Hopefully, one day, Lizzie will understand that we were only trying to protect her. But she can't know who you are until she's safe and knows the location of the relic."

"Even if we wedding crash these people at the inn, this doesn't get Lizzie there. And there's no way, if her boyfriend is as crazy as you say he is, that he'll let me take her there as my plus one."

"I'm still trying to figure that out. But you must plant the idea in her head to go to the inn that weekend."

"There's no guarantee that she'll go."

"The thing about the inn, Brody, is that it's a true speakeasy. It's located in a remote location, and it's a good place to hide. What I'm banking on is Lizzie mentioning the inn to Miles, and him taking care of the rest for us. If he thinks he can hide Lizzie there safely, he might do it. He just needs motivation."

"And are we giving him that motivation?"

"Yes, but I'm not sure we'll have to."

Brody didn't like this plan, not one bit. There were too many variables that could go wrong. Too many lies.

But the part that rattled him most?

Some magical pendant could open an ancient portal to a

dangerous supernatural realm.
    He wasn't ready for that.
    None of them were.

chapter 8

"Who was that?"

"A classmate."

"A classmate," Miles repeated, drawing out the word class. His tone was even, seemingly composed, but Lizzie knew he was anything but.

Miles didn't ask any more questions. He kept his eyes focused on the road, but Lizzie knew by the deep crease between his brows that he wasn't happy.

As they reached the traffic light that would lead them out of Camden and onto the highway, Miles' mood improved. His eyes softened, and he loosened his grip on the steering wheel. And then Lizzie exhaled, realizing she'd been holding her breath for far too long as she assessed Miles' mood.

"I got you a little something," Miles said, breaking the silence. He reached his hand into the back seat as he drove and pulled out a small, black box.

"What is this?" Lizzie asked.

"Open it."

Miles didn't grin, but he smiled in the way only mysterious men could smile, with a half-drawn-up lip that crinkled one of his eyes.

"What is it for?" Lizzie asked.

Miles ran a hand through his slicked, thick black hair and gazed at her, his five o'clock shadow filling out his beard frame and accentuating his chiseled jawline.

"We've been together for almost a year. I'm madly in love with you and want you to have nice things."

"Oh," Lizzie said, offering him a warm smile. "Well, thank you."

The proper response should have been, "I love you, too," but she wasn't ready to say it. Not yet. She did love Miles, but whenever she thought about saying it to him, an invisible force kept her from speaking. Her shoulders tensed. Her breath became shallow. And the words just wouldn't come out.

She blamed it on "dad" issues, which Miles claimed to understand, but that was only half the truth. Lizzie had always sensed something dangerous underneath Miles' mysterious, calm demeanor. Something angry, feral, and unruly. The phone call she witnessed the other day had confirmed her suspicions.

He was hiding something.

That was the real reason she couldn't say it. Her inner voice kept nudging, "Not yet."

Lizzie opened the box and found a small card and two tickets.

"Sandalwood Owl tickets?"

Miles had gotten her tickets to see her favorite boy band, Sandalwood Owl, who had finally reunited after twenty years and was coming to Philadelphia for a long weekend; the shows were already sold out.

"Oh my," she said, reading the ticket. "I can't believe you got these! Wait." She frowned. "They're for tomorrow night."

"That's right," Miles said, raising his eyebrows as he grinned.

"But I have plans with Misty tomorrow after work. She's having a girls' night. I told you about it weeks ago."

"I'm sure she'll understand if you cancel, Lizzie."

Lizzie did her best to stay composed. No, Misty would not understand. The tension was already thick between Misty and Miles. According to Misty, Miles was a "love-bombing control freak" whose sole aim was to alienate Lizzie from all her loved ones.

Misty and Miles' personalities clashed so badly, Lizzie felt ill whenever they were all in the same room. Her boyfriend and best friend misunderstood each other completely, like water meeting electricity. Every interaction ended in a short circuit. Miles did love-bomb Lizzie to a degree, but it was only because he was financially well-off. He bought her things because he could. That didn't mean he was buying her love.

As children, Lizzie and Misty fought about almost everything, from what activity they would do that day, to what other girls could hang with them, to eventually, as they hit puberty, boys. But after Lizzie's mom died, Misty and Lizzie stopped fighting. Misty was Lizzie's rock, the only person who got her through most days.

Now, Lizzie hated fighting with Misty because she needed her more as an adult than she ever did as a kid. The problem was that Misty could be overly opinionated and judgmental. Still, despite Misty's flaws, Lizzie loved her friend, and she *hated* when Misty was angry with her.

She was torn between disappointing Misty, yet again, or disappointing Miles. She didn't want to disappoint either. On the one hand, as nice as these tickets were, Lizzie had been looking forward to spending time with her girlfriends. On the other hand, Sandalwood Owl would only be in town this weekend. They weren't coming back to Philly—she wasn't even sure if they'd be doing another tour. And tickets were incredibly difficult to come by.

"Yeah, yeah okay," she said finally, trying to hide her uneasiness. "This is Sandalwood Owl's last time in Philly. Misty will understand."

"Look, if you don't want to go…" he said.

"No, I do. It's fine." Lizzie read Miles' deepened stare, his raised eyebrows. He was questioning her without saying anything. "Really, it's okay."

"Good," Miles replied. "We'll have a nice evening out. You deserve it. We deserve it."

When Lizzie and Miles arrived back at her apartment, she immediately sent a text message to Misty, who replied with a phone call. She lectured Lizzie on how this situation was a perfect example of Miles, yet again, pulling Lizzie further away from her friends.

Lizzie would never mention this to Miles—she knew better than to add gasoline to a fire, but she couldn't help but feel Misty had a point. Lizzie's life unraveled after her mother died, and the only way she kept it stitched together was through laughing and experiencing joy with the people she loved. Now, being with Miles was tipping that fragile balance. That lonely despair again had found its way back into her soul.

Lately, she felt like a shell of the happy-go-lucky, independent person she used to be. And the icing on that eggless, flourless, gluten-free, sugar-free, fun-free, soul-sucking cake was that now she was canceling plans with her best friend because of her boyfriend. But Miles wasn't purposefully scheduling trips, events, and dinners so Lizzie wouldn't hang out with her friends.

He was just being a nice boyfriend. Right?

Misty ended the conversation by hanging up on Lizzie.

Tears streamed down Lizzie's cheeks as she pulled her long hair into a ponytail. She wiped her eyes, knowing that she would have to call Misty, apologize again to her, let her know she loved her, and wait for Misty to be ready to speak to her. *If Misty ever wanted to speak to her again.* Meanwhile, Lizzie needed a distraction to take her mind off the argument, and she knew just what to do.

First, she called her father, yet again. When he didn't pick up, she left a voicemail that said, "Lizzie, look up? The least you can do is stop whatever crazy scheme you're involved in and explain yourself. Okay... Bye."

Lizzie's father would take her to the park almost every week when she was younger. She was too young to realize he was grooming her for a life running from the "bad guys." *Lizzie, look up* was his way of getting Lizzie to drop everything and pay close attention to her father's next instructions. *Run. Hide. Keep quiet, and don't say a word until I tell you.* Lizzie didn't realize that other children were not raised that way until her father left the family for good. Thank God for therapy.

Lizzie flung herself onto her bed. The only thing that could take her mind off how lousy she felt was other people's misery. She could watch a reality TV show or listen to a murder mystery podcast. Instead, she opened the case file she received in class that day to see how screwed up the people in her case were. According to the file, her task was to investigate a murder at some place called The Speakeasy Inn.

```
    The Real 'Pearl in the Shadows'
  by Rufus Patterson, October 1929


    It's  October  1929,  and  Richard
  Baker  and  his  production  company,
  Lexington-Gold  Productions,  visit
  the  Speakeasy  Inn  in  Beechville,
```

Pennsylvania. Many people are cozying up at the inn, including the famous 1920s author, Gerald Westin. Westin has just finished his masterpiece fantasy novel, *A Pearl in the Shadows*. He sips on brandy, one leg crossed over the other as he smokes a pipe, arguing with Richard Baker about the best way to script his new novel, which has been received well. All seems well between the two men until later in the evening.

According to Westin, Baker and his then-wife, Claire, are found arguing with the owner of the inn on the verandah that leads to the gardens. The inn owner and Baker's wife take off, and Westin realizes they are arguing with Richard. Suddenly, a horrific sight appears, an amber-eyed beast that claws Richard Baker to death. Westin fears the beast so deeply that he is unable to sleep and drinks heavily every day. He is so distraught by the beast that he can no longer write.

When the body is examined, claw marks are indeed found, yet they appear to be human. Westin is considered a top suspect, with much evidence against him, including Richard's blood on his shirt.

Claire Baker and the owner of the inn, Paul Watson, are cleared by guests who saw them at the time of the murder. No one has been tried

> for Richard Baker's murder. Westin is
> admitted to a psychiatric hospital,
> where he eventually suffers the
> unfortunate fate of a failed liver.

Lizzie knew Westin to be the male Agatha Christie, an incredible writer. She had read in high school that he'd died of liver failure, but she had no idea about the murder. Her task was to determine if Westin killed Baker and if it was due to a psychological illness. How was she supposed to do that?

A ping from her phone broke her away from thinking about the case.

BioDad: *How far are you from Kentucky?*

Lizzie: *WHAT?*

Nothing more. Another cryptic message from her father and then radio silence. Nice. Just like him. Sometimes Lizzie envied dads like Misty's, who were always there; Mr. McConville was always in Misty's business, enough to annoy Misty. But at least Misty had a father who cared.

Not like Lizzie's dad.

Chuck Degan was probably off on some job, scamming people for money or doing some drug deal. She had no idea what he did. He never told her, so she would make up stories about who he was.

He was an assassin with a specific skill set.

He was a secret agent who was saving the world.

Things like that. But in her heart, she felt he had hooked up with the wrong people and done terrible things. That's why he didn't want to be in Lizzie's life.

She closed the case file and dialed Misty's number once

more. It went to voicemail, as expected, and Lizzie pleaded for forgiveness and then hung up. Lizzie had done all she could do.

Misty: *Meet me for breakfast on Friday. 9 a.m.*

That was all she said. Misty was still angry, but the invite was an olive branch.

Lizzie: *Okay. Hissock's?*

Misty: *Yes. See you then.*

Lizzie crossed the room to grab a sweater but paused. Something blue shimmered in the mirror. But it wasn't light. It was...

Her fingers reached for her neck, half expecting to feel a necklace with a glistening pendant. But when her hand touched bare skin, her stomach dipped. There was nothing there.

"Okay...that was...weird," she muttered, trying to brush it off. Nothing was there, but a faint tingling lingered on her chest where she thought she saw the pendant. She lay on the bed, consumed by thoughts of the strange experience.

Before she could process it further, Lizzie felt Miles' hand on the small of her back and jumped. She hadn't heard him come in. She rolled over on her side, meeting his stare. He caressed one of her hands in his as he spoke.

"I have to go home tonight," he said. His hand moved up her arm and reached her hair, and he gently stroked it.

"Of course," Lizzie said. "I don't expect you to stay with me all the time."

"But I want to," Miles said. "I would stay here all the time if you wanted me to." He didn't give Lizzie a chance to respond. "But my mom needs me."

"Then you should go home," Lizzie said.

Lizzie hadn't met Miles' mom yet or any of his family. The rule was that Lizzie would meet them when she said "I love you" back to Miles. Lizzie and Miles both agreed on it.

"I'll be back tomorrow to pick you up for the concert," he said. "And I'll pick up your car on Friday."

He pulled her in close to him, so their bodies were touching. Then he ran his fingers over her lips.

"I know you can't say it yet," Miles said tenderly. This was the Miles she knew, the one others didn't see, the version of him she *could* say those three words to. "But I want you to know how scared I am to lose you."

"You're not going to lose me," Lizzie said, caressing his face. She kissed his nose, and he lowered his head.

He let out a low, audible sigh, something of defeat.

"Please, don't abandon me, Lizzie," he whispered.

"Miles, why would I abandon you?"

His split-second pause of silence felt like hours.

"Because we both know I'm not good enough for you."

"Where is this coming from, Miles?"

Miles shook his head. "It's nothing." Then he whispered, "Without you, there is no me."

Lizzie placed her lips on his, and then he pulled back.

"I have to go," he said.

"Yeah, okay," Lizzie replied.

"I love you, Lizzie."

"Thank you," she replied, a familiar tightening coiling in her stomach, and the little voice in her head that repeated, "Not yet."

chapter 9

"Nobody said anything about boy bands," Brody said.

He said it half-jokingly, half-seriously. It's not that he didn't like their music, but he would rather go to a Swift concert than watch four old dudes dancing around like they were teenagers.

"Lizzie and Miles will be there tonight," Nunez said. "So, you're going."

"Alone?"

"No. Shay is going with you."

"What are we supposed to be…husband and wife or something?" Brody asked.

Shay grimaced. "In your dreams, Brody."

"Hey now," Dale replied.

"This is serious," Nunez replied. "Juarez said that Miles returned to the farmhouse last night. He had an argument with Remy Baker. Juarez couldn't tell me everything, but he says Lizzie isn't safe, and Miles is being cornered from a different angle."

"What does that mean?" Brody asked.

"That it's not just Ludwig and Remy Baker that we have

to worry about. Someone else is involved and pulling the strings here."

"How? Why?" Shay asked.

Nunez shrugged.

"But Miles isn't going to hand her over," Brody said. "Right?"

"Like I said, Juarez didn't tell me everything, but whoever is in charge just threatened Miles Corrigan enough to make him scared. And scared people do rash things."

"So what exactly am I doing at this concert?" Brody asked.

"Just keep tabs on Lizzie, make sure Miles doesn't hand her off to a Baker or cart her off to the farmhouse. Or take off to Mexico."

Nunez nodded goodbye, and Brody listened to the click of her heels as she exited the warehouse. Dale sat on his computer—he was attempting to hack the Bakers' computer systems.

"Dale, doesn't your grandmother still live in Mexico City?" Brody asked.

"She does," he said, not looking up from the computer. "But she still doesn't forgive you for letting the dog eat the last tamale, so she won't be helping you should you need to cross the border."

"It fell out of my hand, Dale."

"That isn't what she said." Dale changed the subject. "Oh, the Bakers are good. Whoever they're working with might even be better than me."

"No one is better than you, honey," Shay said flatly as she perused documents on her laptop. Brody sat with his elbow on one of the fold-out tables, twirling a pencil and occasionally tapping the eraser on the table.

"Brody," Nunez called. "Can I see you for a moment?"

Brody met Nunez in the hallway, who kept her voice low as she spoke.

"Juarez told me some information about Miles a while ago. I didn't want to share it then, but I think it's important now. The reason the Bakers have been lenient with Miles is that Remy Baker is his stepfather. Remy's twin brother, Ludwig, is the loose cannon, and Remy has had to talk him out of killing Miles on numerous occasions. But Juarez said last night that even Remy seemed frightened and warned Miles to back out of it, bring Lizzie in, or they all might die."

"Do you think Ludwig's about to burn the whole house down?" Brody asked. "Or is something else going on?"

"I think someone else is controlling the operation. And whoever it is, has scared one of the most feared mafia bosses on the East Coast. My gut tells me it's about more than the inheritance. It's about that pendant."

"Well, that's not good," Brody said, considering the implication.

"At some point, we're going to have to push this along. You'll wait for my signal, but when I say to, we'll have to get Lizzie to the inn however we can and as quickly as we can. Do you understand?"

"I hear you."

"Now do what you have to do to get ready for tonight." Nunez started to walk away. "And tell that Finn Broder, I still have his poster."

chapter 10

"Right this way," a bouncer said, escorting Lizzie and Miles into the ultra-famous, yet small, Philadelphia venue. Sandalwood Owl was the first concert Lizzie ever attended with Misty when they were fourteen. Lizzie could still remember her stepfather Dan driving them to the Tweeter Center; they each wore a Finn Broder crop top and spent an abnormally long time fixing their hair in high ponytails. Tonight, Lizzie's look was much different. She wore high-waist jeans with a bare-shoulder bodysuit. Instead of a ponytail, her hair fell in soft waves down to the middle of her back.

Sandalwood Owl had sold out in the first hour that tickets went on sale, leaving lots of disappointed fans. But Miles was able to get tickets; he worked in wealth management and dealt with some of the richest people around, and there were perks to having that kind of privilege.

Miles and Lizzie grabbed a drink at the bar just as the concert began. It was standing room only, and as Lizzie listened to the music, she was suddenly transported back to that time when she was fourteen, and Misty and she were giggling girls, crushing on Broder. Lizzie's excitement didn't last long, as a pang of guilt washed over her; she was supposed to be at Misty's house tonight. Not only had she ditched Misty, but she had come to the one concert featuring their favorite group. Lizzie knew she would have been equally disappointed if Misty went to the concert without her.

Lizzie didn't expect Miles to have the same enthusiasm as Misty would have, but when she glanced over to see him scanning the crowd, not invested in the concert at all, she couldn't help but feel annoyed.

"What's wrong?" she asked.

"Nothing," he said casually.

"You're not having fun."

"I *am* having fun."

Miles' intense eyes continued to scan the room for something, but of what, Lizzie had no idea.

"You're looking around like you're a bodyguard protecting his client."

"No, I'm not," he said over the music. "I'm just enjoying myself."

He produced a tight-lipped smile and wrapped his arms around Lizzie. The guilt of being at the concert churned her stomach, and soon a nauseous feeling overtook her. She needed a minute to gather her thoughts, and she didn't want to burst into tears in front of Miles.

"I'm going to the ladies' room," Lizzie said, attempting to wiggle free.

"I'll come with you," Miles said.

"Don't be silly."

His grip tightened around Lizzie.

"Miles, you have to let me go."

"Wherever you go, I'm coming with you."

"Why are you being like this all of a sudden?" Lizzie pressed.

"Like what?"

"Overprotective. I'm just going to the bathroom, Miles."

"I'm not being overprotective. I'm just... Fine. *Go.*"

"It's okay," Lizzie said, squeezing his arm to reassure him.

The lines between his brow reappeared, and he turned away from Lizzie as if to hold himself back from saying something he might regret later.

"Everything is okay," she repeated.

Was it okay, though? Lizzie wondered as she headed off to the bathroom. She made her way through the crowd, not looking back at Miles, even though she could feel his glare burning into her back.

The only conclusion she could come up with for his behavior was that he was afraid of something. Of what? She had no idea. But the nausea was turning rancid, and there was a chance she was going to hug the porcelain throne. Miles didn't know fear, so if he was afraid, did that mean she should be afraid also?

And if so, of what?

chapter 11

By the time Brody and Shay arrived at the venue, the line to get in wrapped around the block. Thanks to Nunez, Shay and Brody walked through the back entrance. Nunez said to text her with any problems, but Brody hoped he wouldn't have to. *Smooth, easy night, then go home,* he thought. He was supposed to keep out of Lizzie's way as best he could. "Don't interfere," Nunez had said. And he hoped the night would go exactly that way, especially since Lizzie made him nervous, and if he saw her with her murderer boyfriend, it would take every bit of willpower he had not to tell Lizzie how awful Miles was. His phone buzzed, and he checked his text messages.

Nina: *Can we talk?*

He clicked his phone shut. What the hell did she want? The answer was no. They could not talk. He wasn't inviting her back into his life.

Nina: *Have you heard from Hemmy? I haven't heard from him in days. I'm worried.*

"He probably left you for some other woman because he's a backstabbing asshat," is what he wanted to say but he would never say it; he was angry with Nina still, but he wouldn't disrespect her... at least not to her face.

Brody: *Haven't. Sorry.*

Nina: *Can I call you, please?*

Brody: *I'm busy, Nina.*

Brody followed Lizzie from a healthy distance as Shay kept an eye on Miles. She was walking through the double doors toward the common area, and Brody had a feeling he knew where she was headed.

"Bathroom," he said softly into his earpiece. "What's Miles up to?"

"Looking around. He looks angry. Just pulled out his phone and texted someone. Might follow her."

"Okay. I'll keep my distance. You keep yours. Let me know if he comes my way."

"Understood."

Lizzie entered the bathroom, and Brody dipped into a hallway leading to the green room. From where he stood, he could see the bathroom clearly, and he leaned against the wall pretending to look at his phone. He didn't want her to see him, but he needed to stay close.

Enough people were in this common area that Lizzie wouldn't see Brody. He surveyed the crowd from his vantage point; most of the Sandalwood Owl fans were aged 40-50, but there were a bunch of teenagers, too. How was it that some crowds could be as diverse as could be but still look uniform? That was how Sandalwood Owl fans were. He couldn't explain it exactly, but it was almost as if their lighthearted, catchy music brainwashed these fans into their cult.

Still, the uniformness was why Brody went on high alert when he saw a man scuttle toward the bathroom. The man was in his thirties, tall, dark-haired… definitely not Miles. He was pacing back and forth like he was waiting for something or someone, and Brody knew this guy was up to no good.

Lizzie exited the bathroom a few minutes later, and as suspected, the man cornered her, pinning her against the wall. Anyone looking may have felt he was her horny boyfriend. Besides, everyone seemed consumed in their own worlds, oblivious to the situation playing out right in front of them.

Who was this guy? Was he one of the Bakers? Brody couldn't tell, but Miles was nowhere to be found, and he could sense that Lizzie was uncomfortable—the way her eyes darted around, her shallow breaths that tensed her shoulders, making her chest rise and fall unevenly. She was scared.

Brody watched from a distance, assessing the man and Lizzie's every move.

Don't intervene unless necessary…

Nunez's words rang in his head. But restraining himself from intervening was difficult. He'd been raised to protect women, something his father instilled in him since childhood.

Don't go over there, he told himself. *Not yet.* Lizzie hadn't seen him, and he wasn't sure she'd remember him anyway, as they'd only met once. He shifted from one foot to the other, his hand over his lips, antsy, waiting. All he needed was for this guy to do one thing. One. Thing.

When the guy closed his hand around Lizzie's wrist and pulled, Brody made his move. Nunez could yell at him later. He didn't care. He wasn't going to let this asshole hurt Lizzie, the woman he was hired to protect. There was no time to alert Shay. He had to act now. Within seconds, he reached Lizzie and did the first thing that came to his mind.

"Lizzie?" he said, looking from the man to her. The prick

tried to pull her away, but Brody put his hand on Lizzie's bare shoulder and gripped firmly enough for her to know she wasn't going anywhere.

She was safe.

A flicker of something dark crossed the man's face as Lizzie pulled herself away and into Brody's arms. Whoever he was, oddly, he wasn't willing to make a scene. Brody wrapped his arms around Lizzie in a tight embrace, glaring over her at the man as if to say, "Take one step closer; I dare you."

Brody held Lizzie close, so tightly that there was barely any breath between them. He could feel her chest against his, her deep breaths, her fast-beating heart. Brody wasn't going to let go, so the guy had to. And he did. Then the man hurried out of the double exit doors and into the night. He disappeared as quickly as he had appeared, but Brody didn't let go of Lizzie. He held her close and whispered in her ear.

"You're safe. He's gone. I've got you."

He could feel her trembling against him. Her warm amber-vanilla perfume drifted toward him, and he drank it in, savoring the sweet aroma for only a few seconds before reality pulled him back.

Someone had tried to kidnap her. If he had any doubts before, tonight had confirmed that Lizzie was *definitely* in trouble.

When he was sure her attacker was gone, he pulled back from her slightly, tipped her chin upward, and gazed into her warm brown eyes. Once again, he saw her pained look of loss and loneliness. He knew that feeling all too well.

"What the fuck is this?" he heard a voice say, and he knew it was Miles Corrigan without even looking up. In the heat of the moment, he'd forgotten to tell Shay what was going on. If he had, she would have alerted him that Miles was headed his way. When Brody finally did look at Miles, he saw a creature incarnate, a seething brute, ready to kill for what he thought was his. Lizzie, still shaking, transferred from Brody's arms into Miles', but Miles didn't let up on Brody. "Why were you touching my girlfriend?"

His woman. His *possession*. If only she knew who Miles was. A *killer*. Brody had the choice at that moment to tell Lizzie the truth and pull her away from Miles right then and there. But he thought of Nunez—how angry she'd be with him—and he decided if he was going to help Lizzie, he couldn't have Miles nipping at his heels every step of the way. Or worse, pulling Lizzie away.

Brody put his hands up in a surrender position.

"Some guy got handsy. I just stepped in to help."

"It was him," she heard Lizzie tell Miles. Her voice trembled as she spoke, and Brody wanted to run to her, fold her back into his arms, and keep her safe. "The guy from campus. I think he… he was going to kidnap me." Her eyes met Brody's again, the invisible thread connecting them growing brighter, thicker. "If Brody hadn't stepped in…"

"Oh," Miles said, backing off Brody, but still with narrowed eyes that signaled he was pissed off and ready to fight. He scanned the room. "Where the fuck did he go?"

"He left," Brody replied, signaling to the double doors.

Miles was his enemy, but the guy who tried to hurt Lizzie tonight was their common enemy. *The enemy of my enemy,* Brody thought. Befriending Miles was one avenue to explore, even though he hated him.

Brody tried to make eye contact with Lizzie and read the emotions brimming in her eyes. Why was he having such a hard time watching her with Miles? He hardly knew her, but he had felt something when she was in his arms—that need to protect her again, yes, but something more. This palpable connection, like she was already his, had been his for thousands of years before this lifetime. He wanted to be the one to wrap her in his arms and tell her everything would be okay. Her eyes met his again, those pools of honey stirring a flutter in his chest. But quickly, he was drawn away by Lizzie rubbing her wrist.

"Let me see your wrist," Brody said gently. He could feel Miles seething next to him.

"It's fine," Lizzie said.

"What happened to your wrist?" Miles demanded. "What did he do to your fucking arm?!"

"Nothing. He just tugged me, like tried to pull me away."

"Please, Lizzie," Brody said, holding out his hand. Gentle. That's what she needed. She had enough demands and arrogance with Miles in her life. He kept his eyes fixed on hers, ignoring Miles' trigger reactions.

The way she rubbed it over her long sleeve suggested it hurt. She lifted her sleeve to reveal a set of four red indentations. Not nail marks, but a burn.

"There you are, *bro*," Shay said. *Brother? That's what she was going with?* She widened her eyes as if to say she'd seen everything.

"I'm going to fucking kill this mother fucker," Miles said. Miles was pacing now, and Brody could see he was like a kettle ready to whistle.

"You poor thing," Shay said, reacting to the marks on Lizzie's wrist. Directing her attention to Miles, trying to calm him down, she asked, "What the hell happened?"

Miles relayed the story, and Shay kept his attention by asking questions so Brody could get Lizzie alone for a few seconds.

"Are you going to be all right?" Brody asked Lizzie, keeping his eyes fixed on hers. He wanted one reason to stay, one reason to remove Miles from the equation and take Lizzie somewhere with him.

"I'll be fine," Lizzie said, returning his gaze. "Miles will calm down. Look, I'm so thankful you were here. Really."

"Okay, well, I expect you to still meet me tomorrow morning. One little attack isn't going to get you out of doing this project."

Lizzie smiled, but it didn't reach her eyes. Meanwhile, Miles had calmed down, but he was glaring at Brody.

"We should go," Brody said, sensing that if they stuck around longer, Miles was going to pick a fight. The less he was around Miles, the better. He didn't want to "accidentally" punch the dick in the face.

"Yeah," Shay agreed. "Good idea."

"I was so worried," Miles said, wrapping Lizzie in his arms with almost crushing force. "I should've never let you out of my sight tonight. That's on me."

"It's okay," Lizzie said, and then, turning to Brody. "Thank you. Again."

"No problem. Anyone would do it."

Brody wasn't so sure about that, but he needed Miles to think it wasn't personal.

Nina: *Please, Brody.*

Another text message had buzzed through, and then a phone call. And then another. When Shay and Brody were safely in the car, Shay eyed Brody suspiciously.

"New girlfriend?" she asked.

"Old baggage."

"Hmm," Shay said, sitting back in her seat. "Nina."

"Yep."

"What the hell does she want?"

"Oh, you know," Brody said, "Hemmy got bored like he always does. Seems he's disappeared."

"You think it's serious?"

"Going to bet it's not." Brody didn't want to talk about

Hemmy, so he changed the subject. "Think Nunez will be angry I intervened tonight?"

"Was there any other way?"

Brody shrugged.

"I didn't think so at the moment," he replied. "So, I'm prepared for her to chew me out."

"You should know I did try to warn you Miles was coming your way. Didn't hear any confirmation."

"I was caught up in the moment. It's all good."

"Brody, can I be honest with you?" Shay said. Those words were never the start of a good conversation. He didn't bother responding; Shay was going to "be honest" whether he wanted her to or not. "You're putting too much blame on yourself, not just for what happened to your uncle, but what happened between you and Nina."

"Nah." He deserved the blame for at least that; no one would tell him otherwise.

"When Hemmy decided to put himself in harm's way, you did what any best friend would do. And your uncle did what any good uncle would do. Both of you were heroic."

"Tell that to my father," Brody replied, a tittering laugh escaping his lips. "He still blames me. And Nina blames me for our marriage. They're not wrong. I wasn't there for Nina. I wasn't."

Shay shifted uncomfortably in her seat.

"The one factor in this whole situation is *Hemmy*, Brody. He's the one who defied Nunez's orders. He's the one who put himself in harm's way, knowing that his best friend would come to the rescue. And he's the one who slept with his best friend's wife without a second thought."

He gave her a side glance before focusing his eyes back on the road. The bright lights from opposing traffic shone on Shay's dewy brown skin.

"What are you saying?"

"I'm *saying,*" she drew out the word, "he owes you an apology, Brody. Look, we can't control what happens to us. There's a good chance your uncle was one job away from suffering the same fate. But, in all of this, all of your dark days, all the times you blamed yourself, not once did Hemmy reach out and say, 'I'm sorry.' To me, there's only one person to blame for what happened."

"It doesn't matter anymore," Brody said. "What's done is done. It's just time for me to move on, and that begins with not taking Nina's calls."

"Fair enough," Shay said. "Fair. Enough."

Brody's thoughts drifted back to the incident at the concert.

The marks on Lizzie's arm.

Maybe he was reading too much into it. Would he have felt the same about them if Nunez had never mentioned the relic? Probably not. He would have thought the guy had a damn good grip on Lizzie's wrist and caused a rug burn or…a sleeve burn in her case.

But what if it wasn't his grip that did it?

What if it was something else that caused that burn?

Something older.

Like magic from another realm.

He shook off the thought. No one had found the relic yet, and the portal hadn't opened yet. That was the point of all of this. Still, he pondered whether or not he should tell Nunez what happened. If there was a chance, even a slight one, that Lizzie's attacker wasn't human, then Lizzie was in a lot more danger than they realized. And not just Lizzie… all of humanity.

chapter 12

Lizzie had lied to Brody, told him Miles would calm down, and everything would be okay. But she had no idea if that was true. Lizzie had never seen Miles so unhinged. Her intuition had told her, time and time again, that one day she would see the side of Miles he tried so desperately to hide, and now, that day was here.

Lizzie and Miles were silent on the way home. She could see he was still fuming—his knuckles gripped the steering wheel so tightly they were almost white. She rubbed her wrist. The marks were quickly fading, and she assumed the burn came from the fabric of her shirt rubbing against her skin.

Adrenaline still coursed through her, and she felt her body shake slightly. Her stalker knew she would be at that concert and was willing to attempt to kidnap her in front of so many people. Her intuition knocked again, letting her know this stalker wasn't some rando; her father's warning popped into her head.

Lizzie, look up.

What had her father done? Whatever it was, it must have been awful, and someone was out for blood to make her dad pay. She cursed being his spawn at that moment—wished she could tell whoever wanted retribution that he should pick on someone or something her father *actually* cared about.

Because it wasn't her.

"I'm so mad at you, Lizzie," Miles said, jolting her out of her thoughts.

"What?" Lizzie had expected Miles' anger to be directed toward her stalker, not her. "You're mad at me?"

"Not just mad. Fucking furious."

"What did *I* do?"

"I told you to stay by my side, but you just *had* to break away."

"I went to the *bathroom*, Miles. I hardly call that breaking away."

"You forced me to give you space because you're so damn stubborn." He hit the steering wheel, making her jump. "I should have followed you."

"No," Lizzie said. Was he serious right now? "I'm sorry, but that's ridiculous."

"Is it? You could have gotten hurt, Lizzie. You could have been kidnapped. Normal people don't have stalkers that show up at multiple locations…"

"How is this my fault, Miles?"

"You're irresponsible."

"Irresponsible?"

"You don't listen…"

"Who do you think you are?!"

"FUCK!"

He banged the steering wheel again, and Lizzie drew in a deep breath. She was one more shitty comment away from telling Miles to pull over. She would rather walk home from Philadelphia than deal with his irrationality and outbursts.

For the first time, Lizzie didn't feel safe with Miles. He was driving erratically, had sped up so much that they were going 80 in a 45. She wanted to yell at him, but didn't want him to do anything else crazy.

"Miles," she said, attempting to calm him down. "I know you're upset. So am I. But nothing happened to me. Brody was there, thank God, and…"

"Yeah, of course he was. And you fell right into his arms."

"What is your problem?" she asked, throwing all her attempts to stay calm out the window. "Would it have been better if he didn't help me?"

"You wouldn't need protection if you weren't so helpless and pathetic."

His words cut like a knife. Lizzie didn't grasp how much his comment angered her until a few seconds later when she realized her mouth was still agape.

"Is that what you think about me?"

"Right now? Yes."

Lizzie scoffed. The sting of his words matched the tears pooling in her eyes. Her voice cracked when she spoke. "Well, it's nice to know you think so highly of me."

"There are women who can defend themselves, Lizzie, *strong* women, and then there are women who need defending."

"Screw you, Miles. I don't need you to defend me. Or anyone for that matter."

"Tonight was a perfect example of just how wrong you are."

Lizzie shook her head. His insults were too much for her. No woman wanted to be viewed this way, and Lizzie didn't think she was some weak, helpless damsel. But Miles had said it, was unapologetic about how he felt, and it made Lizzie feel like an ant under a giant's boot.

They didn't speak for the rest of the ride home, nor when they reached her apartment. Once she was ready for bed,

Miles was already asleep, or pretending to be, which was fine with her. She was too angry with him to say anything. They had argued before, but this fight felt different. Usually, the dispute was over in minutes. Most of the time, it was she who did the apologizing.

Still, this fight was their first major one, and she wouldn't be the first to say "sorry." Not after what he'd said. As she lay in bed, she realized she hadn't felt this angry in years and wondered how long she had stuffed this rage inside. Maybe she and Miles were the same—that fury brimming below Miles' composed exterior matched her own.

A text message buzzed through right before she placed her phone on her nightstand.

Brody: *Are you okay?*

She hesitated before answering. Did Brody also think she was pathetic? She put the thought out of her mind. This was a single occurrence. Brody didn't know her—he was helping out in a real threat instance and probably would have done that for anyone.

Lizzie: *Yes. Thank you again.*

Brody: *You got it. We old people need to look out for each other, you know?*

His comment brought the slightest smile to her lips, but she was too upset about her fight with Miles to respond further, so she placed her phone on her nightstand and quickly fell into a deep sleep.

There she was. The bright, amber eyes, the big smile. "We'll get tea after work."

"Thanks for the ride, Mom."

"That's what moms are for."

Lizzie's mom winked.

Suddenly, they were in the car.

Laughter filled the car as they drove along in the soft-falling snow. Lizzie felt the temperature dropping quickly, even the heat from the car was not keeping them fully warm.

Then... impact.

The slowing down of space and time; her mother's face turning from laughter to fear as the car spun out of control.

Hot tea burned Lizzie's skin. The blackout. Her mother, a soft whisper...

"It's coming. Lizzie, I'm scared."

Lizzie woke with tears streaming down her cheeks. The dawn light sprinkled through the windows, shedding a bluish hue onto her bed. She hadn't had a dream about her mom in so long, and she felt that familiar, intolerable sensation surge from her stomach and catch in her throat. She needed her mom right now, more than anyone.

Miles was already up when she woke; her dream had halted her memory of their fight. But as the memory of what happened returned, she felt a deep wave of sadness. The feeling didn't leave her when she showered; nor did it leave her when she walked out of the house and down a few blocks to Hissock's tavern, her stepfather's restaurant.

She told Misty she would meet her at the tavern at 9 a.m. Lizzie had suggested Hissock's, not because she wanted to be at her place of work on her day off, but because she felt safe there. Between what happened last night and her dream, she needed that feeling right now. Knowing her stepfather, Dan, was in the back office and she was only two blocks from her apartment made her feel a little more protected from the recent chaos.

As Lizzie left the apartment, she saw Miles' car was gone, but hers was parked out front. Even though she was still furious with him, she felt thankful he had made good on his word. With everything going on, she could feel her anxiety growing like water dumping quickly into a bucket, and she couldn't afford for it to overflow—she knew how destructive that force was to her happiness. What she needed was to spend time with people who made her feel happy and loved and to do things that kept her grounded.

chapter 13

Lizzie bit the inside of her lip as she picked at her eggs and French toast. Was Misty going to say anything?

"I can't say I'm sorry enough," Lizzie said.

"But you know it's not about that," replied Misty. She sat with her arms folded, her back against the red seat of the oaken high-back booth. The corners of her thin lips tipped slightly downward in a permanent frown. Misty gazed at her food, at her phone, out the window—everywhere except into Lizzie's eyes. Anyone in New Jersey knew this face was called "resting bitch," and it could mean a girl was angry, she was lost in thought about something, or it was a day that ended in "y." In this case, Misty was angry.

"I messed up, Misty."

"This is like the fifth time in a few months. And whatever. I get it. Your boyfriend surprises you with some experience that's more fun than hanging with your friends..." Misty rolled her eyes. "He's more fun than me. You can just say it."

"Stop."

"The thing that gets me, Lizzie, is that it was a Sandalwood Owl concert. Our boys. Finn freakin' Broder, Lizzie. How would you feel if I did that to you?"

"I know," Lizzie replied in a low, soft voice. "If it makes you feel any better, it was the worst night of my life."

"That doesn't."

"And the shit train just keeps on running," Lizzie said under her breath. Then she let out a deep sigh. "I was wrong, Misty. I was. And I see it now. I hear you. I'm not going to do that to you again. I love you too much, and your friendship is too special to me."

Misty didn't respond right away, but when she did, she replied, "Okay. Apology accepted."

"Thank you."

Unavoidable tears stung Lizzie's eyes, and she dabbed them with her napkin.

"Okay, I didn't mean to make you cry or anything," Misty said. "I just wanted you to beg a little for my forgiveness."

"I'm not crying because of that."

"Oh, no. What's wrong?"

"Everything."

Lizzie dropped her fork onto her plate and folded her arms across her chest. She wasn't hungry, not even for Dan's famous French toast.

"Okay, well, start with the first thing that's bothering you."

"I had a dream about my mom last night." Lizzie looked around the tavern. She wanted to be sure Dan wasn't going to pop up out of nowhere. He still struggled with her mom's death, too, even though it had been almost seven years, and she didn't want to upset him should he overhear her story. "I haven't had one in a long time, maybe not for a year or two."

"What was it about?"

"The accident." Lizzie leaned back against the booth and gazed out the window, trying to hide the tears that trickled down her cheeks. "Felt those same emotions tormenting me in my sleep, like they're hidden in there, just waiting to erupt. It felt the same way as it did the day it happened. When I woke up, I… felt like it was the day after."

"I'm sorry, Lizzie." Misty offered wide, sympathetic eyes.

"It's fine," Lizzie said, wiping her eyes and fixing her gaze on Misty. "It's not just that. Miles and I got into a huge fight last night. I've never been so angry. I'm starting to realize that this anger has been inside me for a long time."

"What happened?" Misty asked, her face stern.

Lizzie relayed everything that happened, from the first encounter on campus with the strange man to Brody saving her at the concert to what Miles had said about her. Lizzie knew how Misty would react, and right now, she needed the support of her friend.

"Ew." Misty scowled, a deep crease forming between her eyes. "How dare he say those things to you."

A moment of silence passed between them before Lizzie asked,

"Well, am I?"

"Are you what?"

"Am I some helpless, weak, damsel in distress?" Lizzie asked. "Am I pathetic?"

Misty leaned forward and pointed her finger at Lizzie.

"Hell no." Misty didn't curse, so Lizzie knew she was furious. She spoke in a low, animated tone. "You are Lizzie *freaking* Degan. Your father is an assassin who hunts bad, bad people and takes them out. You were trained by the best. You're no damsel. You're a warrior, and don't you forget that."

Lizzie couldn't help but smile. She and Misty looked at each other and then broke out into a fit of laughter.

"It's nice to see you two here and laughing," Dan interrupted. "Reminds me of old times."

He had come out of the back to say hello.

"Mr. Ortiz, your French toast is surely the best in the state."

"You're too kind, Misty," Dan said. He turned his attention to Lizzie. "I hate to ask you about work-related things on your day off, Lizzie Bear, but is there any chance you can come in on Monday morning? I know you have class, so you can leave early, but Pauline is taking her grandmother out for the day. Says she isn't doing well and would like to spend some time with her."

"Yeah, of course," Lizzie said.

"Perfect. Thank you. All right, girls, enjoy the rest of your day."

"Bye, Dan. Love you," Lizzie said.

"Bye, Mr. Ortiz!" Misty seconded.

"Love you, too."

"Thank God for Dan," Lizzie said after he walked away.

"The man is a saint… to raise an assassin's daughter."

Lizzie laughed as Misty continued.

"I think it's funny he still calls you Lizzie Bear."

The rest of Misty and Lizzie's conversation felt like old times. They laughed as they discussed their favorite reality show drama and shared excitement when Misty announced that she and her husband, Frank, were officially trying for children. When Lizzie checked her watch and saw it was 10:30, she told Misty she had to leave.

"Have fun," Misty said. "Don't make Miles too jealous."

Lizzie wouldn't dare. Miles could be sweet, even tender, but when he felt threatened, something darker surfaced. Once, when Miles and Lizzie had been in the middle of a phone argument, she hung up on him, and he didn't speak to her for two days. No phone call. No texts. She hated to think of what he'd do if he thought she was messing around.

She and Misty said their goodbyes, and Lizzie was off to school in good spirits. The energy around her had shifted—

less dense, weightless. Time with her best friend made her feel lighter. But her stomach twisted at the thought that these days, she mostly felt a heavy feeling when she was with Miles.

Speaking of… he hadn't texted her at all. She needed a break from him, didn't want to hear from him right this minute anyway. She turned her phone off as an act of defiance. He shouldn't think he could reach her whenever he wanted. She wasn't a precious flower that needed protection.

Misty was right.

She was Lizzie FREAKING Degan, the assassin's daughter. And she had been trained to, at the least, hide from the bad guys.

chapter 14

Brody couldn't believe he was actually researching Scottish lore on fairies and elves. Or was it *faeries?* Was he researching Tinkerbell or ancient demon-sprites that cursed bloodlines? Maybe it was both.

The overabundance of information gave him a splitting headache right between the eyes, and none of it brought him any closer to answers about some hidden world. Earlier that morning, he met Nunez at the warehouse and informed her about what had happened the night before. He described Lizzie's wrist burn and questioned if there was *any* chance the portal had already been opened and immortal beings were wreaking havoc on Earth, or at least in the tri-state area.

"I just don't know," Nunez had replied. "But I don't believe so. I really don't. You said Miles didn't see the attacker."

"No, he didn't."

"Then it's possible this guy works for the Bakers."

"Yeah, probably." Brody shrugged.

"We need to eliminate that possibility for sure before we start looking into otherworldly issues."

"How am I supposed to find out if that guy works for the Bakers?"

"I'm sure you'll figure something out," was all Nunez said.

Nunez's answer should have satisfied Brody, but it didn't. So here he was at the library researching faeries on a Friday. He checked the time on his phone before picking out the next book. He had about twenty minutes before Lizzie would be here. Twenty minutes to research the elusive Fae, elves, and beasts like some schmuck gearing up for a mythical creature convention. But first, he had to acknowledge his four new text messages. Without looking at his phone, he knew who sent at least one of them.

Text message one (last night, 11:45 p.m.):
Nina: *I get why you're ignoring me. I do. I hurt you. I don't deserve your respect. But if you cared about me at all, in the time we were together, could you at least CALL ME back?*

Text message two (just now):
Nina: *Damn it, Brody. You're not the guy I married. You're turning into such an ass…just like the rest.*

Text message three:
Roberto: You coming in at 4 today?

Text message four:
Jessica: *Just wondering if you can still watch the kids on Sunday? FYI, DAD WILL BE HERE.*

He replied to his sister, Jessica, and to his boss, Roberto. Yes, he could watch his niece and nephew on Sunday. His stomach lurched as he typed back to her. She was going on a date, finally, almost three years after her husband left her for his receptionist. But the uneasiness Brody felt had nothing to do with his sister dating again. The contention between Brody and his dad was still thick, and Sunday meant navigating it. Brody's dad still only addressed him with grunts, yeses, and noes ever since his uncle's murder, and Brody was getting used to it.

His second text message reply was to Roberto. Yes, he would be in at 4 p.m. Nunez had permitted Brody to tell Roberto he was contracted for a special ops job, but Brody wasn't allowed to reveal any of the details. Brody's shifts were reduced to once a week, and thankfully, he'd trained his team well enough to run the place without him. Still, Roberto wanted him to meet with the team once a week and discuss any issues they may have with clients.

He stared at Nina's messages, debating whether he would reply. How was he supposed to let what happened with Nina go if she was still text-messaging him? And to her point, of course, he wasn't the same person she married—that guy died when he found out his wife was screwing his best friend and then left him for said best friend. Just thinking about the whole ordeal fired him up, and he started typing.

Brody: *What do you even want me to do, Nina? You and I both know how Hemmy is. Did you think he wasn't going to do to you what he does to all the ladies? You want me to clean up his mess. Not going to do it. I don't owe you anything anymore.*

What goes around comes back around, he typed, and then he erased it. He didn't need to go one hundred percent asshole on her. He told himself he didn't care if anything happened to Hemmy, that's how deep-seated his anger was. Yet, there was a part of him that wondered if he would ever be the guy who truly didn't care.

"Fuck," Brody said under his breath as he scrolled through his contacts. He was going to help because that's just who he was, and it made him want to punch a wall. But he didn't tell Nina yet; he didn't want to give her the satisfaction of thinking he was doing it because she asked him to.

Brody found Hemmy's number and wondered why he hadn't deleted it already. He dialed, and the phone rang until it went to voicemail. So, he sent a text.

Brody: *Let me know you're alive, and we'll be done with it.*

Hemmy hated Brody, too. He saw the bubbles show up, then disappear, show up again, then disappear. Finally, Hemmy answered, but only with a thumbs-up emoji.

Brody shook his head. He wasn't getting in the middle of this. Nina deserved whatever she got. Brody had done his due diligence to make sure his ex-friend wasn't dead. He contemplated not telling Nina, but that pull in his gut told him it wasn't the right thing to do. Fuck his stupid conscience.

Brody: *Hemmy is fine.*

Nina didn't respond right away, but when she did, she wrote, *I'm sorry, Brody. I'm sorry I called you an ass. You're not. And I'm just sorry in general. But I know you aren't ready to forgive me.*

He wanted to tell her he was working on forgiving her but decided not to. The truth was, he might never be able to.

Brody picked up his next book, *A History of Faerie Lore, Culture, and Origin.* After reading a few paragraphs of the book, Brody realized many people out there truly believed that faeries were real. Faeries were magical, ethereal, and mischievous. They might be spirits or demons. They were rooted in the elements. The information alone in this one book was enough to make a believer out of a poor soul desperate for some connection to another realm. It was too much to process, but Brody did have a few thoughts.

What if there was another world out there?

A hidden civilization.

What if they're already here?

And...

What if they're dangerous?

chapter 15

"What are you reading?"

Brody nearly dropped the heavy book, caught it just in time before it fell onto his foot. Lizzie stood in front of him, her brown hair falling in waves over her maroon sweater. He hadn't heard her enter. Had he been that engrossed in the material?

"This? It's a…" *What the hell was he going to say that would get him out of this one?*

"I love fairy stuff," Lizzie said, a grin spreading across her face. She took out the case file and placed it on the table.

"It's not for me…" Brody defended. "I'm not reading this."

"Looks like you are…reading it. Unless you're a clone of Brody Woods, reading a book he would not read."

"No, I mean, I'm not reading it for me. I'm babysitting my niece on Sunday, and she's obsessed with fairies. I thought I'd learn something because I know she'll fire a ton of questions at me."

Nice save…ya jackass.

"Oh," Lizzie said, nodding her head. "What did you learn?"

"I'm still stuck on whether to spell the word f-a-e-r-i-e or f-a-i-r-y," he said.

"Aren't they interchangeable?" Lizzie asked.

"I think it's the difference between cute wings and blood curses." He gave her a dry smile. "But anyway, I'd much rather work on what we came here to do." His voice became serious. "But first, how are you doing after last night?"

"I'm fine," Lizzie said.

The brightness in her eyes, relaxed shoulders, and that beautiful smile. He believed her. She seemed happy. Genuinely happy.

"Your wrist?"

"It's fine today. No big deal."

"I couldn't help but hear you say that you saw that guy before."

"Yeah, he cornered me here on campus."

"What did he say to you?"

Lizzie recounted the details of her first encounter with her attacker. After listening to what Lizzie told him, Brody still wasn't sure if Lizzie's attacker had something to do with the Bakers or was about something else entirely. It didn't matter. The point was, he knew now she needed him. Miles wouldn't be enough. The Bakers were too powerful, and who knew who or what else was out there looking for Lizzie?

"Well, you're safe as long as I'm around," he said. Without thinking, he placed his hand on hers and felt the softness of her skin beneath his. A raw, physical longing surged through him, and Brody quickly withdrew his hand. He cleared his throat and adjusted himself in his seat as if that would take the feeling away. *Now is not the time*, he tried to argue with his 'other' self. Today, he needed to focus and put the Speakeasy Inn on Lizzie's radar.

Think of anything else, he told himself. *The case. Focus on the case.* He took the file from Lizzie and pretended to read it over. He already knew most of what it contained, thanks to Nunez. The mysterious death at the inn had never been solved, even though authorities had accused Gerald Westin of going insane and clawing Richard Baker to death.

Brody hadn't thought the murder was important. Until now. Maybe he was reading too much into it, but the terminology "human claw marks" stood out to him. Brody had a few ideas about what may have happened, but he hoped he was wrong. He prayed Baker was mauled by a bear, and poor Gerald Westin had been at the wrong place at the wrong time.

If he could only figure out a way to make the inn sound enticing. He wished he could just tell Lizzie that her grandfather, William "Harold" Yates, had been born Oscar Watson, and the speakeasy owner, Paul Watson, was her great-grandfather. But telling her that would raise red flags. She'd wonder why she'd been given this case, and Nunez would have Brody's head. So, he went with an alternative plan. He had to make solving the murder enticing.

He looked up from the file to see Lizzie observing him with wide eyes, pink cheeks, her plump lips slightly parted, and he felt that sensual feeling stir inside of him all over again. She immediately looked away, and he wondered if she felt the same electricity he did. He forced his attention back on the case.

"Dune mentioned this murder was never solved, so I guess we need to determine if Westin was crazy and killed this Baker guy, or if Baker went into the woods for a piss and got himself mauled by a bear."

Classy, Brody.

"How are we supposed to figure that out?" she asked.

He handed the file back to Lizzie. Their fingers touched again, briefly. This time, she didn't pull away. Neither did he. The first touch was accidental. But this one meant something. That was undeniable.

Brody looked down, forcing himself to focus.

"We could visit the inn. I mean, you could…with me, or not with me, but we could be there at the same time."

Brody realized his social skills were null when it came to Lizzie. But he had to close this deal.

"Interestingly enough, I'm going… next weekend," he continued. "For a wedding. Turns out this place is a popular wedding venue."

"Is it?" Lizzie said. "I've never even heard of it."

"Yeah, it is. My friend Shay's husband can't go, so I offered to be her plus-one."

His lies poured out easily now.

"Is Shay your friend from the concert?"

"Yes." He nodded before adding, "She's like a sister to me."

"You don't seem like a Sandalwood Owl fan," Lizzie remarked.

"I'm not, but Dale and Shay had an extra ticket," Brody lied. He paused before bringing the subject back to the inn. "You should come that weekend." He raised his brows. "We could investigate a murder on Halloween."

He knew he was reaching, knew Miles would never let Lizzie off his leash, but even if Miles was there, Brody would deal with it.

"I don't know if I can go. Miles probably wouldn't want to. Besides, Halloween weekend with a wedding seems busy. I'm sure the inn is already full."

"That's exactly how we want it," Brody said, reaching for any detail that might sway Lizzie's decision. "Busy."

"Why?"

"Well, after I agreed to go to the wedding, I did some research, and I learned that there's an old, preserved library at the inn. You need permission and a key just to enter it. And the original inn owner kept journals. I'm thinking that at least one of them contains something about the murder."

Nunez had snuck in that little detail earlier that morning, and Brody realized it might be the only thing that could get them to the inn.

"Intriguing…but wouldn't the authorities have scoured those journals already looking for evidence?"

"If they could get access to them, which I happen to know most people couldn't."

"And you can?"

"Shay's a detective." *One shred of truth in this whole sea of lies.* "Besides," Brody continued. "The authorities closed the case when they decided Westin was the one who did it."

"And they determined he was insane."

"Yes, but… was he?" Brody asked.

"I guess that's the question we are trying to answer," Lizzie replied. "And you think there are answers about this murder at the Speakeasy Inn?"

"I think there's a lot we can uncover there," Brody said. *Not a lie, either.*

"Well, it certainly sounds like fun. But again, I don't know if I could even get a room."

"I can get you a room," he offered. He didn't want to sound too desperate, but this was his only card trick.

"You can get me a room?"

"Yes. Shay can get you the wedding room rate. They have to fill the block. I think they were panicking that they wouldn't."

Brody L. Woods, pathological liar.

He cursed Nunez in his head for this awful plan. Why did she think this would work?

"I'll think about it," Lizzie said.

"Yeah, of course," Brody replied.

Nunez wanted a "yes" confirmation by today, but Brody wasn't willing to push Lizzie any further. If he had it his way, he would have told her everything. Lizzie was intelligent;

Nunez didn't give her enough credit.

"I think you're right, though," Lizzie said. "I don't think it would be a bad idea to put some distance between my stalker and me."

Little did she know, Brody thought, *just how many people were after her.*

chapter 16

Misty and Lizzie had come up with a code phrase for dilated pupils that glistened with a mixture of excitement and sensual softness. Hungry eyes. Lizzie couldn't help but wonder if Brody had been flashing those eyes at her. *No. I'm just imagining it,* she told herself. *But why are you imagining it? Stop.*

She refused to think about Brody that way, even if he was so damn hot. Even if she'd felt a flutter in her gut after their embrace last night, his muscular body pressed against hers.

No. She pushed any suggestive thoughts about him out of her mind. She was with Miles, and that was that.

Still, she couldn't help but stare at him as he perused the case file. She quickly turned away when she realized she might be the one dishing out the "hungry eyes." When their fingers lingered against each other, she knew the connection was undeniable. The less time she spent with Brody, the better, which was why his proposal for them to go to a remote inn and determine if some insane author mauled a guy to death was ridiculous.

Brody did have a point when it came to Lizzie, though. Besides distancing herself from her attacker, Halloween was coming up next weekend, and she couldn't remember the last time she enjoyed the holiday. Still, she couldn't think about going to the inn with Miles right now. She needed distance from him, too.

Someone knocked on the study door, and Brody answered it—a man in his thirties with blonde hair and blue eyes stood there. He fixed his gaze on Lizzie and then back to Brody.

"How much longer do you think you might be?" the man asked in a British accent.

"I think we have the room until 12:30, so ten more minutes."

"I'll wait out here."

"Guess that guy doesn't realize you *reserve* the study rooms," Brody said.

"I guess not, but I need to go anyway," Lizzie said. She didn't really, but anxiety about her fight with Miles had crept its way back into her mind. She felt guilty for being there with Brody when she should be doing all she could to mend her relationship with Miles. She felt the happy energy from the last few hours slowly fading, knowing that she and Miles would have to talk, eventually.

"I'll walk you to your car," Brody said.

"You don't have to," Lizzie said, unintentionally defensive. But she wanted Brody to know she wasn't what Miles said. Those words still persisted in her mind—*pathetic, weak.*

She knew Brody picked up on her tone when he replied, "You do not need me. I know you're a perfectly capable woman. And I respect that. But if my mother knew I wasn't walking you to the car, especially after last night, she might kill me. So, if you'd like me to live..."

"Fine. For your mom," Lizzie said.

Lizzie and Brody left the study room and headed out of the library into the brittle October air. The skies were on the cusp of turning Jersey gray, which would settle in for the next several months. Lizzie turned on her phone, the cold air numbing her fingertips. Within seconds, she heard endless chimes, signaling a slew of text messages that had come through.

"Someone really wanted to get in touch with you," Brody said as they walked. The air was almost too biting to have a decent conversation.

"Yeah, well, sometimes a girl just needs to be alone."

"I get that," Brody said, "the need to be alone part."

Lizzie cracked a smile and said, "I had fun today."

"Who knew school projects could be fun?" Brody grinned. "The company was okay, too."

Lizzie said goodbye when they reached her car, then got in and shut the door. Brody gave her a wave and then turned back to the sidewalk. He didn't leave right away; she watched him checking around, no doubt making sure her stalker wasn't anywhere in the vicinity. She decided to check her messages before she left, even though she was sure who they were from.

Miles: *Where are you?*

Lizzie didn't respond right away. She didn't want to let go of the happiness she felt today, and the density of Miles' attitude could weigh her down in an instant. She hadn't realized how much she missed hanging with Misty and connecting with people who weren't so serious all the time.

Lizzie: *School. Working on a project.*

Miles: *Alone?*

Lizzie: *with Brody*

Lizzie saw bubbles appear and disappear. She didn't owe Miles an explanation of where she was, but she had always been an honest person who tended to overshare.

Miles: *We'll talk about this when you get home.*

As soon as Lizzie walked inside her apartment, she saw him sitting on the couch. He fixed his eyes on Lizzie with a glare that made her feel like a child about to be disciplined by an angry parent.

The fury that fumed off Miles on this day was the most intense she'd ever seen, but hers was equally palpable. He'd grown so accustomed to her apologizing, even when she wasn't wrong, that she was sure he assumed it would be the same this time. But she had already resolved to stand her ground.

"You turned your phone off," was all Miles said.

"I did."

"You spent the entire day with some guy and turned your fucking phone off."

"I turned my phone off because I wanted to; it had nothing to do with Brody."

"Are you fucking him?"

His accusation infuriated her.

"You're unbelievable, Miles."

"You didn't answer me."

"I do not need to explain myself, yet again, but as I said before, we are working on a school project!"

"Yeah, okay."

Miles leaned his head back against the sofa and closed his eyes. She wasn't going to entertain his jealousy, not when she hadn't done anything wrong.

"You never apologized for last night," Lizzie chided.

"I have nothing to apologize for."

Lizzie scoffed, her anger bubbling up like lava.

"I am *not* weak."

"You can keep telling yourself that if you want to…"

His biting tone and the way he raised his eyebrows as he made his snide comment were too much for her. That heavy, dense energy was all-consuming, like a cloud of thick black smoke from a fire.

"Why are you being so mean?" She threw her hands up in frustration. "It's like you flipped on a jerk switch overnight."

"You're just taking it that way. I'm just calling it as I see it."

"Screw you, Miles!"

"I don't need to be here, you know," he said. "There are people who care about me. People who love me. I could go be with them, instead of wasting my time with you."

"Are you serious?" Lizzie sneered.

"We've been together a year, Lizzie, and you can't say it, can you? I've given you everything, more than you could ever know, and you can't fucking say it. And do you know why? It's because you don't love me, Lizzie."

"Yes, I do, Miles. I do love you, I just…"

"You're not in love with me."

"I didn't say that," Lizzie said.

"Maybe you'll say it to *him*, since he has your attention."

"Will you just stop with him, Miles?" She was losing her patience, turning into something ugly, quickly. "You know I would never cheat on you. You know it."

He laughed with a manipulative sneer that he used when he knew he was getting to her. This behavior was typical of Miles. Push Lizzie until he knew he had made a fool out of her. Make her look like she's crazy, even though he was the one who was rude, insensitive, and cold. Their fights had never been this bad, but he'd done this in the past on a few occasions. Lizzie never realized how calculating Miles could be until now. She gave in to the draining feeling as she always did, allowing any joy of that day to bleed out from her. That incessant need to reclaim the parts of her life she felt were missing, like joy and peace, nagged at her, and she knew if she continued this path with Miles, she would never get it.

"This relationship is sucking the soul out of me."

She hadn't meant to say it out loud, but the words had escaped her, her voice barely above a whisper.

"And the truth finally comes out."

"Miles," she said. "I love you. I do." Miles didn't say a word, but she couldn't stop talking. The words spilled out of her now, and she knew whatever she said, she couldn't take back. "But you're smothering me. You're angry all the time, and last night was awful. And my friends miss me. I just think we need some space from each other," she said.

Miles shifted his eyes toward her.

"You want to break up?"

"No." The word barely escaped her lips. Tears flooded her eyes now, and she fought the frog feeling in her throat. "I just need a little space… to get back to myself."

"Whatever you want, Lizzie."

His words were cold as if he wasn't affected in the least. He cracked his neck and stood.

"That's it?" she asked. "No emotion, just…Whatever I want?"

"Yeah," he said, still showing not one ounce of feeling. "It's like you said, I'm sucking the soul out of you, so there's no reason for me to stick around."

"I don't want to break up with you, Miles. I just want a little space. That's all."

"I'm leaving, Lizzie."

The way he said it… so final. Even though she was angry, his words tore her insides apart.

"You talk a lot about me not saying I love you," she said,

her voice cracking, "but your coldness right now speaks louder than anything I haven't said."

"Well, maybe I was just pretending, Lizzie."

"What?"

"All of this," he said, motioning between them. "It wasn't real."

"If it wasn't real, then why did you bother?"

He shrugged, making his way into the bedroom, where he grabbed his already packed bags.

"You already packed?" Lizzie cried.

The realization settled over Lizzie slowly. Miles had resolved to leave long before she mentioned needing space.

"You planned this," she said.

Miles didn't say a word. He wouldn't even look her in the eye. He showed zero emotion as he walked out of the bedroom and toward the door.

"I hate you," Lizzie said. She wanted to shout it, but it came out as an emotional wince of pain. "Nothing I would have said today would have mattered, would it? You were just looking for a way out, and I handed it to you. So, all of it was just bullshit." She felt the tears well in her eyes. "Or are you just mad because I stood up for myself, finally? Oh, what, as long as I was your stupid helpless puppet, you loved me, but as soon as I grew some confidence, you couldn't handle it?"

If eyes could spit ice, Miles' would have right then.

"I hope you're happy," he said. "Really. I do."

With that, Miles walked out the door, leaving Lizzie to grieve alone.

chapter 17

Brody arrived at his sister's house at 6 p.m. His parents were already inside, and he braced himself for awkward interactions with his father. The kids were good, and they probably would have been fine with just his parents babysitting, but Jessica always felt better when Brody was there because, unlike his parents, he followed her rules. For instance, Brody's mom ignored Jessie's requests numerous times by feeding Ryan whatever he wanted and then complaining when the kid was diving off the armrest of the couch onto the hardwood floors. Or when Jessie said his niece, Ava, wasn't allowed to eat cookies before dinner, his parents would buy her her own box and ask her only to take one. *Like any kid would do that.*

Brody could have watched them on his own, but his parents insisted on being there. They wanted to spend time with their grandkids, and they considered Sundays "their" day. So here they all were on this Sunday, acting like a normal family and being anything but.

As soon as Brody walked inside, Ryan and Ava jumped with glee. He was their "fun" uncle. He loved spending time with them too, and as much fun as they had together, the interactions between Brody and his father were painfully awkward. Brody had received two grunts, an eye roll, and a "no" from his dad. That was more conversation than they'd had since last Christmas, so that was an improvement. It hadn't always been that way; Brody and his dad had a great relationship before the accident. At least now his mom was speaking to him.

Brody fed the kids, and afterward, they retired to the family room where they watched a movie with his parents. The kids had a burst of energy when the movie ended, and as Brody's dad chased them around a coffee table, pretending to be a dinosaur, Brody checked his messages. Nunez was pressing him to push Lizzie to this inn, but there was only so much he could do.

"Uncle Brody, will you be the dinosaur now?" Ryan asked.

"No way. That's Pop-pop's job."

His dad's eyes briefly met his, and Brody thought he might see a slight reaction, but his dad quickly turned away. Brody left the family room and took a seat at the dining room table. He hated how his stomach churned in his father's presence. Brody hadn't cried since he held his uncle in his arms and watched him bleed out, but that didn't mean the feeling didn't well up in him anytime he thought about how his dad used to love him the way he loved his grandchildren.

"You okay, honey?" Brody's mom asked, interrupting his thoughts.

"Fine."

Brody knew she only asked as a formality. She knew it wasn't fine. Not in the least. At least she didn't blame him. She was just happy he was safe. Alive. He didn't want to think of what it would have done to his mom if he'd been the one to die that day.

"You've got that look."

Brody shrugged. She knew. He knew. There was less of an elephant and more of a T-Rex in the room, and it was hungry for blood.

"Okay, honey," she said. "Well, you know you can always talk to me."

Except he couldn't. Because then she'd talk to his dad, and they would argue, and he didn't want to put that on his mother.

A text message saved him from any other awkward conversations.

"I gotta take this," he told his mom, who then left him to it.

MEET ME DOWN THE STREET BY GUNNER AND SOUTHBROOK.

The text was from an unknown number. Just then, he heard the front door open; his sister walked in, looking flushed.

"How was it?" Brody asked.

Jessie and Brody were bonded through their messed-up marriages. At least their father was talking to her, though.

"Great," was his sister's only response, but he could tell it'd been better than great for her, which made him want to find the guy and threaten his life for touching his sister.

"All right, sis," he said. "All right."

"How were they?" Jessica asked as she removed her hat and coat and hung them in the hall closet.

"Kids were perfect, as always."

"And mom and dad?"

"Mom was fine. Dad was… dad." He stood up from his seat and made his way toward the door. "Your kids didn't overdose on the sugar, if that's what you're asking."

"Yeah," she said, offering him a sympathetic smile.

"Anyway, I need to take a call," Brody said. "I'll be right back."

chapter 18

Brody's teeth chattered as he walked down Southbrook toward Gunner Street; a bitter wind whipped against his cheeks. He hated short days and long nights. Summer couldn't come fast enough.

Brody kept his eyes focused on his surroundings, but the night obscured his visibility. The text wasn't from Nunez, Punk, Dale, or Shay, that was for certain, but whoever it was, they had Brody's attention.

Finally, he reached the intersection of Southbrook and Gunner, a dead end by a small neighborhood park. He turned right onto Gunner and felt a surge of adrenaline, the kind that got him all fired up for a fight.

Miles Corrigan leaned against a streetlamp, picking at his teeth with a toothpick. And next to him was Lizzie's attacker from the concert. Brody stopped short. He tried to keep his cool, but all he could think was, *what the fuck are these pieces of shit doing here together?*

"You've got to be fucking kidding me," he muttered.

"Just here to have a little chat," Miles said.

"What are you doing here with him?" Brody said, pointing to Lizzie's stalker. Nunez had been right that Lizzie's stalker was working for the Bakers. At least he wasn't some psycho Fae who had escaped from another world. Brody could kick himself for thinking so ridiculously.

Both of these men exuded the kind of cockiness Brody liked least, and he had to tell himself to stay cool, calm, and collected, or Lizzie might pay the price.

"This… is Cedric," Miles said, rolling his eyes.

Brody could see both Miles and Cedric's faces illuminated under the streetlamp. Cedric, with one tousled brown curl in front of his forehead, had folded his muscular arms across one another. Brody thought he looked like an entitled frat guy who didn't get the memo to graduate and clung to his college years as his only hope for recognition. He wore a permanent frown with a creased brow. The guy was trouble.

"Stay away from Lizzie," Cedric growled.

"Don't think so, Buddy," Brody quipped.

Brody leaned back against a wooden fence that backed up to the park area. He crossed his arms, wondering how long the losers would take to try something.

"Lizzie and I share something sacred," Cedric said, voice low.

Odd thing for a guy to say.

"Is that so?"

"We're destined to be together," Cedric said.

Brody darted his eyes to Miles. "I thought she was *your* girlfriend. Pretty sure relationships don't work like that, Miles. You can't just give your girlfriend to someone else. But I guess if destiny calls…"

"Shut up," Miles said, matching Cedric's indignation. Miles turned to Cedric. "Leave us alone."

"No," Cedric responded. But then his narrowed eyes shifted to Miles, his jaw pulsing before he spoke. "Fine. I'll let you have your little chat." Turning back to Miles, he said, "But this is all meaningless. I don't like it when people touch my things. Not him, and not you."

Miles didn't reply. He waited to address Brody until Cedric was gone.

What was Brody witnessing here? Whatever it was, it was some fucked up shit.

"You can see how strange this is, right?" he said to Miles. "Touching his things? But I'm confused. Is he your errand boy? Or are you his? And what kind of shit boyfriend are you?"

"Shut up."

Brody decided to answer Miles' arrogance with his own. He wasn't intimidated by Cedric or Miles.

"Maybe I'll just call Lizzie and tell her what a great boyfriend you are."

"This is bigger than you, Woods."

"I don't care. You and the Bakers are a bunch of lowlife cowards. Bullies who think they own everyone and everything. The lowest trash scum out there. But here's the thing. I'm not threatened by bullies, and I'm sure as hell not afraid of you and McCaveman over there."

"You should be afraid, Brody."

The way he said it… it wasn't exactly a threat. If anything, it seemed almost sincere, but Brody ignored that.

"Why are you here, Miles?"

"Do I really have to spell it out?"

"Yeah, you do."

"Fine. Like Cedric said, stay away from Lizzie."

"Or what?" Brody asked.

"Let's put it this way. You won't walk away from this."

Brody smirked. "And exactly who's gonna to take me out? The Bakers? Or the President of Alpha Omega over there?"

"Me."

"You? Hmmm. Oh, okay," Brody replied, throwing his hands up.

"I mean it, Woods. You can't help her now, so just back off." He paused, and through gritted teeth, said, "She's Cedric's now."

"Unbelievable," Brody said. "There's something wrong with you, man."

Miles' voice dipped into something calm. Too calm.

"You don't get it, do you? There's no stopping what's in motion. Not by you. Not by anyone."

"Lizzie doesn't belong to anyone. Not to you or to that circus clown, Cedric." This guy was making it difficult for Brody to restrain himself. "Lizzie is her own person. And you're a twisted person for saying otherwise. Now, get out of here, Corrigan. And take Curly with you."

Miles backed up, a sinister grin spreading across his face. Brody must have looked murderous because Miles continued with, "I tried to be nice. I did." Miles paused before continuing. "I'll tell you what. I'll play nice if you play nice. Okay?"

Brody grunted as Miles continued.

"You don't get near Lizzie ever again, and I'll stay away from your sister. How about that?"

Brody felt the blood pumping harder, his body trying to keep up with the surge. He prayed that Miles didn't say what he thought he might.

"What did you just say to me?"

"I knew you wouldn't listen, so I needed some reassurance that you would. How did your sister enjoy our date? It was lovely for me. I took her out for a nice steak, and then we got hot and heavy in the car. Mmmm, I think she really needed that release, you know?"

Brody didn't think as his fist met Miles' face. Miles stumbled backward, blood dripping from his mouth. The rage surging through Brody was insurmountable, enough that he thought he might hurt Miles badly enough that he wouldn't get up. He punched him again, and Miles stumbled to the ground.

Cedric was there in a flash, grabbed Brody by the throat, and pinned him against the fence. Brody felt a stab of pain followed by his breath escaping him. This guy was fucking strong.

Too strong.

"Let him go," Miles said to Cedric. He was still on the ground, breathing heavily, bleeding onto the cold mulch.

"No," growled Cedric. He glowered at Brody. "I could crush you now."

"Let. Him. Go," Miles repeated, this time with a little more force.

Cedric released his grasp, and now it was Brody gasping for air.

Miles let out a slow, jagged laugh. "We're not as different as you wanna believe," he said as he stood to his feet and wiped more blood away from his mouth. "That's what makes this so hard to watch." Miles pretended to "shoot" a gun at Brody with his finger and clicked his tongue. "Hair-trigger. You're a beast. Just. Like. Me. Now, I'll say it one more time. Stay away from Lizzie. And I won't mess with your life."

Brody only saw red, but he didn't attack Miles again.

He stepped in close and then side-eyed Cedric. "If I see you again…" Brody stepped close, his voice like gravel. "You won't walk away."

"We understand each other, then," Miles said. With that, Miles stood, and he and Cedric left, leaving Brody with a seething anger coursing through his veins. His neck burned and was warm to the touch as he hurried back to Jessica's house and paced the porch for several seconds. Brody called Nunez and left her a voicemail. He balled his hands into fists. Should he go after them and beat those pieces of shit down?

He sat on Jessica's front porch swing and put his head in his hands. He had words for his sister, too. Honestly, she had shit taste in men. But if Miles Corrigan ever touched one hair on any of his family's heads again, he'd fucking kill the guy.

He heard the front door creak open but didn't look up.

"Brody?" his mom asked. "Everything okay?"

"Everything is just fine, Mom. Just fine."

But Brody's fist stayed clenched. Because *nothing* was fine.

chapter 19

"You okay, honey?" Dan's wife, Gloria, asked.

"Not really," Lizzie said as she let out a sigh.

"Now, sugar," she said in her thick Southern drawl. "I wanna see you eat every last bite of that sandwich. And don't think I'm goin' anywhere 'til you do." She gave Lizzie those raised eyebrows that signaled she meant business.

Lizzie hadn't eaten for almost two days. She was tormented by her breakup with Miles, by the gut-wrenching feeling of waking up and knowing he wasn't hers anymore. *Maybe it wasn't over*, she told herself. *Maybe they could salvage this.* But in her heart, she knew it was. The threads of love they had carefully woven together were cut and now unraveling fast and final. She hadn't told anyone, except for Dan and Gloria. Lizzie spent the last few days watching reality shows where the drama was worse than hers. Her cats curled up with her on the couch, soothing her pain with each purr. She had thought about calling Misty—knew that she would come right over and bring the rest of the squad, too. But Lizzie didn't need to hear what she already knew; she needed the space to grieve the parts of Miles she loved and would miss.

Lizzie's Sunday morning shift at the diner had been

slow, so Dan let her leave early. By Monday, her mood had improved slightly, enough to eat.

"I have to say, Lizzie," Dan said, emerging from the kitchen, "out of all the guys you've dated, I disliked Miles most."

"You and everyone else," Lizzie said.

"I didn't like that he wouldn't come to Family Day."

They had been celebrating Family Day, gathering at Tacos and Tequila, ever since Dan married Gloria. Lizzie, Dan, Gloria, and Lizzie's stepbrothers, George and Len, would all meet for brunch and enjoy the day together. Dan was right. Miles always had an excuse to get out of it.

"I guess I just thought he was different," Lizzie said. "But I was wrong."

What stung the most was that he'd been lying the whole time. Every kiss, every tender touch, every time they had made sensuous love. Every gift, every trip. All lies.

"It happens to the best of us," Dan said with a shrug. "But the good news is, now you can meet someone who deserves your time and beautiful, loving energy."

"Yeah," Lizzie said, drawing in a deep breath. She felt the tears sting her eyes again. "I get that he wasn't right for me, but I still feel sad."

"'Course you do, darlin'," Gloria said as she rubbed Lizzie's back. "But this feeling will pass one day. All heartache does, just like a summer storm."

"You know what you need, Lizzie Bear?" Dan said.

"What?"

"A vacation. You work at the restaurant all the time. You go to school. When's the last time you did something for yourself, something Miles didn't plan for you, or something you didn't feel obligated to do?"

Lizzie shrugged. She couldn't think of the last time she planned to do something. Her thoughts drifted to the

Speakeasy Inn. Of course, the trip would technically be for school, but investigating a murder and celebrating Halloween at a remote inn sounded more fun than sitting around moping.

Lizzie explained the inn and her project to Gloria.

"Let's look this inn up," Gloria said, typing it into her phone. She held out the screen so Lizzie could see it. A black screen appeared, and then words in creamy white writing began to fade onto it. Gloria read them out loud.

Are you ready for the most seductive experience of your life?

The words faded as new words appeared.

From 1920 to 1933, America was in a period of prohibition.

Again, the words faded out, new words appearing on the screen.

Prohibition was the constitutional ban on producing, transporting, importing, and selling alcoholic beverages. But that did not stop people from having fun. During prohibition, speakeasies sold illegal alcohol to those who frequented them. That is, if they could find the establishment. In 1929, Paul Watson opened the Speakeasy Inn. In this place, select people who knew of the inn could come to enjoy the pleasures of drink, rest, and social interaction. Today, the Speakeasy Inn maintains its cryptic location. Will you join in on the fun? Click now to book a room.

"Aw, honey," Gloria said. "You've gotta go. And would you look at that? They've even got *two* Halloween dances. Spooky fun might be just what the doctor ordered."

"I don't know," Lizzie responded. "Sunday, there's a wedding. My partner for the project at school is going to it. He told me he could get me the wedding room rate if I decided to go."

"He asked you to be his date?" Dan asked.

"No. No. He just mentioned we could work on this project there. And since he would already be there for the wedding, it was just convenient."

"Oh, I get it. Well, ask Misty to go with you, then," Dan

said. "And go. Have fun. Pauline is itching for your Saturday shift."

"Okay…" Lizzie contemplated the idea for several seconds. The inn did kind of sound like fun.

She took out her phone and sent a text to Misty.

Lizzie: *What are your plans for Halloween? Want to get away for the weekend?*

Misty: *Umm… with whom?*

Lizzie: *Calm down. Just me. A girls' weekend.*

Misty: *Why? What's up?*

Misty knew her so well.

Lizzie: *Miles and I broke up. I DON'T want to talk about it right now. It happened on Friday. I didn't tell you because I needed time to process it. But I think a mini vacation is what I need.*

She explained to Misty that she would be doing a little investigating there and mentioned the events taking place that weekend.

Misty: *Sounds intriguing and fun. Can I help investigate this murder, or is it reserved for you and the hot guy?*

Lizzie: *Stop… Of course, you can help.*

Misty: *I'm in…*

Lizzie: *Frank won't be upset?*

Misty: *No. And just like you, I don't want to talk about that right now.*

Lizzie: *Uh, oh…*

Misty: *Let's just get away, okay? I think we BOTH need it. Can we even get a room this close to Halloween?*

Lizzie: *I'll see. I can't make any promises, but I think there might still be rooms available.*

Misty: *This is exciting. Just what I needed. Let me know when the room is booked. I'll send you money for it. And let's discuss outfits. I might need to do some shopping.*

Lizzie: *You and me both!*

Misty: *And Lizzie…I'm sorry about Miles. I know I hated him (still do), but I never want you to be sad. Know I'm here to talk. Promise I'll just listen.*

Lizzie: *Thank you. Love you. And SAME.*

Misty: *Love you, too.*

Lizzie sent a text message to Brody.

Lizzie: *Any chance you can get me that special room rate at the inn for the weekend?*

Brody took half an hour to reply, but when he did, he said, *Yes. Call and ask for the Hackney wedding rate.*

Lizzie: *Okay, thanks. See you in class.*

Brody: *Yes. See you then.*

Lizzie finished her shift at 12 p.m. She had just enough time to walk home, shower, and then head off to class. The wind picked up as she walked out the door, and she hugged her sweater close to her chest. That's when she saw a note folded under the windshield wiper of her car, soaked by the rain. When she opened the note, even though the words were smudged, her heart sank in her chest, and an uneasy feeling coursed through her. She immediately went on alert, looking around for *him*.

Miles had been here, left her this note.

This… *warning*.

A warning that said, *They're coming for you.*

chapter 20

Brody and Lizzie were both quiet in the auditorium during Monday's class. His mind was still reeling after his visit from Miles and Cedric. "They know," Brody spouted off to Nunez's voicemail on Sunday. "They know who we are and were willing to use my sister to get to me." He'd wanted so badly to handle them himself, but Nunez had called him and convinced him to back down.

"Sorry if I'm out of it today," Lizzie said suddenly, breaking him from his thoughts.

"Me too."

Another several seconds passed before Lizzie asked, "Can I run something by you?"

"Of course."

Their voices were low and serious, much different from their lighter banter the Friday before.

"I guess I should start by telling you that Miles and I broke up…" Lizzie began.

"You did?"

He didn't mean to sound insensitive, but all he could think was thank God she was no longer with that piece of trash. He gritted his teeth just thinking about Miles but refrained from telling Lizzie what happened.

"Yes," Lizzie said. "But that's not what I wanted to talk about. Today, I found a strange note on my car, and I know it was Miles' handwriting. He writes in all caps all the time, and he does this weird thing with his G's, whether they're lowercase or uppercase, where he slashes a line through it where the G ends." Lizzie shook her head. "I don't know what to think about it or do about it."

"What did the note say?" Brody asked.

"They're coming for you."

Miles' words rang in his head. *No one could save Lizzie now. She was Cedric's.* He wanted to come clean with Lizzie so badly, tell her everything, and then pray she forgave him for lying and withholding the truth all this time. But he knew Nunez would be furious. So he played further into the lie, knowing he was digging himself into an endless abyss.

"I know it might be uncomfortable to do this, but you could text him and ask him what he meant by it."

Of course, Brody already knew.

"I can't," Lizzie said. "I just can't. We ended things so badly."

"I'm sorry," Brody said. He didn't like to see Lizzie hurting, but knowing Miles was out of the picture, at least for now, made him feel better.

"I think the breakup was coming; I just kept ignoring the signs."

"Hmm," Brody said with a nod. "Don't we all?" Not wanting to elaborate on his own breakup, he said, "You could go to the police. At least have something on record. Your stalker. A warning note. Shay is a detective, so we can always run it by her."

Lizzie nodded and breathed in deeply. She fidgeted with her pen, not meeting Brody's eyes.

"You've been through a lot this last week," Brody said.

"And I'm glad you're talking to me about it. Have you told anyone else about the note?"

She shook her head.

"Okay, well, if anything else happens, Lizzie, I want you to call me." He rested his hand gently on her shoulder. "I'll be there in a heartbeat, okay? You don't need to worry about anything."

She looked up at him, and his eyes lingered on her mesmerizing gaze.

"I appreciate that," she said softly. "I do."

"I mean it," Brody said, keeping his eyes fixed on hers. He could feel that longing for her flickering to life, so he changed the subject. "On a more positive note, were you able to book a room at the inn? Or are you not going now because of everything going on?"

"Oh, no, I'm still very much going," Lizzie said. "*Especially* because of everything going on. Going with my best friend. Honestly, I think it might be the best thing. I just need to get away from all this mess."

"I get that. And hey, look, I understand if you don't want to work on the project while we're there."

Said as a formality, of course. He needed her to be involved and would have to convince her in case she backed out.

"No, I want to," she said. "I think it'll be fun. My friend Misty wants to help."

"Sure," Brody said. "What day are you guys getting there?"

"Thursday…"

"Shay, Dale, and I will be there Thursday, too."

"Will you be going to all the other festivities?"

"Maybe," he said, locking his eyes back onto hers. "But only if you are."

Brody saw Lizzie's cheeks flush and felt that spark again, hotter, steadier. He allowed the faintest smile, which Lizzie returned.

Professor Dune walked in then, and Brody and Lizzie stopped talking. Brody prepared himself for another long, boring lecture. He liked Dune, but damn, if he had to sit through one more pretend class, he was going to lose it. *One more class*, he told himself. *One more.*

A text message buzzed through to Brody's phone from an unknown number, but he knew who it was right away.

Don't forget our little chat from yesterday.

Nunez would say don't answer. Block his number. Get a burner phone. Don't antagonize. Stick to the mission. Think about your sister and how Miles might retaliate. But Brody hated this fuck so much, and the guy already crossed the ultimate boundary.

Brody: *Why'd you leave her the note, Miles? Still have feelings, don't ya? Don't think you're getting her back, though. You really are a FUCKING IDIOT.*

Miles: *FUCK YOU. YOU DESERVE WHAT'S COMING TO YOU.*

Brody: *Back at ya, bro.*

Brody knew he shouldn't have dug the knife deeper, but he couldn't help it. He knew Nunez would not be pleased with him and would tell him he needed to keep his pride in check. They were undercover. This was a job, not a personal quest. But the thing was, Miles had made it personal when he involved Brody's sister. And Brody couldn't help that he was starting to feel things for Lizzie he hadn't felt for anyone since Nina. He hated feeling vulnerable. It made him do rash shit like provoking a hitman. Brody went to click his phone shut, but one more text message popped up, one he couldn't ignore.

Miles: *I never miss. Watch your back.*

chapter 21

"Nice work." That's what Nunez had said after Brody confirmed Lizzie would be going to the inn after all.

Brody met Nunez at the warehouse on Monday evening. He didn't mention the text message exchange between him and Miles, mostly because he knew what she'd say, but he did fill her in about the warning note on Lizzie's car.

"Keep your tabs on her," Nunez said. "We need to get her to the inn safely." Nunez pursed her lips. "But we have to discuss another problem."

Dale had his headphones on, trying to hack the Bakers' security systems at the main site of their operations, an old farmhouse in Hammonton, New Jersey. The site was just a cover; word was they built underground rooms to hold their meetings and do some of their business, which included, but was not limited to, murder, drug trafficking, illegal gambling, arson, extortion, and loan sharking. Nunez was worried because she hadn't heard from her inside agent, Juarez, in days. Even though Dale was making headway with the security systems, he hadn't cracked the code yet.

When Brody walked into the warehouse, he saw a

standing corkboard on rollers. With Shay's help, Nunez had pinned several photos to the board, including a pyramid of the Baker family. The left-side pyramid began with the don, Ludwig, followed by the underboss, Remy, and the capo, Dean Corrigan (Miles' older brother). Their pictures were strategically placed with small captions on index cards tacked next to their names. Miles was one of their made men. A soldier. *After disobeying their orders, there was no way he'd ever rank higher*, Brody thought. The rest of the board contained photos of people he didn't know. On the right side was a new family tree; at the top, a grainy photo of a gray-haired man with sinister eyes, and below him, Cedric.

"What is this?" Brody asked. "You think Cedric is part of another family calling the shots?"

"Juarez gave us some intel before he went silent. I don't know what to make of it, but it doesn't sound good." Nunez took a deep breath and then glanced over at Dale, making sure his headphones were still secured on his head. She spoke in a low, deliberate tone.

"I sent the others home, except Dale. I thought it better that we discuss this alone. I don't think they're ready to hear it." She hesitated before adding, "Juarez said that a few weeks ago, *this* man," she pointed to the man at the top of the second family pyramid, "who goes by Redcap, showed up with Cedric. At first, the Bakers were unaffected by the men, but that changed overnight. I've done multiple searches on both men and have personally overseen the searches. There's nothing in our databases about them."

She paused, and her silence said it all.

"They don't exist."

Brody felt his insides twist—this situation wasn't looking good.

"What do you think made the Bakers change their tune?" Brody asked.

He couldn't help but think about Miles, who had abandoned Lizzie after spending so much time keeping her from the Bakers.

"Whenever I think of men like Ludwig Baker, I'm reminded of a story my father used to tell me about a sordid beggar. The beggar finds himself in the presence of a genie who will grant him any wish. 'Would you like to become king?' the genie asks. 'You would be wealthy and rule over the entire kingdom.' 'No,' the beggar replies, 'there isn't enough *power* in that.' 'What if I made you an emperor?' asks the genie. 'Surely that would satisfy you. You would be rich beyond your wildest dreams and rule over not just one, but *many* kingdoms.' 'No,' replies the beggar, 'there simply isn't enough *power* in that.' 'What is it you wish for then?' asks the genie. 'I wish to rule over all the lands and all the people,' the beggar says. 'I want them to grovel at my feet, beg for me to spare their lives. I want them to sing my name in praise. I want to whisper a single command and watch them obey.' 'I'm sorry,' the genie replies. 'But no one man can hold that kind of power.' 'Then let me stay a beggar,' the man says.

"The point of that story, Brody, is that most people think money is the driving ambition of dominating and manipulating people like Ludwig. But it's not. It's the pursuit of power, of control over others, that consumes a person. Money is simply a means to gain that power. The Bakers' pursuit of the inheritance was never really about the money; it was about power and revenge, about taking back what they believed was rightfully theirs. That pursuit began before Ludwig formed The Family, even before Richard Baker's time. And it's worsened since Redcap and Cedric brought the pendant to Ludwig's attention."

"*The* pendant?" Brody said. "The one from Harold's inheritance?"

Nunez nodded as Brody continued.

"So, now he thinks, what, that Lizzie can open a doorway to some world," he formed the possible story as he spoke, "and now they need to keep her alive?"

Nunez didn't reply right away, so Brody kept asking questions.

"How did Redcap and Cedric even know about the pendant?"

"I didn't want to tell you before and overwhelm you with this, but it appears the Bakers got hold of Harold's research about the scrolls. Juarez reported that, when Redcap arrived, he told Ludwig he had been searching for them. He was easily able to translate the scrolls, kept telling Ludwig if he helped him, he'd promise him '*Donum vitae aeternae.*'"

"Which means?"

"The gift of eternal life."

"Nunez," Brody said, addressing her for the first time in his life by her name, "What exactly are you saying here?"

"I never thought I would say this, but it's time we considered that your hunch may have been right. Redcap and Cedric are not human, and whoever Redcap is, he's offered Ludwig everlasting immortality if he helps him."

Brody let the words sink in, as Nunez added, "We both know Ludwig is just crazy enough to do it."

"If Cedric and Redcap aren't human," Brody continued, "doesn't that mean they already opened a doorway to get here?"

"Unfortunately, yes."

"And we could reason that if they're here, others like them could be here."

"Yes."

"And they may be trying to use Lizzie to open the portal back to their world. Or worse." He swallowed deeply, his jaw tightening at the thought. "They might take her with them."

"Possibly. I don't know," Nunez said, shaking her head.

"The only thing that's clear is that they were searching for the scrolls, and now they've found them. The last thing Juarez said to me was, 'They know where the relic is…they're going to the inn.' I have no way of knowing anything more because Juarez is gone. But this operation just got a lot more dangerous. For you and your team. For all of us."

"And we don't know what kind of torture these freaks would put Lizzie through if they thought she could assist them in opening this doorway."

"That's why she has to find that relic before they do," Nunez said. "Look, I know I told you that if things got bad, I would pull the plug. If that's going to happen, then it has to be now. Once we get to the inn… there's no going back."

"We stick with the plan," Brody said immediately, nodding more to himself than Nunez. "Lizzie is in danger, but we have the advantage right now. I'm not letting her down. I'll protect her, and I'm not afraid of Cedric, the Bakers, or this Redcap guy. Anyone."

"Your courage is admirable," Nunez said, her voice cracking. "But Jaycen Juarez was one of the most fearless men I've had the pleasure of working with, and you should have heard the fear in his voice."

Once more, stone-faced Nunez was showing emotion, and Brody didn't like it one bit. But if he thought that was bad, with her next words, he felt tension curl in his stomach.

"Maybe it's time we exhibit a little fear,." she said, "or at the least, not make promises we can't keep."

chapter 22

Lizzie dropped her cats off at Dan's apartment after school on Wednesday. The rain had returned, and it was already pitch dark at 5:30.

Dan poured a cup of tea for himself and Lizzie as he grilled her about the note and her stalker. He begged her to speak to the police, and she promised she would when she got back from her mini vacation.

"It's good you're getting away, Lizzie," Dan said. "You need this. But you'll have to deal with this either way when you return. And I'm a little concerned about the remoteness of the inn. How are you getting there again?"

"They text you the morning of check-in with instructions to drive to a lot just outside of the inn and then shuttle you there. The inn is in Beechville, but they don't disclose where. But there's no need to worry. The hotel clerk said that even though the inn is remote and doesn't share the location with guests, the police and emergency personnel know the location and can easily get there."

"I feel better about that," Dan replied, "but still… if anything weird happens, I want you to call me or Gloria right away."

"I will."

"I know you're a grown woman, but you're still a little girl to me. I still worry."

"That's because you're a good dad."

Dan grew quiet for a moment.

"Speaking of dads… have you heard from yours since the email?"

"Nope," Lizzie said. "But I'm not worried. He does this."

Dan took a sip of tea and then formulated his words carefully. "Have you been able to get an address for him?"

"No," Lizzie replied. "For all I know, he could be living in a commune in California."

"You ever swing by his old house?" Dan asked.

"I did, once. Someone else lives there now."

"You don't think that whatever is going on with this stalker or the warning has to do with him, do you?"

Lizzie shrugged.

"I have no idea, but if I had to guess…"

Dan sighed as he shook his head.

"That man… I know I don't say it often, but your mother would be so proud of you." His words caught in his throat, and immediately Lizzie felt tears fill her eyes.

"Thank you," Lizzie said, giving Dan a hug.

"Now you call me if you have any trouble," he said. "I'll come get you."

"I will," Lizzie said, offering a smile.

"And don't worry about Tink and Belle. They love Gloria. And Lenny is bringing his girls over this weekend, so they'll have lots of attention."

"Thanks, Dan, as always."

"I love you, Lizzie Bear."

"Love you too, Papa Bear."

Lizzie returned to her apartment, which felt eerily quiet without the cats and Miles. She couldn't remember the last time she'd felt so lonely. At 6 p.m., she ate the dinner that Dan's new restaurant cook had prepared for her. Then she started sifting through the new clothes she and Misty had bought on Tuesday night.

So close to Halloween, the costume selection was slim, but they found feathered headdresses, long black gloves, and fake cigarette holders at a Halloween store. Afterward, they stopped by a department store where Lizzie purchased a black sequined spaghetti strap dress and black stiletto heels. For the Zombie Dance, she bought an emerald-green dress that set off her hair.

She loved how the dresses hugged her curves, and since she was single now, she didn't mind that they showed more skin than she was used to. Misty opted for more conservative dresses that were still stunning.

Lizzie packed the dresses, jeans, a few sweaters, pajamas, and her favorite sweatpants. At 7 p.m., as she was zipping up her suitcase, she heard muffled noises outside her bedroom window. Her blinds were closed, and she didn't pay any mind to the voices, assuming it was her neighbors. Hearing a car alarm going off, she peered out of her front blinds and saw it was *her* car triggering the alarm. Panicked, her mind immediately drifted to Miles' warning.

They're coming for you.

She grabbed the car remote and turned off the alarm from inside her apartment. Then Lizzie got out her phone and typed in a text message to Miles.

Can we talk about the note?

She typed and then erased it.

Why did you leave that note on my car?

She typed, then erased it again.

Miles, I know you hate me, but I need to talk to you.

She was about to send it when she heard them—male voices, louder, right outside her front window, followed by a banging on her door.

There was no way she was going to answer that door, not after everything she'd been through. At first, she didn't move.

There's no reason to panic, she thought. *They could be neighbors; you're just overreacting because of recent events.*

But then she saw the door lock jiggling and knew someone was trying to break in. Simultaneously, she heard a banging at the window. She immediately called the police. She gave them her address and a play-by-play of what was happening. They told her to stay on the line; they would send someone over. But then her trembling fingers accidentally hit the end call button. She fumbled through her contacts and called Misty. It went straight to voicemail. Then Dan. Then her stepbrothers. Then Gloria. Then even her dad. But every call went to voicemail. She thought about calling Miles. But she couldn't. He thought she was pathetic. She was too proud to prove him right. The door lock was giving way, and they were using something to pry open the window. She prayed the police would be there soon.

She dialed Brody—needed to hear someone's voice that made her feel an ounce of safety. She thanked God that he answered right away.

"Someone is trying to break into my apartment." She got right to the point.

"All right," Brody said, calm, composed. "Take a deep breath, Lizzie. Did you call the police?"

"Yes. They're on their way."

Her voice cracked out of fear, but he kept her engaged.

"Do you have anything you can defend yourself with?"

"I… I think so."

She clung to his peacefulness as he guided her through chaos. In the kitchen, she found a knife, but it wasn't sharp enough to do anything, so she checked her storage closet.

Miles had forgotten to take his baseball bat. If they were going to break in, she was going to take them down as much as she could.

"I have a bat," she said, her voice still trembling.

"Okay, what's your address, Lizzie? I'm coming."

"2132 Main Street, Spring Hills."

"I'm not too far away. Stay on the phone with me, okay?"

"OK," Lizzie said.

Crack. Crack. Crack.

The window glass crumbled inward, and she let out a small cry.

"I'm coming, okay?" Brody assured her. "But I need you to find a space to hide. Do you have anywhere you can hide?"

"Bedroom closet."

"Go there now," he ordered.

Lizzie made her way into the bedroom and moved some boxes around so she could squeeze into the back with her bat.

"Are you in the closet?" Brody asked.

"Yes," Lizzie said, barely above a whisper.

"Stay put. I'll be there soon."

Brody didn't speak much but stayed on the line and occasionally updated her on how close he was. She heard voices louder now—they were in her apartment. Her heart thumped loudly as she heard things crashing, banging, and clanking. They were looking for something.

They're coming for you was all she could think, and she closed her eyes.

"She's here, I know it," she heard a man's voice say. "Find her, and the letter. Enough with this shit."

Lizzie held her breath and closed her eyes, praying they wouldn't open the closet door.

But then the door handles turned.

They were out there, about to find her.

Lizzie carefully placed the phone down and tightened her

fingers around the bat.

Lizzie, look up, her dad's warning rang in her mind.

This is what her dad had been preparing her for.

I can do this, she told herself. *I can do this.*

chapter 23

Brody sped along the rain-slicked roads as quickly as he could to reach Lizzie. He'd been at the gym in the middle of a pretty intense workout when she called, and he high-tailed it out of there immediately. Thankfully, he'd been working out at his gym close to Spring Hills. After what Nunez shared with him, his instinct told him he needed to be closer to Lizzie, just in case. And his instincts had paid off.

As he pulled his big silver truck onto Main Street, he saw blue and red police lights in front of Lizzie's apartment. Quickly, he hopped out of his truck and ran to her apartment door. Glass was everywhere; whoever had been there—Brody had a good idea of who—they had busted through the windows and trashed the place, too.

"Excuse me, you can't be in here," a male police officer said, and Brody feared the worst.

"Where is she?"

"Sir, do you live here?"

Without answering, Brody pushed past the officer and into Lizzie's apartment; his heart pounded at the thought that he was too late. He hoped and prayed nothing bad had happened to Lizzie; her call had disconnected in the middle of their conversation. He'd heard her breathing heavily, and then nothing.

Subdued voices came from down the hallway, and he hurried toward them, the officer yelling at him to 'stop right there.'

He found Lizzie in her bedroom, alive and well, dressed in a tank top and sweatpants, a female officer taking her statement.

"Sir, I said…" said the officer trailing Brody.

"Wait," he heard Lizzie say, "This is my friend, Brody. He stayed on the phone with me." She fixed her eyes on Brody. "They were inside my apartment. If the police hadn't shown up when they did…"

"It's okay," he said, pulling her into his arms. As her skin pressed against his, his racing heart began to settle. "I'm here."

"Well, we have your report," the officer said. "We'll let you know if we find out anything, and you'll contact us again if anything else happens."

"Thank you," Lizzie said.

The officers left, but Brody continued to hold onto Lizzie.

"I'm sorry you had to come out all this way," she said, looking up at him.

"It's no trouble. I told you to call me."

"No one else answered me. I know they're busy, but…"

"It's okay, Lizzie. I'm here now." His brows pulled together slightly. "And I'm not leaving."

Lizzie nodded, and he released her from his embrace. He followed her into the living area, where she let out a defeated sigh before saying, "Everything's a mess."

"I'll help you clean it up," Brody said.

"Thanks, but you don't have to do that."

"Lizzie, I'm here." Brody looked around at the wreckage,

wondering where to begin. "Do you have a broom?"

"Yeah."

"All right. Well… Let's take pictures first," he said. "Then, let me get to work. Why don't you relax, take a shower, or take a nap? Call someone. Whatever you need. I promise this will all feel a little less devastating if you're not looking at the mess."

"Okay. I have to call my landlord and tell him about the window."

As Lizzie explained to her landlord what had happened, Brody cleaned up all the glass and anything else he could find that was broken. He put the cushions back onto the couch and closed open drawers and cabinets. Lizzie's stepdad called, and she spoke to him for several minutes. By the time Lizzie hung up the phone, the place looked relatively back to normal.

"Wow," Lizzie said, making her way into the kitchen. "I can't believe you did all of this so quickly."

"I'm happy to do it," Brody said, turning to face her.

Lizzie's landlord showed up five minutes later and took a look at the window. He told Lizzie he'd get new locks for the door and have someone repair the window while she was away. Then he suggested she stay somewhere else for the night; he would return later, board up the window, and change the lock.

Once he left, Lizzie said, "I talked to Misty. She said I could stay at her place for the night."

"I think that's a good idea," Brody said. He'd had every intention of staying with Lizzie if she needed him, but he knew her staying at Misty's was the better option. The *safer* option.

"Misty isn't off work for another hour," Lizzie said. "Any chance you want to get out of here for a little bit? The last thing I want to do is sit around here and relive what just happened."

"I get that," Brody said. "And I am down to go somewhere, but do you mind if I shower first? I was at the gym when you called."

"Of course I don't mind," Lizzie said.

Brody had a change of clothes in his gym bag. It was only a white zip-up hoodie and sweatpants, but that was better than his gym shorts and tank. Lizzie showed Brody the bathroom, gave him a towel, and left him to shower.

When he came out, she was dressed to go out in jeans and a scoop neck bodysuit with a sheer netted shirt on top. Her hair fell in soft waves, and she'd applied makeup and red lipstick. She'd also finished packing her bags for the trip and had them waiting by her front door.

"I look like I'm about to watch a movie on the couch, and you look like you're going out on the town," he said.

Lizzie smiled and gently flipped her hair.

"Maybe," she said, "But not everyone can make a sweatshirt and sweatpants look that hot."

Brody tried not to react too much to what Lizzie said, even though knowing that she thought he was hot made him want to grab her and kiss her. Instead, he kept himself composed and cracked a smile, letting her know he appreciated her playfulness.

"So where are we going, pretty lady?" he asked.

"There's a bar down the street. Anywhere but here," she said.

"Let's go then. I'll drive you. I'll put your bags in Misty's car when she gets there."

"Sounds like a plan."

Brody and Lizzie left the apartment and climbed into Brody's truck. They arrived at a little dive bar called Alden's a few minutes later. The place was empty except for locals. Some bars had dim lighting, but Alden's was mostly dark except for neon green lights that hung over the bar and pool table.

No one paid any mind to Lizzie or Brody as they slid into an oaken booth by the bar and waited for Misty, who said she and Kallie would be there in thirty minutes. They were looking over their menus in silence when suddenly, Lizzie spoke.

"Why do you think people are after me?" she asked softly, looking up from her menu to meet Brody's eyes.

He wanted desperately to tell her the truth, considered telling her everything right then and there. But then he thought, *what if what he told her made her too afraid to go to the inn? What if by telling her, he ruined the whole plan, and she was so furious with him that she didn't want to see him anymore?* He couldn't protect her then. They were so close, and now the stakes were higher than ever. He had to keep up with the lie for a little longer and pretend he didn't know anything.

"I don't know," he said.

"I can think of one reason," she said as her fingers played with the peeling corners of the laminated menu. "My dad."

"Why your dad?" Brody asked, pretending he didn't know who Chuck Degan was.

"I think… I *know* he's involved with bad people, and I think they might be coming after me."

He turned to her and intertwined his fingers with hers, letting their joined hands fall against her thigh. With his free hand, he moved a strand of her hair away from her face and told his biggest lie yet. "I don't know why they're after you, but here's what I do know. No one is ever going to hurt you again."

Nunez's words played in his mind. *Don't make promises you can't keep.*

chapter 24

Lizzie felt Brody's thigh pressing against hers. He didn't move it, allowing an unspoken stream of sensual heat to pass between them. Then he threaded his fingers through hers, her hand the only barrier between his hand and her upper thigh. A desire throbbed deep within her, a soft ache building for his touch.

The night had been a disaster, except for this, except for *him.* She hoped she wasn't reading his signs wrong. Lizzie realized she didn't know much about the handsome guy sitting with her. Did he have a girlfriend, wife, or family? Did he have a job? Almost every conversation they'd had was about her.

"I don't want to make light of tonight," she said. His thumb tenderly moved in circular motions around hers, and he gave her "hungry eyes" but didn't kiss her, even though she wanted him to. "But I don't feel like I know anything about you."

"What do you want to know?" he asked.

"Do you have a girlfriend?"

"No," he said.

"A wife?"

He hesitated. "No wife."

Something in his pause made her question it. *Was he telling the truth?*

"I get the sense you break a lot of women's hearts," Lizzie said. She knew she shouldn't judge him based on his body and looks, but he also had that magnetic personality, the one some women were instantly drawn to. She couldn't help but pry.

"Not if I care about a woman," he said.

Exactly what a heartbreaker would say, she thought.

They'd been lost in each other's eyes for several minutes now, interrupted only by a waitress who wanted to know if they wanted drinks.

Lizzie ordered a glass of red wine, and Brody a beer.

"Who's Cliff?" Lizzie asked as they waited for their drinks.

"What?"

"I saw your tattoos at the apartment when you were wearing your gym tank. I saw you have one on your upper arm that says, Cliff."

"Oh," Brody said, looking down at the table.

"It's okay if you don't want to tell me," Lizzie said, realizing she may have gone too far with the questions.

"Cliff was my uncle."

"Was…"

"He died." Brody offered her an unreadable smile.

"I'm guessing you don't want to talk about that," she said. She could tell he was uncomfortable. He'd moved his leg away and sat up straighter in the booth.

"I don't usually like to talk about it, but…" He let out a deep sigh. The waitress put down their drinks, and immediately Brody took a sip. "The truth is, I used to work for the FBI."

"Oh," Lizzie said. "Wow."

She hadn't expected that.

"It was a difficult time."

"Look, you don't have to share," Lizzie said. "I get it. We all have painful memories."

None as much as me, she thought.

"No, I think you should know. Just…" He wiped his brow with his free hand. "I haven't really told anyone like this," he said, pointing from her to himself. "I was new at the Bureau. Still on probation. They had me doing surveillance mostly. Low-risk stuff. I was monitoring a drug operation. Nothing major. All I had to do was sit tight in a van and gather some intel. But what we didn't know was that another unit had been working a human trafficking case in the same area.

"My uncle was deep undercover in the trafficking case. As I said, none of us knew. Different teams, different jurisdictions. The Bureau keeps things compartmentalized sometimes, even from their own agents. There was just no way we would know, ya know?"

Lizzie nodded. Brody's eyes fell to the table, and he hesitated before continuing.

"Anyway, we're surveilling this drug situation, when suddenly some guys show up, and we hear them talking. My buddy Hemmy realizes that one of the guys is his sister's husband. It then becomes clear it isn't a drug bust we're monitoring but a human trafficking situation."

"Oh geez, Brody."

"Yeah, there was a girl there, couldn't have been more than fifteen. After my friend Hemmy recognized his brother-in-law's voice, we started arguing. I was trying to keep him put, but he got out of the van and went after this guy. Meanwhile, I wasn't going to move because the rules were to stay in the van." He ran his fingers over his mouth. "But then I heard them say they were going to kill Hemmy, and I couldn't let that happen, ya know. So I hopped out of the van and ran to save my friend. And within minutes, I found myself with a gun to my head, and I knew that this was it. I was going to die."

Lizzie squeezed Brody's hand tighter as he spoke.

"I didn't know my uncle was working undercover, and he blew his cover to save me. Jeopardized his whole career, his life." Brody swallowed deeply. He was holding back the emotion, but Lizzie heard his voice cracking. "He should have let me die there. That's what a good agent would have done. But instead, he gave me enough time to get out of the way before they shot him right in front of me. He, uh, died in my arms seconds later, just as a SWAT team got to the scene."

"I'm so sorry," Lizzie said. "I'm so so sorry." She hugged him tightly then. Several seconds of silence passed before she asked, "What happened to your friend?"

Brody let out a small laugh, then took a healthy sip of his beer.

"Oh, Hemmy. He walked off mid-op. If it were anyone else, they would've been terminated. But Hemmy's got connections, so he got a slap on the wrist for disobeying orders." Brody paused. "And then... he slept with my wife."

"So, you're..."

"Divorced."

Lizzie nodded her head. She couldn't believe what she'd just heard, but she wasn't going to let the mood stay somber.

"I thought that I was broken. I mean, all I have is a dead mom, a criminal dad, and a psycho stalker after me, but you... you have got me beat."

Brody gave her a slight smile.

"I'm glad," he said. "I was worried, you know."

"So, if you were in the FBI, did you ever hear of my father, Chuck Degan?"

Brody pondered the question for a few seconds.

"Nope, can't say that I have."

"Oh," Lizzie said. "That makes me feel a little better, I guess."

"But I wasn't there long. I mean, it's possible that if your dad is involved in bad stuff, he's a wanted person."

"Yeah, of course. Do you still talk to anyone from there?"

Brody mulled over the question, and Lizzie could tell he struggled to answer. She guessed it was because of the tragedy he experienced.

"I'm sorry if I'm being too forward," she said.

"No, it's all right," he said, taking a sip of his beer. "I…do know a couple of people. Look, if I can help you in any way with your situation, I'll try."

"Thank you."

"Yeah," he echoed, an awkward moment of silence passing between them, each taking a sip of their drink.

Just then, Misty and Kallie walked through the door, a happy interruption to a heavy conversation.

"Oh, honey, I am so sorry I didn't answer," Misty said, grabbing Lizzie into an embrace. She looked over at Brody. "Thank you for helping my friend. You're the best."

Brody answered with a short nod and smile. When Lizzie glanced at Kallie, she saw her eyeing Brody as if he were a New York strip steak cooked to perfection.

The girls took a seat opposite Brody and Lizzie, and for the next hour, they discussed Lizzie's stalker and the attack.

Eventually, the mood lightened as Misty grilled Brody about his life, and they discussed the inn and what they might find there.

All the while, Brody kept his thigh pressed against Lizzie's as if to say, I enjoy the nearness of you, and once in a while, he'd squeeze her hand under the table.

"We should probably leave soon," Misty said. "We're leaving early tomorrow morning."

"Same here," Brody said. "I can move Lizzie's bags into

your car if you want."

"Yeah, let's do that."

While Misty and Brody were outside, Kallie leaned into Lizzie and said, "I'm sorry about Miles, but he turned out to be an ass, didn't he? And anyway, it looks like someone better has come along. I hope you're fucking that guy, because if you're not, I'm totally going to."

Lizzie wasn't sure how to respond, and she hid her irritation with a nervous laugh. Even though Brody wasn't hers to claim, and she was still processing her breakup with Miles, Lizzie hated that Kallie always felt she could move in on whoever she wanted. Even when Lizzie started dating Miles, Kallie told Misty that if Lizzie didn't appreciate the gifts and the trips Miles constantly showered her with, then she would happily take Lizzie's place as his girlfriend.

Lizzie would have ended her friendship with Kallie if they hadn't been friends for so long. She wasn't loyal, and her need for attention worsened as she got older.

But supposing Lizzie did want to pursue something with Brody, so soon after ending her relationship with Miles, she didn't feel guilty about it. Miles wasn't coming back, and even if he did, Lizzie wasn't sure she *wanted* him back.

When only Misty returned several minutes later, Lizzie jumped up, not giving Misty a chance to ask where she was going. Lizzie headed left out of the bar and found Brody opening the door of his truck.

"You're leaving without saying goodbye?" she asked.

"Looked like you were safe for tonight. Figured I'd head out."

"I don't know how to thank you," she said. She lowered her eyes as she walked closer to him, the outside bar lights casting a somber hue as rain gently grazed his face. She thought of Kallie's threat and decided now was her chance to make a move. "But this will have to do."

She didn't overthink it as she gently pulled his face to hers and kissed his lips, softly at first, and then with a salacious hunger. He pulled her body close to his, cupping one hand on her neck, while the other rested on the small of her back. He pressed himself into her, letting her know how aroused this moment made him. She felt it, too, the pleasurable throbbing between her thighs, the rapid breathing, her body aching for more. But he pulled away before it could go any further.

"I have to go," he said, continuing to run his fingers through her hair, keeping her close to him. The rain came down a little harder now; the chill of the cold October air thwarting the warmness of pleasure she'd felt seconds before. He stroked her face, planting one last kiss on her lips. "But I'll see you tomorrow."

"Yeah," she said, offering a smile as she remained there a few more seconds.

Brody winked and said, "You better get inside, pretty woman, or I may never leave."

Lizzie felt something she hadn't in a long time, the promise of excitement brought on by the euphoria of new love. It lingered on her lips and everywhere he had touched her. After a few moments, she headed back into the bar, glancing one last time at Brody before he drove off into the night.

chapter 25

"**P**unk, I need a favor," Brody said as he drove home from the bar. "You know I wouldn't ask unless it was really important."

Punk's gravelly voice boomed through Brody's truck speakers. "What is it, kid?"

"Do you have connections at the Agency?"

"Why?"

"I need Chuck Degan's address."

"Oh, for fuck's sake, Brody. Please don't tell me you're going to do something stupid."

"Can you get me the address or not, Punk?"

"It's bad enough I'm driving hours to an inn where I don't want to be on one of the worst holidays of the year, everybody dressed like idiots, but now you want me to defy Nunez's orders?"

"Punk, please. I wouldn't ask you unless it was important."

"What aren't you telling me, Brody?"

Brody stopped at a red light. The sound of windshield wipers swished against the front window.

"We're walking into an ambush, Punk. I want a backup plan."

"What kind of ambush are we talking about here? And why the *hell* weren't we briefed about it?"

"Trust me, Punk," Brody said. "You don't want to know. The fact that I'm asking you to do me this favor is me briefing you enough."

"Oh, fine," Punk said. "I'll call my old pal Rick. He's just crazy enough to give me Degan's address. But you owe me, kid. And tomorrow, I expect you to tell us all what we're walking into."

"I will." Brody paused before saying, "And Punk. Don't tell Nunez. Please. She won't get it. But I can assure you, we need Chuck."

"Brody, you better hope that house is lined with CIA agents because if Chuck Degan is as bad as they say he is, you'll be dead before you ring the doorbell."

"Yeah, got it. Thanks."

Brody hung up the phone and continued to drive in silence, the only sound coming from the pelting rain and the swish, swish of his windshield wipers. Lizzie's kiss lingered on his tongue. He'd crossed the line tonight, big time. But everything he'd learned about during his meeting with Nunez the other day had him thinking that time was short and precious. He and Lizzie might not get another moment like the one they had tonight. Hell, they might not even make it through the weekend. And besides, she'd made the first move.

The next morning, as the blue hue of dawn cast its beauty, just before the gray hijacked the day, Brody parked his truck several streets away from the address Punk had given him. He carefully slipped out of his truck and quietly closed the door. Donned in a black hoodie, jeans, and a black cap, Brody stealthily navigated through several backyards, careful not to be seen. As he made his way quietly through each backyard, scaling wooden and vinyl fences, Brody hoped to stay undetected by early-rising neighbors or the agents who were watching Chuck Degan's house.

Chuck Degan lived in an unassuming rancher off Copley Road in Williamstown, New Jersey. What Chuck's neighbors didn't know was that he was a trained killer whose skills were unparalleled, even by the sharpest agents in the country, maybe even the world. He'd spent years doing the CIA's bidding, trained in infiltration, assassination, counterintelligence, and black ops. He could slip in and out of high-security targets without leaving a trace. In his younger years, Chuck Degan was untouchable and unstoppable, until he made one mistake.

He fell in love.

Crouched behind a tall bush in the backyard next to Degan's, Brody listened for any signs of life. Brody had his own history of skills, which he developed thanks to his uncle before he ever entered the FBI. For instance, Brody knew that in order to hear the subtle movements of the agents he was tracking, he had to quiet his inner dialogue, close his eyes, and get into a meditative state. Then all he needed to do was to just listen. He didn't have to concentrate hard. In fact, the less he concentrated, the better.

Within several seconds of sitting quietly and taking in his surroundings, Brody heard shoes shuffling along the ground. By the way the agents walked, he could tell there were two of them. They were as quiet as cats stalking prey, and anyone else might not have detected them. Brody dared not make a sound. All he could do was sit and wait, for he knew the agents would switch shifts at some point, and when they did, he would seize the opportunity.

One hour, more daylight, and a leg cramp later, Brody got his chance. He heard one of the agents whisper, "Goat's here. We can go. Lee is inside."

"What about leaving this unmanned?"

"Come on. Old man Degan's been compliant. He's probably still asleep."

Brody heard footsteps and waited until they faded away before peering over the fence separating Degan's yard from his neighbors. The transition would be smooth and quiet, and now was Brody's only chance to reach Degan undetected.

Brody quietly climbed over the fence and quickly ran to the back door. He didn't have much time, maybe five minutes at most. Brody reached the back porch, carefully picked the lock, another valuable lesson he'd learned from his uncle, and was about to slip into the house when he heard the click of a gun, the barrel pressed against his temple. Immediately, he put his hands up in a surrender pose.

"Boy," a deep, gravelly voice whispered. "You better have a damn good reason for tryin' to break into my house."

Brody saw no point in sugar-coating anything. He knew Chuck Degan's reputation all too well. His best chance was getting straight to the point.

"Mr. Degan," Brody said, no louder than a whisper himself. "Your daughter's in danger."

Degan backed up and let Brody inside, but he still kept the gun pointed at Brody's head. Degan held his finger up to his lips, a motion for Brody to be quiet. Inside, the television blared, and Brody could see a completely oblivious agent sitting in what he assumed was Chuck's recliner, feet up on a coffee table, watching an old episode of Everybody Loves Raymond. Meanwhile, Chuck motioned for Brody to head down into the basement quietly. Once they were downstairs, Chuck started.

"Talk, or I put a bullet in your head."

Degan had a Bond-meets-old-western-cowboy vibe, and Brody admired it, even though he felt threatened.

"Can you...put that thing down first?" Brody asked,

motioning to the gun. "How do you even have a gun when this place is crawling with agents?"

Degan looked Brody over and assessed his outfit.

"You're not CIA. Who are you?"

"Special agent," Brody said, his eyes shifting to the gun once more. "Was a special agent. My name is Brody Woods. I'm doing an undercover job, off the books, protecting your daughter."

"Well, Brody Woods, you don't seem to be doing a very good job of that if you're telling me she's in danger. You better talk, boy. Your clock is ticking."

Brody explained as much as he could in a short amount of time. He had hesitated at first to divulge the information about the pendant and his theory that Cedric and Redcap were not human; he seriously thought Degan might shoot him just for that. But eventually, he told him everything, figured he had nothing to lose.

"Shit," was all Degan said.

"Shit?"

Degan didn't say anything more, just headed to the back of the basement. He used his elbow to cave in a piece of the wall.

"I just told you there's another world out there, Fae, magic, all of it, and your first instinct is to punch a wall?"

Degan grabbed a long black bag and unzipped it.

"You want to know how I keep my guns?" Degan asked. "I hide them in the walls. The agents are too stupid to look."

"And... what are you going to do with that?"

"There's a lot you don't know, kid. And I don't have time to explain it all right now. But there's a reason I've kept my guns in the walls. And it ain't for burglars or dodging agents. What I need is for you to get your ass to that inn and protect my daughter. I'll be right behind you once I figure out how to outwit the pricks upstairs. We'll meet there tonight. I'll fill you in on the rest then. Anyone else in your little undercover op know about me?"

"Just one. But he's solid. The rest of my team, too. They won't talk."

"You better hope not."

Brody thought it best not to mention Nunez, but Punk, Dale, and Shay were as loyal as they came.

"No matter what you think you know, boy, you're not ready for what's coming."

"I can handle it," Brody said. "I'm not afraid of them."

"Good. Because to face what's coming… the Shadow Fae… you'll need every ounce of courage you've got. Now get out of my house, and go save my daughter."

Brody swallowed deeply. Chuck Degan, one of the most feared men among criminals and agents, knew about the Shadow Fae. If he was worried, that wasn't a good sign.

"Yes, sir."

"You call me Chuck," Degan said.

"Chuck, got it."

"Oh, and Brody… don't get killed on your way out, damn it."

chapter 26

The next morning, Brody pulled up to his sister's house early and stood outside her door. If he went inside, she'd ask him to sit, have coffee, spend some time—that would break him. He needed to leave without any sentiment weighing on his mind, just in case he didn't come home from the inn.

Jessica wore sweatpants and a T-shirt with her purple fleece robe wrapped around her.

"Coming in?" she asked.

"No," he said, shaking his head. "I have to get on the road."

"Everything okay?" she asked. "Mips is fine if that's what you're here about. She slept curled up next to Ava last night."

Brody let out a deep sigh.

"Look," Brody said, wiping his nose. "I...uh...I didn't want to tell you before because I didn't want to worry you, but I've been working an undercover job, and it looks like it just got a whole lot more dangerous, so..."

Jessica pursed her lips and nodded slowly, narrowing her eyes and crossing her arms against her chest.

"I thought you were done with the FBI, Brody."

"I was..." She eyed him suspiciously, so he tried to sound

more convincing. "I was, Jessie. I am. I just…" He ran his hand through his hair. "Look, I need you to do me a favor."

"Okay."

"And if…" He rubbed his brow before continuing his thought. "If something happens to me…"

"Brody…"

"If something happens to me," he said more forcefully, "I need you to get Mips a golden retriever."

Jessica laughed.

"Brody, that's preposterous. I'm not getting your *cat* a golden retriever."

"Look, she talks to me, okay, and I'm pretty sure that's what she wants. You know? She misses Kado, and I think it would be good for her to have a companion."

Jessica accentuated her words.

"Then get her one yourself when you come home, ya big idiot." Brody's eyes lingered on his sister's; unspoken words exchanged between them. "You are coming home, Brody, right?"

"Yeah," he nodded. "Yeah… sure. I am. I'm just saying if something were to happen to me…"

"Is something going to happen to you?"

"No, I'm just… can you just please make me that promise, Jessie?"

Jessica took in a deep breath and released it slowly.

"Yeah," she shook her head, not meeting Brody's eyes. "Sure."

"There's one more thing," Brody continued. He reached into his pocket and pulled out a letter. "If something happens to me, will you give Dad this letter? Only if… you know."

"Great," Jessica said, rolling her eyes. She snatched the letter from Brody.

"Thank you."

"Hmm," was her only response.

"I love you, Jessie." He nodded his head toward her. "I love you. You know that, right?"

"I love you, too," she said, returning his nod with worried eyes. "But you better come home, Brody."

"I'm gonna come home."

"You better. You hear me?"

"I'm gonna come home, Jessie."

She nodded as if to convince herself he was coming home.

"Okay," he said, giving her a tight-lipped smile. "Okay. Good." He started to turn away, but then looked back at her again. "Um, there's one more thing. I can't leave without telling you this. You have *shit* taste in men. I know I'm not one to talk because of Nina and all, but you deserve better. That guy you went out with the other day. He's a..." Brody stopped himself from saying *hitman*. "He has a girlfriend. Look for better, okay?"

"Okay," he heard Jessie say, heard the cracking of her voice, and he couldn't meet her eyes. He needed to leave now if he was going to make it to the inn on time.

Brody left, not looking back. In a perfect scenario, he'd see his sister again. He'd mend his relationship with his dad, he'd get the girl, and he'd get that damn cat a golden retriever.

Part Two

chapter 27

"Killers aren't born, Miglio, they're raised." That's what Miles' father had said to him in his thick Italian accent before he passed away, before Miglio Alfonso Leone became Miles Corrigan, *hitman*, and before Miles' mother married into another crime family.

For years, Miles had tucked his father's words deeply into his subconscious. Alfonso Leone, known as "the shoemaker," was a capo who died when Miles was nine. Remy Baker wasted no time pursuing Miles' mother, and soon Miles and his brother Dean were part of another made family, known simply as… The Family. The Bakers ran their operations primarily the same as the Italian mafia when it came to crime, but they lacked that deep Italian respect for their mothers, and they didn't indulge in meatballs and ravioli on Sundays.

While Remy tried to protect the young Leone boys from The Family, his brother Ludwig had other plans. Ludwig started grooming the boys for a life of crime at ten and twelve, sending them on small jobs to steal or transport drugs, using them as bait to lure someone to his death, or delivering warnings and messages to other families. Ludwig sent Miles on his first real job at seventeen to kill a drug dealer who had kept some of the money he was supposed to deliver to Ludwig. After all those years of training, Miles had no conscience left. He'd taken the guy out with little remorse.

Time and time again, Miles had done what he'd been trained to do with effortless ease. Until he met Lizzie. That's when small memories of his father, of a life before crime, snuck through the cracks of his sinewy subconscious, torturing his conscious mind.

"This life isn't for you," his father had said. "I want you boys to go to college and stay out of the business."

Miles and Dean had failed their father, and now they were too deep in The Family to ever leave. The only way out for them now was *death*.

Miles stood on the marble steps of Ludwig's mansion, built on an old farm in Hammonton, New Jersey. The house was anything but a farmhouse, but an old farmhouse did exist on the property; it was where most of the interrogations and torture of unfortunate degenerates took place. Miles had grown up in this mansion. His mom still lived there, along with Remy, Ludwig, and Ludwig's son, Liam. The 10,000 square foot house was big enough for the entire family, but Miles spent as little time there as possible.

Miles entered the house as he had so many times before and walked down the front hallway until he reached a set of French doors that led to the grand dining hall. Similar to the rest of the house, the floors were made of white marble. Tall arched windows with cream-colored curtains lined the back wall, and white crown molding bordered the ceiling. Grecian statues were flanked by two lion-headed fountains that poured water into a stone base on either side of the room. Miles had a fond memory of him and his brother using the fountain water to fill their water guns and then being scolded for soaking the dining hall. A large chandelier hung in the middle of the room, and underneath that was a long mahogany table with thirteen high-back chairs carefully placed around it.

No one who wasn't part of The Family would enter during the meeting except Frida, Ludwig's obsequious servant, who poured wine for the men seated at the table. Frida was the only servant allowed, and tonight, Miles breezed by her as he entered the room. He offered a slight nod to Remy, who acknowledged his stepson with a faint smile. Ludwig had invited Redcap, Cedric, and their three beefy soldiers to a meeting. Miles had no idea why. He sat next to Remy, joining in the ongoing silence. The silence in the room during those meetings was always overwhelming, but on this night, it was so thick that even the wooden chair leg scratching across the marble was welcoming.

Ludwig eyed Miles with his sinister glare—the same one he had graced him with ever since Miles disobeyed. The only reason Miles had been kept alive was because The Family's priorities had suddenly changed, and Remy had argued on Miles' behalf. Ludwig had spared Miles' life, but Miles still lost everything in the end. He lost any hope of a normal life, lost Lizzie. So none of it mattered anyway; he'd already given up.

For several seconds, Ludwig and Redcap looked around the room. No one dared to make eye contact with them, except for Liam. Redcap's menacing demeanor as he cast his eyes over the people in front of him, like they were his insignificant subordinates, was more unnerving than any of Ludwig's narrowed eye glares.

"Our guest has somethin' to say," Ludwig said as he looked over at Redcap and nodded.

Up until now, Miles had only taken orders from Cedric or Remy. Redcap spoke in a slow, croaky voice, casting a sly eye over each person in the room. Miles held on to the gold chain horn he kept around his neck, the last gift from his father, protection from the Italian "malooch."

"You want Lizzie's inheritance. We want Lizzie," Redcap said. "Seems a fair deal to trade one for the other."

"It is," Ludwig responded with a nod.

No one dared speak. In their last meeting, Ludwig explained they would be handing Lizzie over to Cedric and Redcap instead of killing her, but no one asked why. No one ever asked why when Ludwig barked an order.

Remy had insinuated that Redcap and Cedric's motives for wanting Lizzie were more ominous than Ludwig's ploy to kill her for an inheritance.

Who knew there was a plan worse than torture or murder?

Ludwig had allowed Redcap to waltz in one day, giving orders. Apparently, Ludwig was batshit crazy enough to believe Redcap could offer him everlasting life. And he was just loony enough to kill anyone who contested his beliefs. Miles felt powerless in this situation, knowing he couldn't protect Lizzie any longer.

Ludwig took a sip of his wine, keeping his eyes fixed on Redcap.

"I'll admit I was disappointed in your failed attempt to retrieve the woman tonight," Redcap said.

"As I said, the wrong cops were dispatched to the apartment," Ludwig countered.

"Of course," Redcap replied, nodding his head. "Misunderstandings do happen." His lip lifted upward in a pretentious smirk.

Redcap twirled his fingers over his wine glass like he owned the damn place.

"About Lizzie's inheritance…" he said slowly, "we'll be taking something from it."

Ludwig stiffened. "What'd you just say?

"We believe a particular item is among her things. And…

it's *ours.*"

Ludwig's fingers curled into fists, and he ran his tongue over his teeth. "Nah. See, that wasn't the deal."

"This… isn't a negotiation," Redcap replied, his voice calm.

Ludwig let out a low, cold, tight-lipped laugh. "You think I give a shit what you call it? We made a deal. I don't know what it's like where you come from, buddy, but here, you stick to the deal made. *You* get the woman; *we* get the inheritance. All of it."

"You're mistaken, and perhaps I have not made myself clear," Redcap answered. "Something among Lizzie's inheritance is *ours*, a simple pendant, and we *will* be taking it."

Ludwig stood slowly, straightening his cuffs. "Over my dead body. Let's go. Everybody out. This meeting is over. And consider our deal null."

Redcap raised an eyebrow. "As you wish."

Before anyone could leave, Redcap flicked his hand, and suddenly, Ludwig stumbled. His knees buckled as if the ground itself betrayed him. His wine glass slipped from his hand and shattered across the marble floor.

"What the…" Ludwig wheezed, clutching his throat as his eyes bulged.

"Father!" Liam screamed.

Ludwig crashed backward, convulsing once before going still. He wasn't dead, but paralyzed.

Miles' eyes shifted to the wine. *Had Redcap poisoned Ludwig?*

"Holy shit," someone whispered.

A beat of frozen silence passed before Cedric snorted.

"I told you. Your 'Don' is just another meat suit."

chapter 28

Miles didn't move. No one did except Liam. "Touch him, and I'll fucking kill you!" Liam roared, jumping up from his seat. "You hear me?! I'll kill you!"

Redcap let out a tight-lipped snicker. His men quickly rose, ready to fight. Dean slowly pulled Liam back down to a seated position. Miles' brother understood the gravity of the situation and gave Miles a glare that said, Don't you dare move.

Even Remy stayed calm, seemingly unaffected by his brother's sudden demise. Remy's eye flickered from his brother back to Redcap. Ludwig still gurgled on the ground as if he were being held there by some invisible force.

Miles knew the drill. Now that Ludwig was compromised, they were to follow Remy's lead.

Redcap rose and brushed imaginary dust from his jacket. "Let this be a lesson. I don't tolerate disrespect." He directed his gaze at Liam. "You want to cross me, you will end up like him, choking on your pride and your own goddamn tongue!"

An impossible silence enveloped the room.

"Enzo, approach," Redcap said, speaking to Ludwig's

consigliere.

Enzo tried to keep his composure as he slowly made his way over, but Miles knew it was an act. Sweat dripped down his face as his eyes darted down at Ludwig's paralyzed body, then to Remy, and finally to Redcap.

Meanwhile, Liam stifled his emotions while Remy glowered at the man who hurt his brother. Redcap whispered something into Enzo's ear, and Miles watched Enzo's eyes widen with an obvious horror. Then the consigliere reluctantly disappeared through the French doors.

While Enzo was gone, Redcap said, "Now, let us return to our discussion. Unless anyone else would like to join their leader." No one dared move, and Redcap continued. "We believe what we are looking for is at a place called The Speakeasy Inn."

"What are you looking for?" Remy asked, still trying to keep his temperament calm. But his eyes drifted several times to his brother's paralyzed body.

"The pendant I mentioned," Redcap said. He stood, looking down at the remaining filled chairs. "It's a very old relic that belongs to us. I want you to find it and deliver it to me."

"And Lizzie," Cedric added.

"Yes," Redcap replied. "You will retrieve the pendant and the woman. Do I make myself clear?"

"You're sayin' they're both at the inn," Remy said.

"Yes," Redcap answered.

"If we do this for you," Remy asked, trying to restore some order to The Family, "will you leave us alone?"

Fulfill the mission, then cut the ties. Remy's willingness to negotiate with men like Redcap was why he was the weaker of the two Bakers. Ludwig had been a kill now, ask questions later kind of guy. If he could hear any of this, he was boiling.

"As long as we don't run into any...problems," Redcap

replied. "As long as Lizzie and the relic are returned to us."

"What's more important to you, the relic or Lizzie?" Miles asked.

"Shut up, Miglio," Dean said under his breath, but he knew better. Miles always stirred the pot. And since Ludwig was on his way out, what the hell did it matter anyway?

"Both are equally important to us," Cedric snapped, glaring in Miles' direction.

Miles saw something glisten in Cedric's eyes, like a flash of heat lightning.

"Why?"

Redcap had one of those grins where the corners of his mouth jerked upward and folded over, like a clown or a comic villain.

"You're the one," Redcap said, registering the part that Miles played in Ludwig's failed Lizzie mission. "I suppose I should thank you for your insubordination, although you would have had your throat slit if you'd defied me. Now, tell me what's wrong? Are you worried about your precious lover?"

Cedric growled, but no one seemed to pay him much mind, except for Miles, who knew that cock wanted Lizzie for some reason, kept saying Lizzie was his. Miles just didn't know why.

"Lizzie's nothing to me anymore," Miles said, his tone cold, indifferent. "I'm just curious."

"Lizzie may be the last hurdle in your way to her inheritance," Redcap said, "but to us, she represents something far greater."

"What?" Remy asked.

"Unimaginable power," Cedric grumbled, casting a dark glare in Remy's direction. "Something you…wouldn't understand."

"Where we come from," Redcap said, ignoring Cedric,

"power is divided into light and shadow. Each commands its own strength. But elemental power, true elemental power, is boundless."

"And Lizzie is the key to that power?" Miles asked.

"Lizzie is that power," Redcap snickered.

"We don't care about where you come from or your delusional ideas," Remy snapped, standing. "You attacked my brother. Now get the fuck outta here."

"Oh, we plan on returning home once we have what we came for," Redcap said. "But you might want to think about the tone you take with me. Perhaps you'd talk less and do more if you had…an incentive. And here it is now."

At that moment, the French doors burst open. Miles swallowed hard as a beast slowly lumbered into the room, unlike anything he'd ever seen before. It was massive with thick muscles and wiry, matted fur. The creature snarled at the men before fixing its harrowing eyes on Ludwig's frozen body. Thick foam slavered from its long snout.

"If you move a muscle, even one, you will be next," Redcap said to the seated men. "How do you say it in Italy? Mangia."

The beast lost no time tearing into its prey. Miles tried to keep his eyes focused on the table, but he couldn't help but steal glances over to the ungodly act. Cracking bones, snarls, wet, tearing sounds. Everyone stayed frozen, like the marble statues around them.

Miles thought he was going to be sick.

And then…Ludwig was gone. The only traces of him were blood staining the marble floor.

But the sounds would echo in Miles' head for the rest of his life.

He'd killed before, a dozen times; this shouldn't bother him, but it did. When it was over, the beast stood there, panting, blood dripping down its mouth. It sat next to Redcap, ready to attack at his next command.

Dean glared at Miles, an unspoken dialogue coursing between them. At that moment, Miles understood that Redcap was an implacable adversary. This wasn't some mafia power shift. Something ancient and wrong had entered their world, and Ludwig's death wasn't the end of its terror. Whatever Redcap had in store for them wasn't good.

They needed to get their mother far away from this house.

"I think that is all for today," Redcap said. "I trust you will retrieve the woman and the relic..." He glared at Miles, "...with no complications." Then, turning back to the rest of the group, he said, "You will leave for the inn as soon as Cedric and I have prepared for our homecoming."

Miles didn't know what that meant, and he didn't care. All he knew was that they were all in trouble, and he had to get to Lizzie fast.

chapter 29

Brody arrived at the inn around 11 a.m., a little later than he hoped. It was a picturesque sight, not at all what he expected. He'd expected a quaint bed and breakfast, but the inn was a towering mansion, three stories high and as wide as some of the Pennsylvania estates along the Delaware River. A long, circular driveway led to the front entrance. A path of red pavers continued from the driveway to a verandah furnished with several black wrought-iron bistro sets.

The main house only had eighteen rooms, but there were several cabins with guest rooms on the grounds as well. The cabins had long, horizontal, sleek, teakwood panels on the outside, with black-rimmed large bay windows. The owner had woven walking and biking trails between the cabins that eventually led to a long stretch of woods. Each cabin had a fire pit outside, and a few benches were scattered along the trails. Brody wondered if he would be in the main house or in one of the cabins.

As soon as Brody stepped inside the inn, he felt the Halloween ambiance: faux spider webbing lined a red-carpeted grand stairway; a skeleton maid stood at the end of the stairs with a broom; fake rubber spiders hung from the ceiling; and Halloween candy baskets were strategically placed around the front hall. At the top of the stairs, a man and a woman skeleton dressed as 1920s masquerade ball attendees were locked in a loving embrace.

The inn owners had converted the house's old dining room into the Speakeasy Café. Contemporary electronic music oozed from black speakers. A few guests sat in white chairs that flanked tiny white tables. Another guest sat in a loveseat, resting her drink on a teakwood coffee table.

After checking in at the front desk, Brody immediately made his way to his room, which was on the second floor of the main house. He needed a quick shower before he met with his team. Nunez had told them to be prompt because she had important information to share.

Brody headed up a narrow set of carpeted stairs with his bag and made his way down a long, taupe-colored, carpeted hallway to his room. The inn had been updated and now used electronic keypads. He tapped his key card against the pad, and the door opened to a quaint sitting room with hardwood floors. From this view, he could see out to the front grounds. A king-sized bed was in the main room, along with a flat-screen TV and a decent-sized bathroom.

Brody: *Let me know when you get here.*

Brody sent Lizzie a text and then took a quick shower. His feelings oscillated between what they'd started the night before and what was to come. He knew that eventually, he would have to come clean with Lizzie, hopefully sooner rather than later.

Even though Lizzie didn't respond, Brody wasn't worried. Instead, his thoughts drifted to Chuck as he hurried down the stairs and out the inn's main door toward the cabins. He and Chuck hadn't discussed how they would communicate should he be able to break free from his house arrest. But if Chuck were to live up to his reputation, Brody wouldn't have to be concerned about that.

Nunez was set up in cabin five, and Brody walked down a long, winding path until he reached the cabin. The shades were drawn, and Brody couldn't tell if anyone was in there, so the cabin was certainly serving its purpose. He knocked on the door, and an agent with dark glasses opened it, nodded to Brody, and let him inside. The inn staff had completely rearranged the room for them, moving the bed against the wall and providing chairs and tables for everyone to sit. Dale had an entire computer system on a long table against the terrace sliding doors. Nunez's whiteboard with the pictures of the mafia families stood in the corner, with orange and yellow sticky notes posted all over it.

Punk, Dale, and Shay were already seated when Brody arrived. An older gentleman with wispy, gray hair in a checkered sweater stood by Nunez's side, engaging in low, amiable conversation.

"You're late," Nunez said under her breath as Brody sat beside Punk.

"My apologies," Brody answered. "Needed a shower."

Nunez held out her hand, palm up, in the direction of the older gentleman.

"Brody, please meet Francis Ermington. He's the innkeeper here, said he will personally deliver Lizzie and her friend to the inn and make sure they're settled. He's put them in the main house with you, third floor."

"Good to meet you, sir," Brody said, extending his hand to the old man.

"I'm here to help," Ermington assured them. "I've been managing this place since Harold inherited it back in the '80s. Had no idea there was something special in the library.

I keep it locked per Harold's wishes. Only people who go in there are cleaning staff, and I don't even have them in there but once a month to keep the cobwebs out. There's a wrought iron casing around the original owner's old journals. I have a key for that, too. Harold was a good man, a friend, so you have my full cooperation. My only question now is… I have quite a few guests and a wedding party this weekend. Do you think we should evacuate them?"

"No need, Mr. Ermington," Nunez assured him. "This is a covert operation that won't require such measures."

"Oh, good. I wouldn't want anything to happen to anyone, you know."

"Of course. Of course. Thank you, Mr. Ermington," Nunez said, motioning to the agent by the door. "But we won't keep you any longer," she added. "Agent James will see you out."

Once the innkeeper was gone, Brody asked, "How much did you tell him?"

"Very little. Just that we needed to investigate something of Harold's that he left for his granddaughter, and that some bad people were after it. I wanted him to know we were pressed for time, which we are." Nunez kept her focus on Brody. "Tomorrow morning, get the library key from Ermington and begin your search for the pendant. I want Lizzie to read those journals carefully. Harold may have left her some clues about who she is and what she's inheriting. Ermington seems to have no idea what kind of situation he's in. I assume Harold didn't tell him much, so let's keep him out of it as much as possible. Stick by Lizzie's side if you make it to the Halloween Ball tomorrow night. I imagine we might finally see some action from the Bakers."

"And if they don't come?" Brody asked.

Nunez's mouth twitched upward, giving away something that Brody couldn't quite pinpoint.

"I was waiting for Brody to arrive before telling you all of this," Nunez said. "Dale was able to get some information about Juarez. Unfortunately, we have confirmed his death."

"Who did it?" Punk asked.

"Not who," Nunez said. "But *what?*" She approached the board and added a grainy photo to it. "Some kind of attack animal. Unclear, but whatever it was, it was two times the size of a wolf and well-trained. It took its orders from Redcap. Seeing as this has become personal for me, we're going to bring every one of those maniacs down."

"What kind of animal could it be?" Brody asked.

"I don't know," Nunez said. A quick widening of her eyes made Brody feel a pit in his gut.

"How are we going to bring these guys down?" Shay asked, oblivious to the silent exchange transpiring between Brody and Nunez.

"Well, for starters, I've brought more of my team to help," Nunez said. "Juarez's death is now an official FBI investigation. If Redcap and the Bakers show up, we'll have a team in place to lock down the inn."

"You called in a SWAT team?" Brody asked.

"Lotta manpower for a what-if-they-show, don't ya think?" Punk said.

"Not a what-if any longer," Nunez said. "I had my mole plant the information that Lizzie is here, that she's looking for the pendant."

"Wait, you what?" Brody said, not bothering to hide his cynicism.

"I told you," Nunez retorted. "It's personal now. We're taking all of them down. I have a team with tranqs waiting to take that beast out. But we need all of them here, in person, to do that. We have enough evidence to put them away for a long time, but we need them unaware that we're waiting for them."

"And you can trust this…mole?" Punk asked.

"I trust him," Nunez responded.

"Director…" Brody warned. "There was always a chance they would come, but now you're handing the pendant *and* Lizzie to them. You're using Lizzie as bait."

"Did you not hear me?" Nunez barked. "This is our chance to take down the largest mafia family we know of in the U.S., Brody, plus whoever else they're working with. They killed one of ours! I'll do everything possible to ensure it goes the way we want."

"Even at the expense of Lizzie?"

She glared at him. "At anyone's expense." Her words were cold, business-like.

"So, we're clear," Brody snapped. "You just told that innkeeper not to evacuate anyone, and then you invited a bunch of cold-blooded killers to the inn."

Nunez attempted to soften her tone but instead stumbled over her words.

"I understand you're upset, but if Ermington evacuates even one person, the Bakers, this Redcap, they'll know it's a sting." Addressing the rest of the team, she said, "All of you go. I need to speak to Brody alone."

Brody's mind reeled as the room cleared. Was Nunez serious right now?

"Brody…"

"Director, before you say anything else, you told me if it became too much, you would pull the plug. Now you're intentionally putting Lizzie in harm's way. All of us, for that matter. Before, there was just a chance, and now you've made it definite."

"Brody, I did what I did, and I'm not going to apologize for it. You knew when you signed up for this that it wasn't going to be a stroll on the beach and some candlelit dinners. If you have strings attached, that's on you. I'm doing what's necessary to get these guys."

"Is this about Juarez, or does catching them make you look good?"

Nunez looked down at her shoes before speaking, and Brody braced himself for her to explode. He hadn't come here for a fight, but he wasn't going to nod and obey when it put so many people's lives on the line.

"I know the situation seems dire," Nunez said, "but I wasn't going to leave you in the trenches without reinforcements. That's why I called in the extra manpower. That's why I made it *official.*" She took a deep breath before she said her next words. "And I'm going to ask for your forgiveness now in case you're too angry with me in the future."

"About what?" Brody asked. He couldn't imagine what else she could say that would make him angrier than he already was.

A knock made him turn just as one of Nunez's agents opened the door. Brody felt a lump form in his throat at the sight before him. There he was, standing, cocky as ever, all five foot eleven of him. His jet-black hair was slicked back, a light stubble coating his chin. He had deep olive skin, large brown eyes, and a big smile, more fake and sinister than ever before. Hemmy "fucking" Giordano.

"Brody, mah main man," he said in his Philly drawl. He winked, and Brody almost lost his cool. He'd played *this* day, the day he would see Hemmy again, over in his mind about a hundred times. Each fantasy had ended with Hemmy badly bruised and begging for Brody to spare him. But now that the moment was here, Brody did not carry out his sick imaginary plot; instead, he maintained his composure, although he was certain his facial expression made his feelings very clear.

Hemmy still wore that smug grin as he smacked his gum in the most irritating way. Nunez gave Brody wide eyes, a warning to remain calm despite the situation.

"I'd prefer it if you don't kill each other, as we have an important job to do, and I need both of you focused and dedicated."

Brody still didn't speak. He just stood, crossed his arms against his chest, and glared at his old best friend.

Nunez was a dick for this move, and Brody wouldn't forget it. She knew how much he hated Hemmy, how this guy was the one guy who could make his blood smolder. He hated Hemmy more than Miles, more than Redcap, the Bakers. If Brody had any enemies, Hemmy was one of them.

"This is your idea of reinforcements," Brody said, nodding toward Hemmy. "You have the coroner on call, Nunez? With this guy in charge, there'll be a lot of casualties."

"Brody," Nunez warned.

"Listen, buddy," Hemmy said. "I'm here to help keep you alive. Why don't you let bygones be bygones?"

Brody snickered.

"*You're* going to keep *me* alive? Do you even know what side you're fighting for?"

Hemmy stepped closer, eyeing Brody with his gum-smacking, arrogant grin, one eye crinkling upward.

"Hey, Brody, why don't you let me handle Lizzie, you know, take her off your hands? She'll cozy up quickly, just like Nina did."

"Fuck you, Hemmy," Brody said. Brody's blood had gone from simmer to boil, and his rage almost got the best of him. Hemmy was an asshat, even now, and Brody wondered why he was ever friends with him in the first place.

"Play nice," Nunez droned on. Then she turned to Hemmy. "Watch your tongue, Giordano, or I'll have your badge."

Hemmy scoffed but didn't say anything else.

"Now, sit down, both of you," Nunez said.

"I'll stand, thanks," Brody said as he watched Hemmy take a seat. Even the way Hemmy sat, with his legs wide apart, his elbow resting on the bed, was arrogant.

"Hemmy's SWAT team will have your back. They'll monitor any activity on the premises. The goal here is for all of us to blend in with the crowd. With any luck, we should see some activity from the Bakers and this Redcap by tomorrow night. When we do, Brody will stick to his plan with his team, and Hemmy, you'll stick to yours. You'll communicate via earpieces that Dale will monitor from the room. I want you to wear them at all times except after hours. We need to be in constant communication with each other. Do you both understand?"

Neither Brody nor Hemmy responded, but Nunez looked back and forth between them until Hemmy said. "Yeah, heard ya loud and clear, Director."

"Yes," Brody responded, refusing to meet Hemmy's eyes.

"Good," she said. "Enjoy your last night of freedom, boys, and please, stay the *fuck* out of each other's way."

chapter 30

"How are you feeling?" Lizzie asked Misty as she drove along Route 476 towards Beechville, Pennsylvania, a little town next to Starlight.

A mélange of colors, warm greens and browns, burnt oranges and yellows, and a spectrum of vibrant to dull reds painted a serene scene that made Lizzie feel like she was dancing along an artist's oil painting. Such were the Pennsylvania hills and mountainsides in fall.

The women had gotten a late start that morning, leaving at 11:00 a.m., but they needed sleep after last night's events. The night before had brought a whirlwind of emotions for Lizzie, ranging from fear to lust. Brody's kiss had lingered on her lips, but when she fell asleep, nightmares enveloped her.

She was dressed in a long, gold gown, standing on top of a tall mountain with her stalker. He was dressed in a long black garb, pointing to thick clouds of fire in the distance that were barreling toward them. His hand touched the small of her back, evoking a pulse of warmth and belonging she hadn't felt in a long time. He didn't speak. Didn't need to. An electric ache moved between them, letting her know all she needed to. They were in danger, about to be consumed by the fire. And the worst part was? Lizzie was madly in love with him.

Lizzie shook off the nightmare, chalking it up to the previous night's events, but it lingered with her, even now, as they traveled to the inn. And while it had been disturbing, it was nothing compared to Misty's current reality.

Misty's husband, Frank, hadn't come home last night and wouldn't be returning for the foreseeable future. He had packed his bags while she was at the bar, and all she had left of him was a perfunctory goodbye letter.

"I'm fine," Misty replied, taking a sip of water from her pink water bottle.

But Lizzie knew Misty better than that.

"Okay, but I worry," Lizzie said, dancing around the topic delicately. "Because I know how much you loved Frank, and I know you seemingly had a good marriage. I mean, Miles and I didn't have a great relationship, but I still cried for three days straight over him. You were with Frank for five years. It's okay to cry, you know."

Misty shrugged, but Lizzie sensed the twinge of grief washing over her friend. The way Misty's shoulders curled forward and how she blinked back tears gave her away.

"I said I was fine, Lizzie."

Lizzie nodded.

"All right then."

She'd told Misty they didn't have to go to the inn, that she would sit with her, cry, do whatever she needed to do. But Misty insisted they go and told Lizzie there was no time for pints of ice cream and tissues. She wanted to get away. Getting away would help.

Lizzie agreed, but with one rule… that *she* drive, just in case Misty needed to have a meltdown. Lizzie didn't want to press the issue, but she needed her friend to know that she didn't have to hide her true feelings, not with Lizzie.

Lizzie took a deep breath, bracing herself for an aloof response.

"I just want you to know you can say anything to me, express yourself however you need to. You can scream. We can pull over on the side of the road, and you can run in circles screaming every expletive about Frank that you want. I don't care how you need to grieve, but I just want you to do it, and do it where you feel safe, because I will never, ever judge you. There's nothing you can do that would make me judge you or view you differently. I love you, and I just want you to know that."

Misty was reticent for several seconds before saying, "I really appreciate that. That's why you're my best friend. But I just feel numb right now, so…"

"I get it," Lizzie said.

"I just want to enjoy the weekend."

"Me too."

"And I'm tired of being the person everyone wants me to be. The person everyone *thinks* I am."

"Okay."

"I'm tired of being the goody-two-shoes do-gooder who never misses a church bake sale and offers to run bingo nights for the elderly every Thursday and Sunday in the summer. I don't want to do it anymore."

"Okay, whoa. Now you're just being cruel," Lizzie said. "Don't take bingo away from the old people!"

Misty let out a short snort.

"My parents will say Frank leaving is my fault," Misty mumbled, her tone somber.

Misty's family was so strict that they thought divorce was an act of the devil. If Frank left, it was Misty's duty to reflect on what she'd done wrong and figure out what she could do to be a better wife. In Lizzie's opinion, Misty's parents could be irrational about certain issues. But she'd never said anything to Misty, and for the most part, Misty's life had been smooth sailing. Nothing so serious had ever happened to her.

"It's not your fault," Lizzie assured. "And I don't want you for one second to think that."

"I know it's not," Misty said, "But they won't care about the truth. Frank left because he didn't want children."

"Frank?" Lizzie said, a wave of disbelief washing over her. "This is the guy who told me he wanted a brood of kids."

"I know."

"All he did was talk about wanting children!"

"Okay," Misty said. "I can see you're in shock, so if you plan on having a stroke, pull my car over and let me drive."

"*Yes*, I'm in shock," Lizzie said. "He literally told me he couldn't wait to have kids."

"Yeah, well, he was lying," Misty said. "Or at least, he didn't want to have them with me."

"No," Lizzie shook her head. "Obviously, Frank is just an asshole. He knew what you wanted when you got together. And now he gave up the best thing to ever happen to him." When Misty didn't reply, she continued. "So what will you do now?"

"I don't know," Misty said, keeping her eyes fixed forward. "But that's why I'm on this trip. To figure out my next move. I married Frank in the house of God, in sickness and in health, the good and the bad, but he wanted to leave, and I don't want to waste any more of my life."

Her voice started to crack, and Lizzie comforted her friend.

"I'm sorry you're going through this, Misty. You know that quote that everyone is fighting a battle, and you should be nice to people because you have no idea about their struggles?"

"Yeah," Misty said. "You butchered the quote, but yes."

"I'm starting to realize how true that quote is."

Lizzie and Misty arrived in Beechville at 2:30 p.m. The area, which bordered New York State, did not have a lot of industry or dense residential areas like South Jersey. Sporadic homes of various sizes dotted the hills; some were trailers, others were two-story homes or quaint farmhouses. They drove by one-road towns and heavily wooded areas—the perfect setting for a horror film.

Misty pointed to a sign that said, *Pick-up point.*

"Here it is, I think."

Anyone driving by might've thought the sign was to catch a bus. Lizzie turned and drove up a long, snaky, wooded path.

She turned into the parking lot carved out into the wooded area. Lizzie surmised it could hold about fifty cars max, and most spots were already filled. She searched for Brody's truck but didn't see it among the other vehicles. Her thoughts briefly returned to their kiss; it had been so hot, and she hoped he wanted to do it again.

"There's an empty spot," Lizzie said, parking Misty's car. They both got out, stretched, and breathed in the cold, fresh air.

"Excuse me," a deep, gruff voice said.

Lizzie was still on edge from last night's break-in and jumped when she saw a tall, bald man dressed in a black suit. He had a coil earpiece dangling from his right ear.

"What are you here for?" the man asked.

Lizzie relaxed when she realized he was there to help them get to the inn. A text message on her phone gave her the verbiage code for when she arrived, and she read it to the man.

"Windows adjust to sunlight or night."

"Come with me," the man said, unamused. He grabbed their bags, and the girls followed him past the parking lot and down a small path in the woods.

Soon, the women arrived at a clearing where they saw a shuttle. The big, burly man held up four fingers to the driver, who nodded.

"You can get on the shuttle here. It'll take you to the inn."

"Okay. Thanks," Lizzie said.

"Enjoy your stay," the man said.

"We will. Thanks," Misty replied.

Lizzie climbed into the shuttle first, followed by Misty. Outside her window, Lizzie saw the brawny man talking into an earpiece. The shuttle began to move up a long, winding path.

"Afternoon, folks," the shuttle driver said. "I'm Francis, your chauffeur to the Speakeasy Inn, where you will enjoy all things from the alluring 1920s era. How long are you folks staying?"

"A few days," Lizzie replied.

"Well, you sure are going to enjoy yourselves. You should know that the phrase you had to tell Brian was the original secret code people had to know to get into this speakeasy back in the 1920s. It's an acronym for the original owner's last name. Watson. You know, the inn is rich with history, and people love that it's still a secret."

"Sure," Lizzie nodded.

"In a world where everything is on social media and the internet, it's nice to have a place cut off from the mainstream."

Soon, Francis pulled the shuttle around a large circular driveway, revealing the impressive inn. The shuttle doors opened, and another man, thinner and taller than Brian, stood waiting for them.

"Good afternoon, and welcome to the Speakeasy Inn," the man said. "My name is Zeke. If you allow me to take your bags, you can enter the lobby and check in. We'll bring your bags straight to your room."

"Great," Lizzie said. "Thank you, Francis." Lizzie tried to give him a tip, but Francis declined.

"Enjoy your stay."

Lizzie and Misty made their way to the front desk to the right of the front doors, and Lizzie marveled at the inn's ornate beauty. The lobby chandelier consisted of circles of sparkling iridescent crystals and twinkling lights that tapered into a point.

"You'll be on the third floor," the hotel clerk said after Lizzie checked them in. She set a pamphlet on the desktop and pointed to it. "Room 313. You'll have to take the stairs, as we have no elevators."

"Thanks," Lizzie said, taking the pamphlet and her room keys. Then Misty and Lizzie headed up the circular stairs toward their room.

The decorators of the inn had doused it in Art Deco. The sharp geometrical patterns in gold, silver, and white gave the inn a regal appearance.

Inside, Room 313 looked just as beautiful as the hallway. Gold, white, and silver tapestry rugs covered the hardwood floors. Heavy white-gold curtains draped the window. A chandelier hung in the middle of the room. Two double beds were neatly made with white sheets and decorated with taupe and gold pillows. Opposite the beds, a flat-screen television was mounted on the wall above a wooden dresser. Secured on the geometrically designed wallpaper were paintings of wooded landscapes.

Misty plopped down onto one of the beds.

"I'm beat. I need a nap," she said.

"Me too," Lizzie replied. "I am happy to be away, though, far from all the drama."

"Amen, sister. Speaking of drama, are you going to text Brody or what?"

"I will. I just need a nap first."

Lizzie sat down on the other bed and let out a large yawn. She lay her head against the pillows, thinking she would only rest for a minute. As she did, she thought about what the weekend might bring. *It was good for them to be away, right?* As Lizzie's eyelids began to close, she thought, maybe, just maybe, she and Misty would experience an incredible transformation on their little trip, one that would allow them to leave the pains of their past in Beechville and return home with a renewed confidence and zest for life. But another thought consumed her, too—a sense of overwhelming dread—that something terrible was about to happen.

Brody fumed all the way back to his room. He drew in deep breaths in an attempt to calm down. *Why Hemmy, of all people?* The enmity between Brody and Hemmy persisted like a raging wildfire. He felt his blood pressure rising as he punched the pillows on his bed and realized he couldn't sit inside, not right now. He was too angry. He headed out of his room, down the stairs, and out the front door into the cold. The late afternoon sky had already begun to give way to the persistent night. Besides Brody's footsteps on the pavement, the only sounds were of rustling leaves. Rain threatened to drip from the darkening gray skies. Brody looked around at the vast nature surrounding him. And then he started to run. He ran through the cabin trails, past Nunez's cabin, and into the woods. He kept running deeper into the woods, letting the cold air slowly snuff the wild flames fanning inside him. And when he was far enough away, his nose too red from the cold, and he was too exhausted to run anymore, he stopped, folded over to catch his breath, and then let out a deep, primal yell. Then he sat in the leaves and breathed heavily, taking in the wooded scenery around him.

The pain inside him wasn't solely about Nina; it was about his family. Hemmy had destroyed Brody's family from the inside out. Nina was just the icing on the cake. And what made Brody most angry was that Hemmy didn't think he'd done anything wrong. He had never apologized… just made excuses for himself, and everyone but Brody seemed to buy it.

Brody stood now, staring into the woods, watching dead leaves slowly fall from a mighty oak. He couldn't think about Hemmy. Not now. Not when Lizzie needed him the most. He would have to put his grievances with Hemmy aside, no matter how much the guy pissed him off. Brody drew in another deep breath of fresh air before heading back through the woods toward the inn. His focus would be on Lizzie tonight, and maybe… *maybe* he might enjoy a little piece of sanity with her before the chaos set in.

Brody reached his room and took a short rest. He dressed in a nice suit and fitted the earpiece in place. As soon as he turned it on, he heard Hemmy's voice.

"All clear around the perimeter," Hemmy's voice echoed. "My guys will keep watch tonight; I'm signing off for now. They'll alert me if there's any more activity."

Any more? Brody thought.

A text message buzzed through from Nunez.

Nunez: *Need to see you. Now.*

Brody knocked on Nunez's door, expecting to see Agent Jimbo. But Nunez answered instead.

"I needed to speak to you alone," Nunez said, "and before you start, it's not about Hemmy."

"I've made my peace, for now," Brody said, entering the cabin. "In case you were wondering." Changing the subject, he said, "I heard there was some activity?"

"Nothing significant," she replied. Her folded arms and guarded stance told him she was hiding something. "But my informant came to see me. He told me some interesting information, and I need you to know it before everything goes down tomorrow."

"Who's your mole?" Brody asked.

"Not important," Nunez replied. "What's important is that this person told me Ludwig Baker is dead."

"What? Who did it?"

"Redcap murdered him in his own home in front of the entire Family." She paused, pursed her lips, and said, "The beast..."

Brody gagged at the thought: the bones crunching, blood pooling, flesh shredded. That beast had probably eaten Ludwig like a dog devours raw meat.

"Well, I can't say Ludwig didn't deserve it."

"Brody..." Nunez scolded.

"What?" *What did she want him to do, pretend he was sad that one more mass murderer was gone from the world?* "Isn't it a good thing that Ludwig is gone?" Brody asked. "One less threat to deal with?"

"My informant told me some horrible things I don't even think I have the courage to tell you yet, but what I *will* say is that Redcap and Cedric have been searching for that relic for a long time." She bit her bottom lip. "Much longer than we thought. And you were right. Now they're hell-bent on getting home, and to achieve their goal, they need that pendant."

"And Lizzie?" Brody asked. "Did your informant know what their plans were for her?"

Nunez shook her head.

"So the plan is the same. We find the relic first; we interrupt their plans," Brody said.

"Exactly, but..." Nunez looked down at the floor, then

back at Brody. "They've made contact with whatever world they came from."

Made contact? How? Brody had questions. He also wanted to know who was giving Nunez this information, but he didn't have a chance to ask her. Nunez seemed to read Brody's mind.

"We don't have time to talk about it right now," she said. "That beast is coming, and I don't think tranqs will be enough to keep it down. The others are sensing that something isn't right. Asking questions. At some point, we'll need to tell them. But I don't want military involvement here. They would lock this place down like it's Area 51. Our whole plan would go to shit. We need to take care of this ourselves, discreetly. I trust you understand."

"I need to tell my team," Brody commanded. "They won't talk."

"I know that," Nunez replied softly. "They're loyal to you." She unfolded her arms and tapped the top of a table with her fingers, contemplating her next move.

"What about Lizzie?" Brody said. "Doesn't she deserve to know the truth? Now, especially? What's the point of dragging this out for her?"

"We're nearly there, Brody. Please, hang on just a little longer. I can't have anything jeopardizing this mission now, and if Lizzie were to feel threatened, frightened…God, if you were to tell her some maniacs from another world were after her on top of the mafia…"

Brody ran his hand over his mouth.

"Yeah, okay. I get it." He hated keeping Lizzie in the dark, but Nunez had a point. Brody turned to leave but stopped just before he reached the door. He had questions about Lizzie's fate, questions he should have asked when he first agreed to take the job.

"What will happen to Lizzie after Redcap and his thugs

are gone? After the Bakers stop their pursuit?" Brody asked.

Nunez didn't respond immediately.

"We have a special program for victims like Lizzie."

Brody waited for Nunez to explain more, but she didn't.

"And?" he pressed.

"It'll be a chance for her to start over."

"Start over?" Brody repeated. "You mean a new identity?"

"It's what Harold wanted," Nunez said, shifting her arms uncomfortably. "It's what his parents did for him." She paused. "Don't give me that look, Brody. It's the only way to ensure her safety."

"Hmmm," Brody said, nodding in disbelief. The idea of Lizzie being erased, replaced by a version of herself she'd never recognize, coiled his gut like a snake. "And what if she doesn't want to give up her identity, who she is?"

"Find the pendant, Brody. We can worry about dotting "i's" and crossing "t's" when it's all over. Your goal right now is to make sure that relic gets safely into our hands, or we're all in trouble."

"Good, no pressure then," Brody said. "What will you do with the pendant once we find it?"

Nunez raised her eyebrows.

"Destroy it, of course," she said. "No relic, no other world, no problem." Brody nodded as he absorbed her words. Meanwhile, Nunez continued. "One more thing. Yesterday afternoon, Chuck Degan escaped house arrest. Took out two CIA agents. There's a manhunt out for him. You know anything about that?"

Nunez lifted an eyebrow, searching Brody's face.

Brody considered her words for a moment.

"Nope," he lied. "Can't say that I do."

With that, Brody left and headed back to the main entrance of the inn. As he did, he couldn't help but notice the innkeeper hobbling out of the woods, seemingly in a dour mood.

"Everything okay, Mr. Ermington?" Brody asked.

Ermington looked up at Brody and said, "Everything's fine. It's just… I'm getting old, and preparations take time, you know."

"Yeah," Brody responded, unsure what the old man meant. "Did you hurt yourself in the woods?"

"Some sacrifices must be made."

"Sure," Brody said. "Sure, but do you need help, sir?"

"No," Ermington smiled. "Enjoy yourself at the dance tonight. The rain is coming."

"I will," Brody nodded. He couldn't help but notice the innkeeper's odd behavior. "Hey, do you think I could get that library key in the morning?"

"The key? Oh, yes. The key. Umm, come to the desk in the morning, and I'll have it for you."

"Thanks," Brody replied.

Ermington walked away, and Brody hung back for a second. He contemplated telling Nunez about Ermington's odd behavior. The man had seemed fine earlier that day, but now…Then again, it was possible, given Ermington's age, that he was simply experiencing some confusion. He would leave it alone for now and check up on the old man in the morning.

chapter 32

Lizzie stirred in bed, her eyes opening slowly, the weight of sleep still clinging to her. She'd dreamt of a stream of flames twisting violently against a pulse of ice. The weight of the elements kept her pinned against a nothingness, unable to breathe. Neither element winning, both consuming.

Suddenly, a sound.

No, a whisper.

"It's coming."

"What's coming?" Lizzie murmured, assuming it was Misty. But Misty was still asleep, and Lizzie's breath caught in her throat.

Lizzie couldn't shake the prickly feeling that ran down her arms, even as she showered and got ready for the night.

It was only when she checked her phone and saw she had a missed text message from Brody that she was drawn away from the strange feeling.

Lizzie: *Yes, we're here. Will I see you tonight?*

Brody: *Yes. Meet you at the dance?*

Lizzie: *See you then.*

A rush of excitement flooded Lizzie at the thought of seeing Brody. Maybe, if the stars aligned, she might end up alone with him again. But she'd already resolved that she wouldn't leave Misty's side, not when Misty was so vulnerable.

Lizzie took her time getting ready, curling her hair into soft waves, carefully applying smoky eye makeup, and then changing into her emerald-green dress. The dress was a lustrous, shimmering satin with a corset-style bodice. Its sleeves draped off her shoulders, and a sexy side slit showed off her left leg.

"Dear Lord, I pray for Brody tonight with you in that dress," Misty teased. She had showered and blow-dried her hair while Lizzie was getting ready. "Meanwhile, I'm going to look like Frumpasaurus Rex. Kind of wish I brought something sexier to wear," Misty said. "Now that I'm a paper's signature away from single."

"You look pretty in everything you wear," Lizzie assured her. Misty had a natural beauty and confidence that Lizzie only wished she had.

Misty bit the inside of her lip and continued. "I just want to be different."

Lizzie sighed. "Misty, you don't need to change who you are because Frank was a jerk. Don't let him get in your head like that. You're a beautiful person… your personality, your style…"

When Misty focused her eyes on the floor and slumped her shoulders, Lizzie knew her effort to cheer up her friend was futile.

"It's amazing how one person can say one thing or do one thing that can suddenly make us feel we aren't good enough." Lizzie paused. "I've been where you are, maybe not in the same way, but you know I have. Remember when I was sixteen, and Jay broke up with me because I was 'too nice?'"

"He was an idiot," Misty said, dabbing her tear-brimmed eyes with a tissue.

"*Exactly*," Lizzie said. "He was an *idiot*, just like Frank. Yet, I still changed my whole personality because of that one experience. I never felt good enough after that. I always felt less than, and *you* were the one who told me I shouldn't change who I am just because someone couldn't handle my greatness."

"But maybe I was wrong," Misty countered.

"You weren't wrong."

"I think I just need a change. I need to feel different, even if it's only for one night."

Lizzie walked over to the closet and found the alternative dress she had brought for tonight's dance. It was a long, black velvet evening dress with a tempting V-neckline. Shimmering gold lace embellished the waist and hem of the dress and continued down into a dramatic sweeping train.

"Why don't you try this on?" Lizzie offered.

"No, I couldn't ask you to do that," Misty said, shaking her head. "You spent a long time picking it out, I'm sure."

"You know I always bring an extra dress," Lizzie said.

"That's true," Misty agreed. "It is beautiful. Would you do my makeup, too?"

"Of course." As Lizzie helped Misty with her makeup, she said, "I told Brody to meet up with us tonight, but I promise I'm not leaving your side."

"Lizzie, so help me; if you do not make something happen with this man, then maybe I will call Kallie up here to kick your butt into gear."

Lizzie shook her head as she sprayed Misty's face with a setting spray. Then she helped Misty into the black dress, the golden embellishments meeting one another as she zipped the back of the dress.

"Well, how do I look?" Misty asked.

"I told you before, you always look beautiful, Misty. But tonight, I think Frank would cry if he were here."

"That's what I was going for," Misty said.

Lizzie smiled.

"Now, let's get to that dance. Oh, wait!" Lizzie said, quickly heading over to her suitcase. She pulled out a pair of long, velvet black gloves. "You need to complete the outfit."

"Yes," Misty agreed. "Now, let's go. I'm starving, and I don't know how long they're passing out free food."

chapter 33

The Zombie Dance took place in the inn's second ballroom, a long drawing room that, to Lizzie, resembled one of the French rooms at the Philadelphia Art Museum. Small, yet impressive, the room had three floor-to-ceiling arched windows, long curtains, and tall ceilings. A marble-mantled fireplace sat under a massive arched mirror. The staff had arranged eight cocktail tables with no chairs around the room and set up a bar in the corner manned by a "zombified" bartender. A mix of Halloween tunes and lively hits pumped into the room via large black speakers that hung over the two entrances. A warm glow emanated from a grand chandelier hanging above a man-made vinyl dance floor in the middle of the room. All the staff were dressed as Zombies in half-cut-up shirts and pants, their faces painted with heavy bruise makeup.

The dance had no formal dinner or guest list, and the room provided no places to sit. It was a place where guests could eat hors d'oeuvres, dance, drink, and leave as they pleased. Since it was Friday night, the Speakeasy Bar would be open late. Waiters and waitresses carried trays of mini crab cakes, shrimp wrapped in bacon, chicken on skewers, potato and spinach puffs, and mini beef and salmon sliders. Waiters floated food and champagne on silver trays around to guests.

Lizzie and Misty entered the crowded room, and Lizzie scanned the room for Brody. He wasn't there, but there were many people their age, no doubt for the wedding that would take place that Sunday. A group of bachelors were ordering drinks at the corner bar. Various groups of people, some dressed in Halloween outfits, were enjoying the hors d'oeuvres. Lizzie grabbed a glass of champagne off a tray and took a sip, letting the cool, bubbling drink slide down her throat. Misty didn't drink alcohol, so Lizzie was surprised to see Misty grab a chute and drink half the glass in one gulp.

"You don't have to drink that to be different," Lizzie said.

"I know," Misty said. "But tonight, I'm feeling… spontaneous."

The last thing Lizzie wanted to do was make Misty feel bad about drinking. This was a woman who may have had three drinks in her life, one being the champagne toast at her wedding. Lizzie danced delicately around the drinking issue, thinking of the best way to word it so Misty understood the potential consequences.

"All I'm saying is alcohol can creep up quickly on you. *Especially* if you have no tolerance, which you have none. So, if you want to enjoy the night, go low and slow."

"Low and slow?" Misty asked.

"Keep the number of drinks low and the amount of time you drink them slow."

Misty let out a snort, which made Lizzie break into giggles. But Misty sipped her champagne more slowly, and soon, the girls were dancing and enjoying the night. Lizzie was finally letting loose—letting go of Miles, letting go of her stalker, letting go of the past year. Lizzie was soaking up the fun with her best friend, something they hadn't done in a few years.

That's when she saw him. He strolled into the room with a confident gait, his brawny body filling out his suit like a gorgeous Norse God. Brody had just enough stubble to give him that rugged look; his chiseled jawline looked like it had been carved out of marble. His slicked-back hair gave him that handsome, old-fashioned appearance. Immediately, Brody's blue eyes scanned the room and rested... affectionately... on her.

"Holy cannoli," Misty said, shaking her head.

Lizzie could barely hear her; she was so fixed on Brody that no one else mattered. She could tell he felt the same by the way his eyes stayed locked on hers. Her heart rate began its ascent as he took confident strides toward her.

When he reached her, she swallowed slowly and deeply. Then his arms wrapped around her for a hug, and he planted a kiss on her cheek. She was just close enough to catch his scent, warm sandalwood that clung to his skin, along with something she couldn't quite place. Maybe vetiver? She felt his breath on her face as he whispered into her ear, "You look stunning."

"I could say the same about you," she whispered back. He squeezed her hands and then pulled away to hug Misty.

"Can I get you something to drink?" Brody asked.

"I think we're okay for now," Lizzie said. "But thank you."

"I'll be right back," he said, giving Lizzie's hand a squeeze.

Brody went off and returned shortly with a drink in hand, accompanied by two people by his side.

"Lizzie, Misty, these are my friends, Shay and Dale. You know Shay," he said to Lizzie. "Although you didn't meet under optimal circumstances. This is Lizzie's friend, Misty," Brody continued, and they all shook hands.

"What, no invite to the party for your best friend?" Lizzie heard a voice say, and she turned to see a man dressed in a suit who was slightly shorter than Brody. He smacked his gum obnoxiously as he looked Lizzie up and down and winked at her. Then he looked at Misty and did the same.

"What are you doing here?" Brody asked. Lizzie could sense Brody's tension, the ticking in his jaw, the subtle lowering of his brow. He knew this man, and he didn't like him.

"Joining in the festivities like everybody else," the guy said.

"I'm sure you have friends here somewhere who would *want* to hang out with you," Brody said. But his words fell on deaf ears. The man had already given Misty hungry eyes and a charming smile. And if this guy were the ocean, Misty was like an anchor sinking to the bottom.

"I'm Hemmy," the intruder said, reaching for Misty's hand. He kissed it.

"Oh," Misty replied, her eyebrows lifting as a nervous laugh slipped out.

Lizzie tucked her hands behind her back, denying him the same gesture.

"I'd kiss yours, too," Hemmy said, glancing at Shay, Dale, and Brody, "but you already know me."

Hemmy? Hemmy, as in, the guy who slept with Brody's wife? The guy who had a hand in killing his uncle? What the hell was he doing here? A pit opened in Lizzie's stomach. Did that mean Brody's ex-wife was here, too?

Lizzie caught Shay's subtle eye-roll and sensed no one liked Hemmy that much, which was not good for Misty because she seemed completely oblivious. If Hemmy was with Brody's ex-wife, Lizzie would interrupt any connection this man was desperately trying to make with her vulnerable friend.

"Were you invited to the wedding?" Lizzie pried.

"Yeah," Hemmy said. "I was… a last-minute addition."

"Did you bring a plus one?" she asked, taking a sip of champagne. She kept her eyes focused on him, attempting to read his body language. He didn't flinch, not even for a second, didn't drop his eyes toward Brody, nor look down at the floor. He kept them fixed right on Lizzie.

"No. I'm single." He smirked, and she realized either he was telling the truth or he was a sociopath. Both were still on the table at this point.

"Oh, okay."

"I'm in the mood to dance," Hemmy said, changing the subject. He focused his eyes on Misty. "You wanna get down?"

"Yeah, I do," Misty said. "I'm down for *anything* tonight."

The way Hemmy puckered his lips, like he was going to devour her friend, made Lizzie open her mouth to object. But before she could say anything, Misty was hand in hand with Hemmy, and they were making their way to the dance floor.

"Brody, can I talk to you alone?" Lizzie asked.

"Yeah, sure."

She grabbed his hand and led him into the hallway.

"Hemmy?" she said.

"Yeah, I'm sorry," he said, scratching the back of his neck. "I didn't know he was going to be here."

"Is he still with your ex?"

"No," Brody shook his head. "I don't think so."

"But he's not a good guy."

"He's not…I don't know," he said.

"Misty's vulnerable right now. Her husband left her, and I shouldn't be telling you that, but if your friend…"

"He's not my friend…"

"If your ex-friend is going to hurt my friend tonight, then I'm putting an end to this right now."

"Hemmy's stupid. And he's a shit friend. But he's not going to hurt her physically or anything like that."

Lizzie nodded, not taking her eyes off Brody. She could

sense the pain behind Brody's blue eyes. Hemmy being here affected him. She decided she would gracefully pull Misty away and tell her about Hemmy in the bathroom. If she still wanted to hang out with him, then she could. Lizzie suspected Misty would run far away when she learned what Hemmy was really like. But when she returned to the drawing room, she saw Misty laughing and letting loose for maybe the first time in her life, and she didn't have the heart to stop her fun. Hemmy was making her laugh, and Lizzie couldn't remember the last time she'd seen her friend so relaxed and free. So she resolved to watch from afar, keep an eye on Misty, and if this Hemmy guy made a move, she'd intervene.

Later in the evening, Hemmy and Misty returned to the cocktail table.

"There's a pool table here," Hemmy said, clapping Brody's shoulder. "In the lounge. What do you say, ol' buddy?"

Lizzie saw Brody flinch and saw his fists ball, but he kept his cool.

"You guys wanna go a round?" Hemmy asked.

"I do," Misty replied. "But I'm on Lizzie's team."

"Oh yeah?" Hemmy said. "I was thinking we do girl, guy, girl, guy."

"I'll play," Lizzie said. She loved a good pool game, but it was also a good way to watch Hemmy and Misty. She looked at Brody, whose cheeks were a shade of pink, his jaw still tight and restrained. He didn't want to play; she read that loud and clear from his face.

"Yeah, fine. Whatever," Brody said.

"How about we switch it up?" Hemmy said. "Lizzie, you can be on my team, and Misty and Brody can be a team."

"NO," Brody said, finishing his drink and slamming it on the table. "If we play, Lizzie's on my team."

"All right, all right," Hemmy said, holding his hands up in surrender.

"Ugh," Misty said as they exited the drawing room and headed toward the lounge.

"What's wrong?" Lizzie heard Brody ask.

"What's wrong is that we have no chance. You guys are going to win."

"Is that so?" Brody replied.

"Yeah, didn't you know? Lizzie is like *freakishly* good at pool."

chapter 34

"Where did you get the name Hemmy, anyway?" Brody heard Misty ask.

He couldn't help but roll his eyes as he followed behind the two of them with Lizzie at his side.

"You might be the first person to ever ask me that," Hemmy replied.

Brody scoffed as he chalked the tip of his cue.

"Something funny?" Hemmy asked Brody, who didn't respond.

Hemmy spoke as he crouched down, eyeing his ball.

"It's a nickname that stuck. I was a bit of a rambunctious kid. So people just started calling me Hemi, after the engine. Over time, it evolved into my name, so I made it my own."

"And what is your real name?" Brody asked.

"Carlo," Hemmy said, taking his shot. "But you already know that." Hemmy sank one of the solids into the pocket and winked at Misty. He missed his next shot, which meant it was Brody's turn.

Brody leaned over the pool table and lined up his cue ball, wondering if it was possible to hit the ball so hard that it would fly off the table and whack Hemmy in his balls.

How did the night come to this? Brody remembered countless nights like these in his twenties with Hemmy, playing pool at a little pool hall called *Hot Shots*. Hemmy and Brody had played so much that they joined a team and even won a few tournaments. The pool hall eventually closed, just like their friendship.

When it was Lizzie's turn, she surprised everyone when she ran the entire table, called the eight-ball, and sank the shot. Brody couldn't help but smile, watching the shock wash over Hemmy's face.

"I told you all," Misty said, giving up.

"It was a good win," Hemmy said. "I say we do best out of three. But first, my partner and I need to strategize at the bar."

"Yeah, okay, you do that," Brody said, his tone slightly cocky. Hemmy didn't like losing—he'd play until he won. Misty went off with Hemmy, and Brody leaned into Lizzie.

"Okay, where did you learn to play like that?" Brody asked. "Not that I'm complaining."

"My dad," Lizzie said, a grin washing over her face. "He wasn't around much, but when he did come around, we always played a game of pool. And he taught me a lot. I guess it was our thing for a while."

"Hmm," Brody said, nodding. His thoughts drifted to Chuck; hopefully, he was on his way to the inn, no doubt on foot. "Well, I'm impressed. Hemmy and I used to play in tournaments. He's probably fuming because he doesn't like to lose."

"Well, I'm glad we won, then. Because any guy who would sleep with a man's wife deserves to be annihilated at pool."

Brody couldn't help but laugh. Being with Lizzie was so easy. He felt comfortable talking to her about his life and wished he could tell her everything.

Hemmy and Misty returned a few minutes later, ready for

a rematch. When they lost again, Brody could see Hemmy's irritation, his fidgety hands, his closed-lipped smile, and the way he ran his tongue over his teeth.

Brody and Lizzie celebrated another win with an excited hug, one Brody didn't immediately pull away from. He traced his fingers along her jaw and thought about kissing her right there. They were still in public; anyone could be watching and report directly to Nunez. *Even Hemmy*, Brody realized. But Brody didn't have time to think any more about it because suddenly, Lizzie broke away from him and searched the room.

"They're gone," Lizzie said. "Where could they have gone?"

Brody felt the sinking in his gut. He didn't know Misty well, but he knew Hemmy, and when he wanted something…

"Want me to look for her? You stay here." Brody said, rubbing Lizzie's shoulders. He didn't want to go but could see Lizzie's tensed brow. She was worried about her friend, and tonight was supposed to be relaxing, fishing on calm seas before a hurricane.

"I just worry because she's not thinking straight right now."

"I know," Brody said. "Do you think Misty is drunk?"

"No, she knew her limit."

"I understand," Brody nodded. Misty's husband had left her, and Hemmy was showing her attention. Lizzie was afraid her friend might do something she would regret. He couldn't control that, but he could make sure Hemmy wasn't taking advantage of the woman.

Brody headed out of the inn into a cold, biting air that nipped at his nose and fingertips. He wanted to put Lizzie's mind at ease, but Hemmy had a certain way with women—

even the most unlikely to fall for his charm usually did. Brody didn't condemn Hemmy for being a veritable Casanova or his relentless pursuit of his object of desire. At one point, Brody even envied it. It was Hemmy's lack of loyalty and the breaking of their bro-code that caused Brody to want to spit venom at Hemmy and inflict a wound that hurt as bad. But now, it all seemed pointless; he had bigger problems, like dangerous Fae people who were headed to the inn for Lizzie.

It was obvious to Brody that Hemmy had already moved on from Nina like a storm passing through a New Jersey summer evening. A cold raindrop kissed Brody's nose, and suddenly he spotted them—Misty and Hemmy tangled in a lust-filled embrace. Hemmy's hands had found their way up to Misty's ass, exposing her bare skin to the stinging cold. Misty had her arms around Hemmy and locked lips with him so hard it made Brody blush. Hemmy was grinding against her, and for a split second, Brody let his thoughts wander, imagining how Hemmy and Nina might have had that same lust. He shoved the thoughts out of his mind and turned away. Misty certainly didn't seem to be in any peril. In fact, it looked like she was enjoying the eroticism as much as Hemmy. Brody was no cockblock, even if Hemmy deserved more blue balls than a teenager obsessed with a centerfold.

Brody didn't want Hemmy to see him, so he returned to the inn as the drops turned to a steady rain. As soon as he was back inside, he saw Lizzie standing in the lobby waiting for him.

"Your friend is sure enjoying herself," Brody said.

"How?"

Brody let out a grunt as he raised his eyebrows, and Lizzie picked up on what he was trying to say.

"Oh…oh, okay." And then softer. "Okay."

Brody felt his desire climbing as he stared at Lizzie, the top of her breasts heaving up and down with heavy breaths.

He took a step toward her, moving a strand of hair from her chest to her back, exposing her breasts even more.

"It'll be okay," he said.

"I know," she said. He swallowed deeply as she bit her lip and took a step closer to him. He could hardly control himself now; he wanted to touch her, to kiss her, but the timing was wrong.

"I think I should head up for the night," Brody said. "I want to wake up early tomorrow."

She grabbed his hand.

"I want to come up with you," Lizzie said. Those doe eyes of hers drew him in, and he forgot about everything. She did that to him.

She took his hand and gently placed it on her neck, letting his fingers trace down her neck toward the tops of her breasts.

"Are you sure?" he asked, his voice soft, breathless.

"Very much so," she whispered. She stepped in close, and their bodies touched just enough to spark a sensual, static heat between them.

Brody didn't need to be told twice.

The curved staircase creaked as he made his way up to the second floor, holding Lizzie's hand tightly. He planned to lie her on the bed, massage every inch of her body, lick and taste her until pleasure surged and broke over her like a crashing wave.

But as soon as they entered the room, his lips were on hers. The taste of mint still lingered on her tongue, sending tingling sensations from his lips to the back of his throat. He kissed her with a growing hunger, a *need* he'd been starving for since he met her that day on campus. His hands roamed her body, slow at first. Then with urgency. He threaded his fingers through her hair, each kiss an insatiable plea.

Without breaking the kiss, he pinned her gently against

the wall, his unmistakable solid heat pressing into her. Bold. Unhidden. She let out a subtle moan, wrapping her thigh around him. His lips gently kissed her bare shoulder before he began to slowly and deliberately unzip her dress. The bodice fell slightly, exposing her breasts.

He paused, taking her beauty in.

She reached for the buttons on his shirt, but her fingers trembled. He gently clasped his hands over hers, eyes stilling on her before he took over and undid his shirt effortlessly. He tossed it behind him, and she ran her warm fingers over his chest.

He leaned down, capturing her mouth in another hungry kiss. From her mouth, Brody's tongue grazed the sensitive part of Lizzie's neck before it traveled downward to her breasts, his fingers gently stroking her free nipple.

When Brody heard Lizzie groan with delight, he slid his hand up her leg and let it settle between her thighs, his fingers finding that bundle of nerves that would bring her to ecstasy. He rubbed her there in slow, circular movements, feeling her building wetness. Then his large fingers slipped inside of her, and she let out a gasp. Her hips arched forward toward him, begging for more.

Her fingers grabbed for the top of his pants, unbuttoning them. She slid her hand inside, and as soon as her hand found his hardness, he bit his lip, reveling in her touch. There was nothing gentle about the way they touched now. It wasn't slow love. They were devouring each other.

But a thought trickled slowly into Brody's mind. It wouldn't release him, wouldn't allow him to continue his throes of passion.

When Lizzie found out the *truth*, that he'd kept so much from her, she would hate him forever.

He ground his teeth in frustration as he gently removed his fingers and then pulled her away from his aching arousal.

"Fuck," he said under his breath, balling his fingers into fists and pressing them against the wall; his balls were bluer than that teenager drooling over a centerfold. "Lizzie. I need to tell you something."

chapter 35

Lizzie had been to Tuscany once, a trip her high school had planned for students taking Italian as a language. She'd seen Michelangelo's *David*, his perfectly chiseled body and face. She'd seen every detail of that sculpted nude figure, but Brody's body was even more beautiful than the most well-known naked man in history. His carefully carved body was like a forbidden fantasy no one dared admit, satisfying, titillating. His big, firm hands caressing her body left echoes of ecstasy rippling through her like aftershocks. Each slow thrust of his fingers sent a fresh ache through her center, warm and electric, making it impossible to think of anything but more. She was breathless, ready to let him have his way with her, which was why, when he stopped touching her, it took her a minute to get oriented.

"I need to tell you the truth," he said. She was still breathing heavily from his touch.

Great, she thought. *This was the part where he confessed that he was still married or in love with someone else.*

"What is it?" she asked.

Brody zipped up his pants, grabbed Lizzie's hand, and led her to the small loveseat in the sitting room of his hotel room.

"What is it, Brody?" Lizzie asked again. No one sat anyone down unless what they were about to tell them was bad.

"I want you so badly," Brody said.

"I want you, too," she said. "So what's the problem?"

"I'm sorry I let it come to this without saying something first. But I couldn't… I couldn't… do *this* with you without telling you the truth."

"What is the truth?"

She watched Brody's chest rise and fall as he took a deep breath.

Then Brody launched into a story, one that made Lizzie fight back the acid threatening to rise in her esophagus. She tried to keep her composure calm as he spoke, but the rapid thumping of her heart prevented her from any hope of that. She tried to compartmentalize all the things he'd just said.

The mafia was trying to kill her for an inheritance.
Lizzie's bloodline connected her to an ancient Elven-Fae people.
Her stalker wasn't human.
Coming to take her.
The pendant, the scrolls.

She laughed bitterly. It had to be a cruel joke. That was what it was. But why would Brody do this? Why now?

"Why are you doing this?" Lizzie asked.

"I'm telling the truth."

"No," Lizzie said, shaking her head. "You're humiliating me. Why?" It was all too much to process. "You're insane," she added.

It was the only response she could muster.

"I know it sounds crazy," Brody said.

Lizzie scoffed. If he only knew the half of it. She didn't believe him, not one word. And how could she?

"I was hired to protect you," Brody blurted. "This… this whole thing. The inn, our class, the project, everything, it was a setup."

"A setup?" Lizzie repeated incredulously. She almost laughed, but the response caught in her throat.

"A mission," he said. "I'm not making this up. I wish I were. I'm an undercover agent, and you're in grave danger. I need you to trust me, Lizzie. I'm telling you because it's important. We don't have much time."

"*Trust* you?" Lizzie said, feeling her cheeks redden. "I don't even *know* you." Waves of regret settled over her as she realized she was still half-naked in this man's room. Brody wasn't the first guy to deceive her, but she felt disappointed and humiliated knowing she'd been so naïve.

"I know you're upset," Brody said. "But you do know me, Lizzie." He tried to reach for her hands, but she pulled away. "I didn't want it to come out like this…" he continued.

She felt tears sting her eyes as she zipped up her dress. *How could I have been so stupid? Because you always are,* she reminded herself. *That's why you have a stalker in the first place. You attract the worst men possible.*

"I need you to meet me tomorrow at the library," Brody said, his tone serious. "We have to finish this."

"I…" Lizzie stammered, standing and collecting her purse and shoes. Like hell she was going to meet this guy… tomorrow… or ever again. "I have to… go."

"Lizzie, wait," Brody said, rising from the loveseat.

"Just let me go," Lizzie said, and she ran out of his room. She ran down the stairs and out into the night. The rain had stopped, but a biting cold nipped at her arms, the top of her breasts, her legs.

Why? She'd let this man touch her. She opened up to him. *Trusted* him.

A fake class? A fake mission? The deception was too

much to take.

She ran toward the back of the inn, through the pathways of cabins, until she reached the woods. She needed to be alone, far away from Brody, Misty, and anyone else who might be part of the elaborate plan to control her life.

The darkness of the night enveloped her, leaves crackling under her freezing feet. *It was stupid to come out here,* she thought. *The ground is wet. I could slip. And no one knows where I am.* She stopped in the dark woods and reached for her phone as the cold rain kissed her bare shoulders. She needed to talk to someone—Dan. But then she realized she'd left her phone in Brody's room. Scattered, fragmented thoughts rushed through her mind as panic blanketed her. She struggled to take deep breaths and sat on the ground, hoping the dizziness that had suddenly plagued her would subside. She thought she might pass out and didn't have her usual remedies, ice on the wrist, someplace safe to lie down. Her fingers trembled along with her body as she sat in that paralyzing fear, and she worried about what would happen if she lost consciousness there in the woods.

Why did she feel this way? It was only a crazy story from an unhinged man, yet another one who tried to use and deceive her. She shouldn't have paid his story any mind—should have just gone back to her room, chalked the encounter up to another bad mistake.

Lizzie had resorted to the fact that she wasn't going to find love. A wave of grief washed over her as she stood there, her bare feet soaking in the mud beneath the leaves. She'd lost so much; her life had felt fragmented and jagged since her mother died. She'd lost a piece of her soul and struggled for years to find some even footing. Some peace. Lizzie's life was like a mosaic, but instead of plaster, each tiny piece was held together by a fragile glue. Whenever she thought she'd pieced herself back together, she experienced a new chaos that tore her apart again.

Brody was crazy, she told herself.

But the way he spoke was so calm. Her stomach churned; Brody believed every word he said. And if there was even a hint of truth in his revelation, then Lizzie knew those fragmented pieces would scatter for the last time.

If what he said was true, there was no putting herself back together.

She pressed her back against the trunk of a wide tree, the cold bark like sandpaper against her skin. Her breaths came out hard and shallow. Maybe she deserved this, this endless betrayal.

That's when she first heard the whispers, drawing toward her like tendrils. They were feminine and masculine voices, calling out to her, "Lizzie. Lizzie…" She felt the tender silvery coils wrap around her, squeezing her tightly, suffocating the last breaths of air from her body. Her body stretched wide; vines coiled around each extremity. They squeezed tighter and tighter until her world faded to darkness. She opened her eyes; blackness surrounded her. Sitting up, she saw her body unconscious on the ground. Then the voices spoke, whispering messages into her ear from the left, then to the right, like binaural beats shifting from ear to ear.

Suddenly, she felt a tug, gentle at first and then stronger, and she had an urge to lie down.

Was this death?

A warning?

Or something else.

She felt her spirit merging back into her body. Then big, strong arms wrapped around her, lifting her as she gently came to, like waking from a long, vivid dream. As she tried to orient herself, she felt herself being carried away from the woods, away from the voices who had no choice but to release their tendrilled vines from her.

The man holding her carried her inside, up the creaky stairs to the third floor. He easily opened the door to her room and placed her on her bed.

Her eyes opened, and as her blurry view came into focus, she saw her savior.

"Miles?" she asked, looking up at the man. "What are you doing here?"

A hand gripped Miles' shoulder, pulling him away. Miles resisted, but the hand was firm, and then he disappeared.

It feels like a dream, she thought, *it must be a dream.* And then she drifted off into a long sleep.

chapter 36

Ahand gripped Miles' shoulder firmly as he stood over Lizzie's bed. Something wasn't right. She was unconscious in the woods, and for a brief moment, he couldn't find a pulse. He had feared the worst when suddenly she'd gently come to. He planned to stay with Lizzie until she woke up, tell her everything, and bring her somewhere safe. But he'd barely placed her in her bed when he heard a voice behind him.

"What the *hell* are you doing here?"

Miles recognized the voice right away. His brother, Dean.

"What am *I* doing here?" he said, turning around brusquely. "What are *you* doing here?"

Dean didn't answer Miles' question. All he said was, "You need to get out of here. Now, Miglio."

"No," Miles shook his head. "I came to warn Lizzie. To come clean."

"You can't help her. You have to let her go. You have to."

"Did you follow me here?" Miles asked.

"No."

"Then what are you doing here one day early?" Miles pressed. Miles ushered Dean out of Lizzie's room. He and Dean moved out into the hallway and spoke in heated whispers.

"It's a long story, but it doesn't matter. We need to go. Now. There are agents everywhere, and if they see you, you're a dead man."

"And you?" Miles asked, folding his arms one over the other. "Why wouldn't you be a dead man?"

"I'll tell you everything," Dean said. "But only after we leave here. I'm staying at a motel five miles down the road. Packing up, heading out. For good."

"What does that mean?"

"There's a lot you don't know about Redcap and Cedric, and once you do know, your life will change forever."

Begrudgingly, Miles agreed to go with his brother. After ensuring Lizzie was safely asleep, he closed her door and followed his brother out of the inn. They walked in silence for a short time through the rainy woods until they reached Dean's truck. Miles hopped in, and they drove five miles north to a small motel off the side of the road. Dean used an old key to unlock the door, and Miles stepped into the dimly lit room, observing the mauve-colored walls, old box TV, and worn patchwork bedspread.

"Sure this isn't the Bates' motel?" Miles asked.

Dean didn't even crack a smile as he threw Miles a towel from the bathroom, and Miles examined it for roaches before using it to dry his hair. Then Dean grabbed a sweatshirt and some sweatpants from his partially packed duffle bags.

"Put these on," Dean said, throwing them to Miles.

Miles changed out of his wet clothes, and once he and Dean were both dressed in fresh clothing, Miles said, "So, are you going to start talking or what?"

He knew his brother was higher up in The Family than he, but did any of it matter now that Ludwig was dead? Now that this Redcap was in charge of their fate.

"You should sit down," Dean urged.

"No," Miles replied, leaning against the motel dresser.

"Please," Dean said, holding his hand out for Miles to sit.

Miles reluctantly sat, and Dean began to speak while he stuffed his belongings into his duffle bag.

"I'm helping them, okay?"

"Who?" Miles asked.

"The FBI," Dean said. "I'm giving them information."

"You're a *snitch*?" Miles retorted. "Are you serious?"

"It's the only thing I could do to help us, man."

Miles scoffed.

"We're in deep shit," Dean continued. "This Redcap guy is fucking mental. Real off. And don't give me shit about going straight because *you* have no room to talk."

"But the FBI, Dean? Why?" Miles asked.

Dean hesitated, and then, after letting out a deep sigh, he said, "Because I can't get us outta this."

"Because they killed Ludwig?" Miles questioned. He stood from where he sat and paced the floor. "The FBI isn't gonna help us, Dean. You know that, right? They aren't going to let us off the hook. Not for all the shit we've done."

"I made a deal," Dean argued.

"I don't care what kind of deal you made," Miles snapped. Dean was losing his damn mind. "They won't honor it. You even said so yourself, so why did you become a plant? Of all things, Dean. You put Mom's life in danger by doing this. You know that, right?"

"Redcap and Cedric aren't fucking human, Miles!" Dean yelled. "Don't you fucking get it? You think that the beast that ate, *fucking ate*, Ludwig in front of our eyes is a natural animal that prowls the Earth?"

"No, but…"

"This situation is bigger than us," Dean continued, "and it's fucked, and I don't wanna be a part of it."

Dean made his way to the front of the motel room. He moved the thick red velvet curtains to the side to peek out the window, a motion Miles had frequently made while on a job.

"You're afraid," Miles said. "You're fucking afraid."

"Yeah, I'm fucking afraid!" Dean yelled, getting in Miles' face. "And you should be, too."

"Tell me what you know," Miles said.

Dean rubbed his hand over his chin as Miles pressured his brother.

"Tell me, Dean. Right now."

"Last night, after the meeting, I went to the farmhouse, needed to blow off some steam after the whole… anyway, I heard them, Redcap and Cedric." Dean took a beat before saying, "I saw something in that farmhouse, Miglio. Redcap communicated with someone. It was…*something*…a shadow figure. It just materialized into an entity, and it spoke. Gave him orders. And trust me when I say that *thing* was something of nightmares even you and I couldn't stomach."

"Is this some kind of Halloween prank?" Miles asked. It wasn't like Dean to make light of…well…anything, and he wasn't the type to engage in fairy tales, but still, Miles had to ask. What really concerned Miles was that Dean only called him Miglio when he was worried. When Dean didn't respond, Miles continued. "What did…*it* say?" He could sense the worry in Dean's face, his tensed shoulders, his darting, wide eyes.

"Everything is playing out according to the prophecy."

"What exactly does that mean?"

"It means all of this is meant to happen. And we can't stop it, so if we're smart, we'll let it happen. And get the hell out of here."

"And you thought telling the FBI this would win you points, Dean?"

"You saw that beast, Miles. You *saw* it. If you saw what I saw in that farmhouse… that thing. It doesn't matter now. We're leaving. Tonight."

"I can't leave, Dean."

"She's one of them, Miles," Dean argued.

"Who?"

"Lizzie. She's one of them."

"One of…"

"Whatever the fuck Redcap and Cedric are."

"No, she isn't."

"Yes, she is, Miles, and you need to let her go. They need her and that pendant to carry out their mission. We're leaving. I've got our passports. The Director is granting me immunity for my help."

"They won't let me leave, Dean," Miles said. "I've hurt too many people."

"And I haven't?" Dean asked.

"You fucking kidding me, Dean? All these years, you never got your hands dirty," Miles said. "Not once. *I* was Ludwig's puppet, Dean. *I* was the one who did the hard work. You sat in a mansion and gave the orders, but I stained my hands getting the jobs done. Maybe they granted *you* immunity, but they'll never let me out of here alive."

"Fuck you, Miles, like either of us had a choice."

The two brothers stayed quiet then, not wanting to argue any further. Miles' mind raced. He knew he should have come clean with Lizzie right away. Of course, there was a good chance she wouldn't have wanted to start a relationship with him.

"Hi, I've been hired to kill you, but don't want to" wasn't exactly a pickup line. But supposing it had worked out, he could have avoided the dozens of times he had to fight off The Family, including Dean, to keep Lizzie safe. Protecting her had been a continuous fight, and a reservoir of frustration had built up as the pressure weighed on him. The outbursts and anger weren't toward Lizzie but toward Ludwig. But Lizzie had taken it wrong, and rightfully so. Leaving her cold and pretending he felt nothing was the last thing he wanted, but it was the best decision he'd made for her sake and his.

Miles knew he couldn't protect Lizzie, so he let her go. He had known Brody Woods was some do-gooder the moment he saw him; the guy wore that broken knight-in-shining-armor guise that only those guys could do. Brody was irritatingly squeaky clean, and some part of Miles knew that Lizzie would fall for him. Brody was the better guy… there was no contesting that, and he seemed genuinely interested in protecting Lizzie from harm. That's why when Miles let Lizzie go, he had to piss Brody off just enough that it would kick his ass into gear and make him serious about protecting her. Even Miles hadn't wanted to stoop so low as seducing someone's sister, but he was desperate. Miles thought he did his job well, but he had found Lizzie alone in the woods, barely alive. He'd been wrong about Brody. And now, Miles was faced with the decision to leave this situation behind and start somewhere new or go after Lizzie.

"You go back there, they'll kill you on the spot, Miles," Dean said, seemingly reading Miles' thoughts. "I need you to stay away."

"You need to go," Miles said. "I get it. Take Mom and go. But I'm staying, Dean. I'm staying. I'm going to help Lizzie."

"I'm not letting you go back there."

"I'm not *asking* for your permission," Miles argued.

"I outrank you, Miles," Dean retorted. "Just because Ludwig is dead doesn't mean you can do whatever you want."

"A little hypocritical coming from the guy who just gave intel to the FBI!" Miles yelled. "Ludwig is dead. And so is this *Family*." Miles softened his tone then. "You have to give this to me, Dean. One thing. One thing I can do right with my life. It's the only thing I can do to make me feel like my life isn't wasted."

"You'll die, Miles."

"So if I die, my life wasn't a waste."

"Fine," Dean said, gritting his teeth and pushing his duffle bag with his hands, letting Miles see his frustration. "But you're not going back alone. I'm coming with you."

"No," Miles shook his head. "Get out of here. I'm going to stay and help Lizzie until the end."

Dean just stood there, his eyes wild and unruly.

"Damn it, Miglio," he said, slamming his fists on top of the duffle bag. "When are you gonna learn you're my brother, and I'm not abandoning you?"

chapter 37

Lizzie's eyes opened in tiny, gradual increments until she adjusted to her surroundings. Caught between asleep and awake, she felt immense inner peace. Sunlight filtered through the windows, giving the room a soft, ethereal glow. She felt warm, safe, and comfortable.

Until memories began to flood her conscious mind.

Then her fingers gripped the sheets as she remembered the events of the night before—Brody's confession, her experience in the woods, Miles...

She threw her covers off to see she was in her pajamas but didn't remember changing into them. All she recalled were firm, familiar arms wrapped around her. She was sure it had been Miles then, but it couldn't have been. Could it? He was nowhere near the inn and had no idea she was there. Her purse and shoes were on the floor. But the phone she'd left in Brody's room was on her nightstand. Had Brody found her in the woods and brought her back? Had he changed her clothing? Had Misty helped? *Misty.* Lizzie glanced at the empty, still-made bed beside her. A chill swept through her. Was Misty safe? Or had Hemmy...? She didn't know who or what to believe after last night.

Lizzie placed her fingers between her brows, a poor attempt to thwart an oncoming headache. She felt her body more fully, the blood flowing through her veins, the beating of her heart. She also felt something else, a sensitivity she couldn't quite explain, a subtle, energetic pulsing like the vibration produced from a gentle flap of a butterfly's wings.

She knew her experience had been more than falling unconscious due to a severe panic attack—she'd seen her body on the ground, entered some altered state where loving beings had enveloped her and imparted wisdom…wisdom that she was only now piecing together. *Did I…die?* she wondered. How would she know?

After her experience in the woods, what she did know for sure was that Brody was telling the truth. A slow, sick tightening spread through her gut. She needed to speak to Brody and find out if anything else had happened to her in the woods. Her inner knowingness confirmed that what the beings had said was true, and she was convinced that she had to help Brody find that pendant. But first, she needed to make sure Misty was okay. Lizzie grabbed her phone from the nightstand and sent a text message to Misty.

Lizzie: *Where are you? Are you okay?*

Misty responded right away, thankfully.

Misty: *I'm fine. I didn't want to disturb you, so I am at the coffee shop…grabbing a Zombielatte if you want one. Happy Halloween, by the way. We have A LOT to discuss.*

Lizzie: *Yes, I need coffee. Thanks.*

Lizzie felt her heart rate slow, knowing her friend was safe and in good spirits. "Happy Halloween," Lizzie said out loud, flatly. Ruefully, she added under her breath, "How fitting! Since my life has slowly turned into a nightmare."

Lizzie stepped into the shower, allowing last night's events to wash away from her. Mud was still caked on her feet, and she apathetically watched the dark brown color swirl down into the drain. She held her hand and examined it. A yellowish glow surrounded her fingers, wrist, and arm—little dots of blue energy shot from her fingertips.

What is happening to me, she thought?

After a nice long shower, Lizzie did her makeup and dressed warmly in jeans, a short black wool sweater, and tall, flat black boots. She still felt the pulsing, couldn't turn it off, and it was beginning to worry her. *Maybe I should see a doctor,* she thought. But when she envisioned herself telling a doctor her symptoms, she realized she was the one who sounded insane. Instead, she sent a text message to Brody.

Lizzie: *Meet me in the library, fifteen minutes.*

He didn't respond, and Lizzie had to accept that Brody might be long gone by now, and she might be alone on her quest to find the pendant. But even if that were the case, she would see this task through.

Just then, Misty entered the room wearing a sheepish smile that quickly vanished once she noticed Lizzie's creased brow and pursed lips.

"Are you okay?" Misty asked as she passed Lizzie her latte.

"I…" Lizzie shook her head. She didn't know where to begin. "Did you help me last night?"

"Help you with what?" Misty asked, taking a seat on the corner of her bed.

"My pajamas?" Lizzie asked.

"N… no," Misty said, narrowing her eyes. "Why are you asking me that?"

"I..." Lizzie let out a nervous laugh. If Lizzie started telling Misty about Elven-Fae and the mafia this early in the morning, she swore it might send her best friend over the edge. "Never mind," Lizzie said, attempting to feign a happy demeanor. She took a sip of her drink. "I was a little worried this morning when I didn't see you, but I'm happy you're in a great mood."

"Well, hold on... before we change the subject."

"It's nothing. I think maybe I had too much to drink last night," Lizzie lied. "Brody must have been the one to help me get ready for bed."

"Yeah, about that," Misty said, sitting on her bed. "The guilt is *killing* me this morning. I don't even think Frank and I have ever had that much sex."

"Oh," Lizzie grimaced, this time from envisioning Misty with Hemmy. "You're spiraling, and I'm going to be sick."

"Like you didn't have a wild time last night with Brody?"

"I didn't," Lizzie replied. *Because a life-altering confession ruined our sensual encounter,* she wanted to add.

"Yeah. OK," Misty laughed, "Is that why your sheets are covered in mud?"

Lizzie glanced at the sheets. She'd been so distracted when she woke that she didn't realize they were stained brown.

"Did something bad happen?" Misty asked, noticing Lizzie's knitted brows.

"Ummm, sort of, but I don't want to talk about it," Lizzie told her. "I just want to work on this project with Brody and then go home."

Project.

Mission.

Setup.

The words repeated in Lizzie's mind, banging the invisible gong in her gut that sent those tremors of worry throughout her body. She hoped Brody would meet her in the library because now that her mind had been opened to the truth, she needed to confront him about concealing it.

"I'd help you," Misty said, "but I'm exhausted from last night, and it's time I tell my parents about Frank and me. So it'll be nice to have the room."

Lizzie gave her friend a gentle, reassuring smile. Misty's earthly issues seemed trivial now that Lizzie knew the world was so much bigger than anyone realized. Still, no matter what Lizzie was going through, her friend's issue was important to her.

"If you need me," Lizzie said. "I'm just a couple of rooms away."

"Thanks," Misty replied. "And if you need me... same."

chapter 38

The desk staff at the inn had told Lizzie that someone had already asked for the library key, and Lizzie sighed with relief, knowing Brody was still willing to help her. As she opened the library door, letting it creak open, subtle sunlight cascaded downward through the windows onto the library's hardwood floors, giving the room an otherworldly glow. Inside looked as she expected it would—medallion-designed cream-colored flooring, a wooden desk, and two tapestry-covered chairs. Books lined built-in shelves that carried to the ceiling. Heavy, navy blue curtains hung from three floor-to-ceiling windows. A dark blue settee and four matching chairs flanked a claw-footed wooden coffee table. To the far right of the room, a skinny, singular six-foot cabinet wrapped in wrought iron bars protected several journals, and in the middle of the room, a three-foot circle had been carved into the floor, a tree etched in the center.

The air had a musty feel, and Lizzie could tell that while the rest of the inn had been updated, the library was well-preserved and most resembled the 1920s era. An old candle chandelier hung in the middle of the room. Except for electrical outlets, the room had no modern technology. There were no computers. Tall rectangular brass lamps with navy blue lampshades provided faint, warm lighting.

Being in tune with her subtle energies now, Lizzie could feel the footprints of the past in this untouched room, waiting for her to uncover something, but what? Silence shrouded the room. Brody looked up as Lizzie entered and closed one of the many journals he had sprawled on the coffee table.

"I didn't know if you'd actually come." He rubbed the back of his neck.

"Same here," she said. Lizzie didn't have time to rehash last night's conversation with him, so she got to the point. "I heard something in the woods while I was unconscious."

"You were unconscious?" Brody asked, worry washing over his brow. "You were in the woods? It was cold and raining."

"Didn't you bring me back to my room?" Lizzie asked.

"No," he shook his head. "I assumed you ran to your room after you left mine. You didn't have your phone. So I put it outside your door, thinking you didn't want to speak to me."

"Miles…" Lizzie said, the words breathlessly escaping her lips.

"What about him?" Brody asked, his eyes squinting from wide to near slits.

"I think he was here," Lizzie said. "I felt him. Saw him." The memories flooded back to her now. "He found me and carried me back."

Brody grunted and sat back on the library's loveseat. He wore his disdain for Miles like a freshly tailored suit.

"I heard something in the woods," Lizzie repeated, brushing over the Miles subject. She would revisit that later. She dropped onto the settee, and Brody perked up.

"What did you hear?" he asked.

"A message."

"A message?" he repeated.

"Yes, from the Elders of Elgoria."

"Elgoria, as in…"

"Yes," Lizzie nodded. "The Elders whispered to me, kept repeating, *Au pwein cu vour.* It all came back to me this morning."

"What does *au… pwein… cu… vour* mean?" Brody asked, struggling to sound out the ancient language.

"Come home." Lizzie pressed her fingers between her eyes as a throbbing headache crept up on her once again.

"What's wrong?" Brody asked.

"It's nothing," she lied.

"What is it?" He kept his eyes focused on hers. "What are you feeling?" He reached his hand out to hers, but she quickly pulled away. "Lizzie…"

"I said it's nothing." She didn't mean to snap at him, but she still resented his deception and needed more time to forgive him.

Brody didn't push her to share; instead, he changed the subject. "Did these Elders say anything else?"

"Yes," Lizzie said. "They told me the pendant's magic is only for the one."

"The one?"

"The *Shadow Breaker.*"

"Which means?"

Lizzie slowly shook her head and watched Brody run his hand over his mouth.

"They said we need to find the pendant, get it to the Shadow Breaker, and no one but the *one* is to touch the magic, or he will die."

"What else?" Brody asked.

"That's all I can remember." She paused. "What do we do now?"

"I've been combing through these journals but haven't

found anything useful about the relic yet. Maybe…I have an idea," Brody said, "but I don't know that it will work. Director Nunez said you received a letter from your grandfather. Have you read it? I mean, it's probably a dead end, but…"

"I have it," Lizzie interrupted. Brody knew about the letter. *What else did he know,* she wondered. *What else hadn't he told her?* She couldn't worry about that now. She had to focus. "I have it here with me."

"You brought it?" Brody asked.

"I've had it in my purse since Miles told me about it weeks ago, but I didn't have the courage to open it."

"Oh, good," Brody sighed in relief. "Harold wanted you to come here and find out everything. I imagine he would have left you clues."

Lizzie reached into her purse and pulled out an envelope the color of tumbled brown jasper. Her fingers trembled around the envelope. If Brody was right, this letter held more than an apology. As she opened it, her mind raced with the possibilities of its contents. She decided to read it out loud, knowing that Brody needed to understand its message, too.

My dearest Lizzie, I love you. I'm old enough to know there's no more important way to begin a conversation. I guess if you make it to my age, you're allowed a certain amount of wisdom. Nothing matters more than love. I had my reasons for staying away, to protect you, and I think you'll forgive me when you know the truth.

They say you can't choose your parents, and you can't choose your bloodline either. Unfortunately, you've been born into a doozy of one. This might not make sense now, but it will if you follow my instructions.

Your life is in grave danger. Do not take this message lightly. Stay vigilant. Find your father. Tell no one except for those you trust completely. Everything I own is yours, including a place called the Speakeasy Inn. The library at the inn holds many secrets. Find Gerald Westin's "A Pearl in the Shadows" and follow the highlighted passages to your destiny. Ask Raymond to give you the letter with the journal entries that lead to the pendant. Do not let it fall into the wrong hands—it can neither be wielded nor destroyed. Only protected. We don't have much time. The shadows are upon us...

Lizzie stood up from the settee and paced the floor. "The shadows..."

"Redcap and Cedric," Brody replied.

"Who is Raymond?" she asked.

"No idea," Brody said. "Nunez never mentioned anyone by that name."

"I haven't been able to get in touch with my dad," Lizzie said. "I can try again, but..."

"Yeah, about that," Brody replied. He shifted uncomfortably on the settee and ran his fingers through his hair. When his eyes drifted to the floor, Lizzie sensed he would reveal yet another secret.

"Seriously, Brody, is there anything else I should know?" Lizzie asked. She lowered her eyebrows and folded one arm over the other.

"I promise that's everything."

"Well?" she asked.

Brody informed Lizzie about her father, and instead of anger, she felt relief. Relief that her father was okay, that he wasn't deliberately ignoring her. She hadn't been far off in understanding her father's occupation but wondered if he knew anything about her bloodline. Given Brody's conversation with him, she was sure that her father knew *something.* Fragments of her childhood drifted into her mind like a stray log flowing along a river's current—her father had been preparing her for years to stay vigilant. *Lizzie, look up;* a memory surfaced, his voice as clear as day as he pointed his fore and middle finger toward his eyes. Maybe, just maybe, he was preparing her for this. *How far are you from Kentucky?* His other cryptic message. *Miles.* That was the answer. He was trying to warn her about Miles. She prayed her father would make it to her so she could ask him questions.

"I didn't tell Nunez about Chuck," Brody said. He sat with his hands together, his shoulders slumped, only meeting Lizzie's eyes briefly before casting them down onto the coffee table.

"You don't trust her completely?" Lizzie asked. She watched him hesitate, a reddish hue pulsing from his body like strings of clouds. Somehow, she could see actual colors pulsing from Brody's skin. She blinked, but they didn't fade. This was a sudden, newfound gift of sight to add to her list of unusual experiences, and while it was not unpleasant, she hoped it would not always be this distracting.

"I don't have a reason not to," Brody replied, "but…"

"Maybe you should trust your instincts," Lizzie snapped. *Maybe if you had, you would have been more honest with me.* Realizing her rudeness, she said, "Look, I appreciate you not saying anything to Nunez about my dad."

He nodded and stood up.

"I would do anything to help you, Lizzie. *Anything.* And from now on, no secrets between us. And whatever you want to do, I'll follow you."

For a second, she forgot about last night as she watched the reds circulating him turn into oranges. She felt lust emanating from him and then watched the oranges transition into a green, the color of dew-tipped ferns. He did care about her, and she knew then, despite all that had happened, she could trust him. Still, she needed to express her feelings first.

"I also appreciate you telling the truth last night," Lizzie said, softening her tone and gazing into Brody's eyes. "But I need some time to…"

"I understand," Brody interrupted.

"You lied to me," she accused.

Brody responded calmly, "I wanted to tell you from the beginning."

"But you didn't," she said.

"I know."

"You lied to me," she repeated, this time softer. That small fact should not have meant much, given everything he'd told her, but then, *why did it sting so much?*

Brody didn't say anything; he just sat there, not allowing his eyes to meet hers.

"What did Nunez say happens to me when it's over?" Lizzie asked. "If we even survive?"

"We get you to safety," Brody said. "Full protection."

"Change my name?" she said, not hiding her sarcasm. "Leave behind all the people I love and care about?"

She waited for Brody to say no, but her heart sank when he didn't.

"I don't know what Nunez's intentions are," he said softly. "But my job was…is to protect you. That's all I care about. And if we can stop these guys, maybe it won't have to come to that."

"What did Nunez say she would do with the pendant?" Lizzie asked.

"She wants to destroy it."

"And you believe that?"

"I don't know. I thought I did, but…I'm more inclined to follow the Elders of Elgoria. Nunez doesn't know much about Fae, only what she learned from your grandfather. She might not know, might even change her mind if she knew what the Elders told you."

"I say we keep Nunez in the dark for a while," Lizzie

expressed. "Maybe she is on our side. If my grandfather trusted her, then we'll tell her about the Elders... eventually. For now, we have to keep our circle close. And there's only one person I'm certain we can trust. Misty."

"All right," Brody agreed. "But I'll have to check in with Nunez. She'll want to be updated."

"That's fine," Lizzie said. "We just won't tell her everything. Meanwhile, I'll have Misty meet us here."

"And Shay," Brody added.

"Shay?" Lizzie asked. "Are you sure?"

"Lizzie, Shay is a detective. She could help us find the relic faster."

"And you trust her?"

"With my life," he said.

Lizzie nodded.

"Then that's settled. So where do we begin?" she asked.

"Now, we eat something," he said. "Meanwhile, I'll check in with Nunez; tell her we're searching these journals Ermington provided me. That will keep her from asking questions."

"I *am* a little hungry," Lizzie said. Hungry. Dizzy. Disoriented. Why was it all escalating? She was different somehow, and the more she tried to feel normal, the less herself she felt. She couldn't tell anyone, not even Brody. Not yet. The fact was that whatever happened to her out in the woods had altered her very essence, and she knew in her heart she would never be the same.

chapter 39

Brody bought Lizzie and himself a sandwich from the café. They quickly ate, and he observed her every expression. He could see that she was struggling internally, but she wouldn't say what she was struggling with. She was different externally, too, even more intoxicating than she usually was. When she was near, he couldn't look away. Her presence pulled him in, no matter how hard he tried to resist. He was glad he'd told her the truth, even if it ruined whatever slight chance they had of a relationship. Although he knew she was angry with him, every once in a while, she'd soften her gaze as she looked at him, as if she were seeing him the way he desperately wanted her to.

After lunch, Brody and Lizzie perused the bookshelves, looking for *A Pearl in the Shadows*, while they waited for Shay and Misty to join them. According to Lizzie, Misty was having a serious conversation with her parents. Meanwhile, Shay assisted Nunez and Punk by examining a map of the area, speculating possible enemy entry points, and then conveying those to Hemmy and his team. Shay had an inkling they'd enter from the wooded area to the west. Meanwhile, Dale worked on intercepting phone signals—he'd tracked one of the Bakers' men fifty miles south. They were on their way; there was no doubt about that. Nunez had met with her informant in the morning, but she wouldn't share her plan. Brody finally understood how both Lizzie and Shay felt. He knew what Nunez learned was none of his business, but it unnerved him when she withheld vital information. What if the informant knew something that could help Brody, but Nunez hadn't shared it?

Conversely, she wanted to know Brody's progress. He'd shared with Nunez, with Lizzie's permission, that Lizzie had finally read her grandfather's letter, and it had pointed toward the journals. He told Nunez they would begin with the journals Ermington gave him. He didn't tell her that Lizzie knew everything, only that she was beginning to suspect something was wrong. Of course, Nunez reminded Brody, yet again, that the faster they found that relic, the better. She wanted to ambush Redcap and Cedric at the inn but hoped it was after they had the pendant safe in their hands. He told Nunez they needed extra help, and it was time he brought in Shay, to which Nunez reluctantly agreed.

Most of the books in the library were leather-bound. Brody watched as Lizzie's fingers grazed the worn covers, searching for *A Pearl in the Shadows*. A wooden rolling ladder allowed them to search the higher shelves, and fifteen minutes passed before Brody found books at the top of one of the shelves with authors like Christie, Poe, Lovecraft, Keats, Huxley, Fitzgerald, Atwood, and Woolf. Next to them were Gerald Westin's books, and immediately, his eyes fell on A Pearl in the Shadows.

"I found it," he said, removing the book from the shelf.

"Oh, good." Lizzie let out a sigh of relief. Brody stepped

down from the ladder and handed Lizzie the book.

"I think it's better you read it. I can search the journals again."

"No," she said, grabbing his hand before he could walk away. "We should do this together."

He didn't let the electricity pulsing from her touch distract him; instead, he nodded toward her and stood by her side as she opened the book to the first highlighted passage. Lizzie traced her fingers over the worn pages of the old book as she read.

"'Genevieve believed the stars would guide her through the places blanketed in the darkness. The moonlight shining on the water's surface paved her path, but she knew the real treasure lay beneath the surface, where no men could travel except for those graced with the gift.' I don't know what that means."

Brody shook his head. If Lizzie didn't know, he assuredly didn't.

"He's referring to the conscious and subconscious minds," a voice interrupted. Misty had quietly entered the library, her eyes spider-webbed with red vessels from crying.

"Are you okay?" Lizzie asked, closing the book so she could hug her friend.

"I will be," Misty assured Lizzie. "But as expected, my parents assume it's my fault Frank left." She attempted a smile, but it didn't quite stick. "Now, why are we reading passages of this old book out loud like we're doing a Hardy Boy, Nancy Drew team-up?"

Even Brody couldn't help but crack a smile.

"Might as well fill me in, too," Shay said, gently closing the library door behind her.

Brody turned to Lizzie.

"I think we should tell them everything before we continue," he said, "but quickly. Every second counts."

Lizzie nodded.

"Shay… Misty," Brody said. "Would you both sit down for a minute? Lizzie and I have something to tell you."

"Wow, that's a lot to take in, Brody," Shay replied after he'd told her and Misty about the Fae world, Lizzie's bloodline, and the real purpose of the pendant. "Why didn't you tell me about the Fae before?"

Yet again, Brody found himself in a position where he'd kept something important from someone he cared about.

"Nunez didn't want me to…" he started. "And…"

"You didn't think I could handle it?" she replied.

"I was just…"

"Being a good agent?" Shay said, finishing his sentence yet again. He noted her sarcasm.

"Yeah… something like that."

"Except you're not an agent anymore," Shay reminded him.

"I get it, Shay, but what did you want me to do?"

"Be honest with your team, Brody. Your team. No, forget your team. Be honest with *me*. You and I are practically family."

"Look, I messed up, okay?" Brody barked, the frustration of his mistakes overwhelming his poise. "I messed up with you, Lizzie, and the entire team. I listened to Nunez and believed everything needed to be kept quiet until I realized maybe Nunez was wrong."

"So, now what?" Shay asked. She'd folded her arms across her chest, blocking him out.

Meanwhile, Misty stayed quiet. She just kept looking at Lizzie and then back to Brody.

"Is this a Halloween prank?" she asked. "Because I'm not

in the mood today."

"I wish it were," Lizzie said.

"Faeries *aren't* real," Misty scoffed.

"I know it's hard to believe," Lizzie said. "I almost don't believe it myself yet, but something happened to me last night. And now, I'm changing."

Misty's glare stayed on Lizzie, who widened her eyes in silent plea. For a moment, they stared at each other, speaking without words, Lizzie's expression a clear confirmation that every word was true. Misty's posture shifted. Her smile faltered, and her eyes searched Lizzie's face.

"Wait... you're serious?" Misty said. "*Great.* Killer Faeries. *Love* that for us."

"Are you growing pointy ears or something?" Shay retorted, breaking the silence.

"Come on, Shay," Brody said. She was angry with him; he got that. She could join the club. Shay was a straight-shooting detective. She cracked cases from concrete evidence and wasn't the type to hold a crystal for good luck or get her tarot cards read. That's one of the reasons he hadn't filled her in in the first place. She definitely wasn't the "dragons once roamed the Earth" type.

"No," Lizzie said, ignoring Shay's tone. "I'm sensing things I didn't before."

"Like ESP?" Misty asked.

"Much more than that. I can see people's emotions."

Shay perked up. "What am I feeling right now?"

Hesitatingly, Lizzie responded. "You have swirls of pink and green, but it isn't love you feel. It's betrayal."

Shay shook her head. "Anyone could see that. You already know I'm pissed."

"All right, come on," Brody said. "Shay, I know you're angry at me, but we don't have time for this right now. We *have* to find that relic. I called you here because I trust you.

So either help us or don't."

"What else is going on with you?" Misty asked Lizzie.

"I'm just not feeling well. There's this pulsing. It's me, but it's not me. I can't explain it. And this headache."

"Okay," Misty said, standing. She reached into a small teal knapsack she had slung over her shoulder. "I have meds for the headache, and we'll figure out the rest."

"So our plan is to find the relic, and then what?" Shay asked. She relaxed slightly, grasping the gravity of the situation.

"Nunez wants to destroy it," Brody answered.

"And you don't think she's right," Shay replied.

"I think… I don't know what I think. We need to find the relic first. Once we have it in our hands and know it's safe from Redcap and Cedric, then we can decide what to do with it. Destroying it might be the best option, but it might not. The Elders told Lizzie we need to get it to the Shadow Breaker."

"And who the hell is that?" Shay asked.

"No idea." Brody turned to Lizzie. "Read the next passage. Misty, can you write down what you and Shay think these passages might mean?"

Lizzie turned the stiff pages until she reached the next passage.

"A cloaked Crone, the mistress of Deep Magic, commanded the woodlands. She spoke to the trees, especially to the Elder, and advised Genevieve on the importance of letting go of her futile quest to find her father and, instead, embracing her destiny. 'Beginnings and endings, birth and death, transform thy ways and leave what has left.' The Crone showed Genevieve the Elder and beckoned her to cross the threshold." Lizzie paused as she considered the passage.

"From what I remember," Misty said, "the Crone tells Genevieve how horrible her journey will be, and Genevieve hesitates to take the journey. You know, the whole hero's journey thing."

Lizzie frowned.

"Well, I don't see how this has anything to do with me, except…"

"What?" Brody asked.

"The mention of the Elder," Lizzie said in a low voice.

"What's an Elder?" Shay asked.

"In the story, the Elder is a tree," Misty said, "It's a gateway between worlds."

"Hey, guys?" Lizzie said. Brody followed Lizzie's gaze as it focused on the tree carved into the wood in the center of the room. Then she read the last line from the highlighted passage. "The Crone showed Genevieve the Elder and beckoned her to cross the threshold. Do you think it's possible…"

"You think the library has something to do with this story?" Misty said.

"That's what my grandfather seemed to imply in his letter," Lizzie said. "And why have a tree carved into the wood without there being some significance? We need to read the next passage." Lizzie lost no time turning to the final highlighted passage.

"The Crone left Genevieve with her sense of purpose before taking off into the forest. Genevieve begged the Crone to let her be and refused to cross a threshold that would lead her to more pain and suffering. But the Mistress of Deep Magic took Genevieve's hands into her own and said, 'Like the mollusk feels the unnerving irritation of its mantle and seeks to undo that irritation, so will you layer your pain and suffering with nacre, only you will call it anger and grief, and you will enclose your pain and suffering over and over in those emotions. But like the nacre changes into a precious pearl, through breaking and building, so will you change your anger, grief, and suffering into strength and resilience. You, my dear Genevieve, shall become a precious pearl of your own if only you accept your destiny. You must die to become who you wish to be.'"

Lizzie skipped to the following highlighted passage.

"Sun rays swept in from the small window, casting a light on the yellow wallpaper, whose patterns morphed with the sun's movement. Genevieve knew that walls held secrets. She gazed upon the sunbeam in the afternoon light, and when her eyes fell upon that yellow wallpaper, she knew she'd found the entrance to the underworld."

"Yellow wallpaper?" Brody asked. "Kind of an odd thing to write about, no?"

"Westin is referencing a book by the 19th-century author Charlotte Perkins Gilman called *The Yellow Wallpaper*," Misty replied.

She referenced it as if everyone should have read it. Brody shared empty glances with Shay and Lizzie.

"What?" Misty said. "I majored in English in college and took an unforgettable Literature of Horror course."

"Clearly unforgettable," Lizzie teased.

"What was *The Yellow Wallpaper* about?" Brody asked.

"The story doesn't matter," Shay interjected, tapping her chin as she perused the bookshelves. "Westin is saying the book's location should align with the sunbeam."

"How do you know that?" Brody asked.

"Because," Shay said, holding out her hand for Lizzie to hand her the book. She reread the passage. "'Sun rays swept in from the small window, casting a light on the yellow wallpaper.' The light would come in from one of the windows at a certain time of day and shine onto that book." Shay estimated where the light from the windows might fall based on the time of day.

"You two are exceptional," Lizzie smiled. Brody hated to

admit it, but he couldn't help but feel a little intimidated by these three women.

"Are you saying Westin came to this inn?" Misty asked.

"Yes," Lizzie replied.

"And Westin knew about your bloodline, was working with your great-grandfather, the owner of the inn."

"It appears that way," Lizzie nodded.

"So, then the attack that killed the director, Richard Baker, it wasn't Westin? It was… something else, which would mean that something might still be here."

Yes, Brody wanted to say, *and that beast is making its way back here right now.*

"Let's just find this book," he said, trying to keep the pace.

Each of the four took a section of the room to search. In just a few minutes, Brody heard Shay call out.

"I found it! I found *The Yellow Wallpaper.*"

Shay grabbed the book excitedly, but her face twisted into a bemused grimace as she held it.

"What?" Lizzie asked. "What's wrong?"

Shay tapped the top of the book. A hollow sound replaced what would have been a solid one. She opened the book, but no sweet, musky smell of worn pages filled their noses and lingered there. Instead, they found the book had been made into a box, crafted only to look like a book. Inside was a key, the color of raspberry cream, mixed with swirls of quartz stone.

"A key," Brody said. "To what?"

Lizzie held out her hand, and Shay gave her the key. After examining it, Lizzie said, "This key is made of Petalite and Rhodochrosite, two sacred Elgorian stones. And before you ask me how I know this, you should know that I don't know exactly, but I think the Elders may still be speaking to me, just not like they did last night."

"Okay, so where do we think this key leads then?" Brody

asked.

"A secret box," Misty offered.

"Or…" Lizzie said, gazing at Brody. "A secret room."

Both made sense, Brody thought.

"If there were a room," Brody said, "then where would it be located?"

"If there were a room, we're standing on it," Shay said.

"A secret room beneath this library?" Brody asked.

"Yes," Shay said. "If I had to make my best guess…"

"If that's true, there must be a hidden doorway somewhere in these bookshelves," Misty added. "You know, one of the shelves will start rumbling and reveal a secret room?" She immediately began to search the shelves.

"Okay, let's all take a section and search," Brody said. But as soon as he said it, he stopped before taking one more step. A sound outside in the distance caught his ear. Was it… screaming?

"Shh," Brody said, holding his finger to his lips. He headed over to the window, drawing one of the long curtains to the side to get a better look.

"What is it?" Misty asked nervously.

Gunshots. Lots of them.

Immediately, his eyes latched onto Shay's, and he nodded toward her. Simultaneously, they put their earpieces on and began communicating with separate people: Shay to Nunez and Dale, and Brody, reluctantly, to Hemmy.

"Kado-1," Brody said, revealing his call sign to Hemmy.

"We have a dozen hostiles. Go! Go! Move!" Brody heard Hemmy shout to his men. "Coming around the… perimeter," his voice cut in and out. "Nun… informed." Brody heard shots, and then Hemmy's voice came in. "They're prepared for a fight. We have men down. Stay where you are. Do not leave under any circumstances."

"Understood," Brody said. Hemmy had muted his comms

device, so Brody couldn't hear what was happening. Brody heard screams outside the window now, no doubt innocent guests feeling the wrath of whoever and whatever was out there.

"Okay, no one panic," Shay said, although even Brody could hear the fear in her voice.

"Dale and Punk?" Brody asked.

"In Nunez's cabin, still." Shay grasped Brody's arm and frowned. "That cabin is exposed. They could bust inside."

"They *could*," Brody said. "But we have to trust that they'll be okay. None of us are safe if we don't find that pendant."

"Yeah, okay," Shay agreed.

"Look," Brody addressed the room. Both Lizzie and Misty were quiet, their faces impenetrable. "This situation isn't ideal, but we knew it would happen eventually. So let's stay calm and keep looking for the entrance to that room."

Brody watched the worry crease over Lizzie's brow. She didn't move, seemed paralyzed in the moment. He put his hands on her arms. "We're safe in here for now, okay? But if there's any chance we can stop this, we have to try. Now is not the time to let fear take over."

Lizzie nodded, calmed her nerves, and headed to one of the bookshelves to begin looking for any signs of a secret doorway. Meanwhile, Brody moved the settee first, pushing it toward the door. They'd have to move a lot more furniture to keep anyone from busting in, and even then, it wasn't likely to keep Redcap and his beast out. Still, it would slow them down, if only for a short while.

Brody had successfully pushed the settee against the door and was in the midst of moving an armoire when he saw the jiggling of the door handle and then a banging. He held his finger to his lips, signaling to everyone to keep quiet as he pushed against the settee. He leaned into the door, every muscle straining.

Suddenly, something slammed into it.

Whoever was out there *wasn't* getting inside. Not on his watch, not when so much was at stake.

Brody's heart thundered.

"Open the damn door, would ya?"

Brody let out the breath he'd been holding. He knew that voice—it was an unforgettable, formidable tone, and he'd never been so happy to hear it. Chuck Degan was here. He'd made it. Maybe they did have a chance of surviving this after all.

chapter 40

Miles crouched down and rested his fingers gently on the exposed neck of the motionless man in front of him. He futilely searched for a pulse; the guy was dead, that much he knew. He looked up and shook his head at Dean, who was leaning against one of the tall, leaf-dropping oaks and quietly scanning the area for Redcap or FBI agents.

Dean had convinced Miles to wait until Redcap and the rest of The Family were closer to the inn. Miles initially resisted, but Dean confessed that he couldn't abandon the rest of The Family, not when Remy had little intention of following through with Redcap's mission.

"You don't think Remy was going to follow through?" Miles asked.

Dean shook his head.

"When have you ever known Remy to engage in a conflict?" Dean asked. "Ludwig was always the aggressor, and Remy sat on the sidelines, observing. Even when we were kids."

Miles sighed. "Then what was Remy's plan? How was he going to protect everyone?"

Dean scoffed. "By doing what Remy does best. Ludwig's always been the outspoken leader type, but Remy, he's the master of manipulation."

"So, he was gonna, what, make Redcap think we were all in and then sabotage the plan?" Miles asked. It was a simplistic idea, but Dean had a point.

"Remy may not be as ruthless as Ludwig, but he's as selfish," Dean said. "When I spoke to him, it seemed he'd made up his mind. He told the guys in private to pack their bags, leave, and get out before Redcap noticed. But the rest of The Family are reluctant to take orders from him. Liam especially. You know how they are."

"Because they think…" Miles started.

"They *know* Remy is selfish. Gola and Mako left, but Laskin, Liam, Enzo, Danva, and Servino all stayed. They're afraid if they run, Redcap will hunt them down before they can leave. And to that point, no one has heard from Gola or Mako since, but could be they don't *want* to be found."

"And I imagine Liam thinks even less of Remy now that Ludwig's dead," Miles added. "Especially since Remy didn't do much to stand up for him."

"The problem with Remy is he doesn't know how to get his hands dirty, and Redcap isn't the type that can be manipulated."

Miles paused, a question lingering on his lips like the stain of dry Italian red wine.

"How did you know the FBI was involved?" Miles asked.

"Juarez was an informant."

The way he said it was remarkably casual, as though everyone should have known.

"Really?" Miles asked.

"Yeah. Redcap must have found out and sent that thing to kill the poor bastard, and I found him bleeding out by the side of the farmhouse. His last words were, 'They're not human. Find Director Nunez.' As soon as he said it, I knew, pieced it all together."

"But Juarez has been with us for two years. Never once…"

"He was good at his job," Dean said. "And we were lucky. Ludwig intimidated enough people to keep us protected from the local police and the Feds. But when Juarez told me that, I knew something bigger was happening."

"Where's Remy now?" Miles asked.

"He left this morning with Mom. They're on a flight to Remy's island."

"Did you confirm this? Is it possible Redcap's after him?"

"Last I heard, Redcap was on his way to the inn, and so was Remy, except Remy took a detour. He wasn't too keen on my idea."

"What idea?"

"After your *insistence* on coming back to this inn, I decided we better have a plan and a good one. I met with Director Nunez this morning, and we came up with something that works out for all of us. Our men are set to follow Redcap to the inn."

"But aren't you condemning them?" Miles interrupted. "Either to Redcap's men or the Feds?"

"I traded information with Director Nunez so I could protect The Family, Miles. She assured me that none of our men would be harmed. She said if we help her with this, she might even cut us a deal."

"And you believe her?" Miles asked. *Cause I don't,* he wanted to say.

Dean just grunted, signaling to Miles he was skeptical as well.

"And how will she know who our people are versus Redcap's?" Miles asked. Sure, there were noticeable physical differences; all of Redcap's men looked like they were WWE wrestlers. "Tell me you didn't give out names and identities?"

"No, what kind of idiot do you think I am?" Dean scoffed. "I told Nunez our guys would be wearing camo-green ski masks. Before I left, I purchased them for the team, but for a different reason. I thought if we were going in, we needed to blend in, but now... those masks might save our lives. And I even confirmed with Redcap that it would help conceal our men since they have their own gear. It's a simple, stupid thing, but it was the only way I could ensure Nunez would know who our men were and who his were. But the other thing is, Redcap knows our guys will be wearing the green ski masks, so if we're wearing them, he won't bother us too much."

"I don't like it," Miles said. He hadn't meant to say that out loud, but it came out anyway. "Do our men know they're going to turn on Redcap?"

"All I told them was to stick with the plan, and when the time came, I might be giving them new instructions."

Miles couldn't help but let out a haughty laugh.

"It'll work, Miglio," Dean said. "Trust me."

Miles did trust his brother, had always trusted him. But this plan? This plan was crazy. Still, Miles didn't have a better one.

"Last night," Miles said, "you were worried the FBI would come after me because..."

"They know who you are—have been following you for a while. And you're after the one person they want to protect at all costs."

"And what is the plan after the crew arrives at the inn, and if they survive the SWAT team?"

"Nunez wants Redcap to get as close to the library as possible. She seems to think he'll be most vulnerable there, close to Lizzie. That's when we all attack. And, with any luck, after this, our lives will go back to normal."

Whatever normal was, Miles thought.

"You really think we can do this?" Miles said.

"If the SWAT can't take them down, we're fucked, Miles. Now, here, put this on." He threw one of the ski masks toward Miles. "It's time to go."

Even though they both had weapons—Dean a gun, Miles a knife—it would do little against Redcap, Cedric, and their men when the time came to turn on them. Redcap and his goons were better equipped, and who knew what else they had on their side? Miles stood, adjusting his ski mask, and then moved a little closer to the inn, where he found another dead agent.

Miles heard screams in the distance and prayed Lizzie was safe. They had to find a way back into the inn, but the timing had to be right. No doubt Redcap was close to the inn, so Dean and Miles had to hurry. Miles was about to pick up his pace when Dean grabbed his brother by the shoulder and pushed him against a tree. Dean widened his eyes and pressed his finger against his lips. Miles turned his head slightly and saw the beast there, feasting on some poor bastard, oblivious to Miles and Dean. Miles felt his heart race. How were they going to get around this thing? The beast was like a lion enjoying a fresh kill, and Miles knew that any sudden moves might make this thing turn and consider them his next prey. They had to keep moving. Redcap might even be inside the inn at this point and already have Lizzie. But if they moved, the leaves would crunch under their feet, and Miles knew there was no way to outrun this behemoth.

Miles held his breath, trying to think of their next move. He shifted his position slightly, trying not to make a noise.

Crunch.

The sound of his muddy black boot crushing a leaf long past its prime made the beast stop, turn, and stare at Miles directly into his eyes. The beast sauntered slowly toward the men.

"Stay back," Miles said, as if that would do anything.

But the beast crept nearer and nearer until it was so close, Miles felt its hot, fleshy breath on his face. Blood dripped from its fangs as it sniffed Miles' mask and then Dean's, and they held their breath, not daring to move.

The creature grunted, let out a long, slow, disgusted snort, and then slowly turned away back toward its kill. As soon as it turned, Miles and Dean began to run toward the inn.

Why hadn't the beast attacked them? Had Redcap trained the beast not to harm anyone wearing the mask? Or was it some otherworldly instinct? Miles didn't dwell on it. All he knew was... he would thank his brother later.

A gunshot from somewhere close made the beast growl, but Miles and Dean did not dare turn to look. No doubt more SWAT team members were in these woods, and Miles and Dean ran as quickly as they could toward the inn, while the beast ran in the other direction, dodging oncoming bullets. Neither Dean nor Miles spoke, and neither looked behind him at the beast. Miles heard a scream in the distance, knowing that yet another person had suffered an untimely fate. When Miles and Dean reached the inn, they entered through one of the side doors closer to the venue.

They were safe, at least for now. But once inside the inn, Miles felt his stomach sink. The scene before him couldn't have been the work of just a few men. Even the combination of The Family and Redcap's men wouldn't have produced the horrific scene before them. No, this was a massacre. There were only a few survivors crying out in pain. Miles knew then they were up against much more than they bargained for. He could turn around now, leave with Dean, meet his mother and Remy on that island, and never look back.

But he wouldn't.

Because Lizzie was *here.*

And despite everything that had happened between them, he still loved her. So he would fight, even if it meant that this inn was where he would take his last breath.

chapter 41

A wrinkle creased Lizzie's forehead as dread surged through her. Just knowing the Bakers and the murderous Fae were here, and they were coming for *her*, made her draw in deeper breaths, a futile attempt to tame the raging fear in her body.

She still hadn't found the pendant. If the library had a secret room, it might buy them some time, but there was no guarantee that the room existed. Lizzie heard the screams, followed by the hollow sounds of gunshots.

Was it a bloodbath? Were innocent people dying?

If they were, was it all her fault? After all, the Bakers were after her inheritance, the Shadow Fae after her pendant. Could all this have been avoided if she had stormed out of the library and surrendered to the people who pursued her? *What was her one life worth when so many others were paying the price?*

"A lot of casualties," she heard Brody tell Shay. His auric field rimmed in swirls of crimson red, like the blood spilled outside the library walls. *Survival.* Guilt tugged at her gut. If anything were to happen to Brody or Misty… Misty wore a worry-crease of her own as she feverishly combed

255

the bookshelves for any sign of a secret room. Lizzie's throat tightened, and she felt that hot feeling that accompanied a panic attack. Losing her mother had been painful enough; Lizzie could not stomach losing another person she cared about, especially her best friend.

Now, someone was trying to get into the library, and Brody was moving the settee away from the door. She didn't have time to yell for him to stop. When he opened the door, and her father stood there, looking angrier than a loose cannon, all Lizzie could muster was an incredulous, "Dad?"

Was it shock, relief, or both that Lizzie was feeling? She couldn't pinpoint the emotion. Looking at Brody, Lizzie saw yellowish hues emanating from his aura now, transmitting his confidence in Chuck's presence.

"You're here," Lizzie said as her father approached her. He was a man of few words and had never been a sentimental man as far as she could remember, so when he wrapped Lizzie in his arms for a hug and said, "I'm so thankful you're okay," she was taken aback. Instead of hugging him back, she kept her arms limply at her sides. She wasn't good at forcing an emotional connection where there was none.

"I'm… okay," she assured him.

Biologically, Chuck Degan was her father, but emotionally, he was like a close friend Lizzie had lost touch with after high school. A bond had existed, but it hadn't been *nurtured*, and now she didn't even know the person who stood before her. She wanted to say mean things to him; it was too late to mend their relationship; he should leave, since that's what he did best. Yet, how could she be angry with him when he was here now, when it mattered most?

His face had weathered since she'd seen him last, the deep wrinkles spread across his forehead like cracks in dry mud. His dark eyes were the same, though, piercing and classically handsome. He'd grown an impressive beard since she last saw him—its salt and pepper gray matched his ear-length hair. "I have so many questions," were the only words she could utter.

"And I'll answer them," her father replied, oblivious to the storm brewing in Lizzie's mind. "But right now, we need to prepare for what's coming." Her father turned to Brody. "You're going to need this," Chuck said, removing a long black bag from his shoulder. He carefully placed it onto the ground, unzipped it, and then pulled out a sleek, long, black barrel.

"Is that a gun?" Lizzie asked.

"Here," Chuck said, handing Brody the barrel. "Came out of my wall. It ain't a person-killing gun. Had a gun specialist in special forces make these for me."

"How does it work?" Lizzie asked.

"Simple," Chuck said. "You point and then spin this little piece right here." He pretended to spin a little nozzle attached to the barrel. "The bullet, if you want to call it that, will shoot out from the barrel."

"Like a cannon?" Misty asked.

"More like a cannon. Yeah," Chuck replied.

"You have any more of these?" Brody asked.

"I do." Chuck pulled out another long barrel and handed it to Shay.

When Chuck tried to hand Misty one, she shook her head and put her hands up in surrender.

"It's best I don't have one," she said. "I'm not the killing type."

Chuck shrugged.

"I hate to be the one to bring you bad news." Chuck's expression tightened. "But the bad guys are here. I tried to throw them off course, but… we're already on borrowed time." He looked at Brody. "You should move as much furniture as you can against the door like you did before. I'll help you. It'll slow them down a little, I hope." Holding up his barrel, he said, "There are only six bullets in these, so use them wisely."

"You said these aren't human-killing. What kind of guns are they?" Brody asked.

"Fae-killing."

Lizzie's father knew something about their family connection to the Fae, and while she desperately wanted to know what, she knew that now wasn't the time to ask.

"What kills a Fae?" Lizzie asked. She wanted to know the answer as much for herself as for their enemies.

"Pure cold iron," Chuck said.

"Iron?" Brody said. "I thought that was just a myth."

"Most myths about faeries are true."

"So, the iron does what?" Brody asked.

"Rusts the bastards from the inside out," Chuck said. "One bullet will disarm their capabilities and then spread like a black mold throughout their bodies."

"You're out to kill with these," Shay said. She examined the gun and checked the bullet chamber as she spoke. "Why not stun and let the law decide what happens to the bad guys?"

"If you knew who we were dealing with, you'd opt for shoot first, ask questions later," Chuck said.

"What do you know of who we're dealing with?" Lizzie asked.

Lizzie watched as her father's eyes narrowed. Suddenly, she noticed something peculiar. Everyone in the room had a hazy reddish cloud about them; all of them were fighting for survival, but her father had *nothing*. No shade of anything, not even a shade of gray, as if… he didn't have any emotions at all.

"Why can't I see your emotions?" she asked skeptically. "And don't sugar coat it." Lately, she'd found the best way to get to an answer was to ask bluntly. Maybe now wasn't the time, but Lizzie's father owed her some answers. "If I'm Fae, then you must be, too," she continued. "Can Fae only see human emotions? Are you able to speak to the Elgorian Elders too, or is it just something I can do?"

Chuck kept his eyes steady on Lizzie and contemplated his next words carefully.

"There's something you should know," Chuck said, his voice a husky murmur. "Lizzie, Elgoria was my home."

"You're *from* Elgoria?" Brody asked.

Even Lizzie hadn't expected that. She'd accepted that she was part of this bloodline but thought her parents had both been born here—on *Earth*. She never imagined her father might be from the Fae world. Now the questions swirled around in her mind like the sky in Van Gogh's *Starry Night*.

Did her mother know? Was her mother from Elgoria, too? Why hadn't anyone told Lizzie this information? How did her father get here? When did he get here?

Lizzie had so many questions, but she knew there was no time to get answers now.

"Then it's true. I can't see your emotions because you're Fae?" she said.

"You can't see my emotions because I'm a Shadow," he said, his gravelly voice as downtrodden as his expression.

"A Shadow?" Lizzie asked. Her father had said it like it was a bad thing. "Like a Shadow Breaker?" *Was her father the Shadow Breaker?*

"What do you know about the Shadow Breaker?" her father asked.

"There's no time for this," Brody said, urgency straining his voice. He stepped in front of Lizzie and gently took her hands in his. In a low voice so only she could hear, he said, "I know you have questions, and your father can explain all of this to you later, but for now, we have to keep on the task at hand. If Redcap and Cedric break down that door right now, all of this will mean nothing."

Lizzie nodded. Brody was right. She needed to stay focused, help find that secret room, or some clue that would lead them closer to the pendant. She would have plenty of time to ask her father questions if they survived this attack. *If…* being the operative word here. Lizzie was tired of being afraid, tired of fearing for her life. She wanted peace so badly that she refused to let anyone rob her of it any longer.

"I want one of those," she told her father, pointing to the Fae-killing gun.

"You sure?" her father asked.

"I've never been surer," Lizzie said. "In fact, I pray Redcap and Cedric come through that door soon. The faster we get rid of them, the faster I get my life back."

chapter 42

"What if Dale needs me? Or Punk?" Shay said.

Her voice was soft, but still it sliced Brody like tiny shavings of glass. They stood by the library door, deciding what to do with the sideboard in the room. They could leave it on its side, so it stood vertically, and push it against the doors, or keep the settee fixed horizontally across the doors. A small wooden curve arched the back of the settee. It was just thin enough to wedge under the curved door handles of the library, creating a makeshift lock. But even if they stacked all the furniture against those doors, Brody knew it wouldn't be enough.

"What if they need to take refuge here?" Shay asked. "We're blocking them out." Shay's eyes pleaded with Brody's now. "I feel like I should be out there with my husband."

Brody heard the fear in her voice and swallowed the guilt he felt for putting them in this position. He didn't allow himself to imagine anything happening to Dale or Punk or even Nunez. But they couldn't risk letting anyone else inside this library. Not now.

Brody patted Shay's shoulder, a poor attempt to console her. "I'm sure Nunez has a trick up her sleeve. She wouldn't leave herself exposed. Dale is probably in a safer place than we are. Punk, too." He maintained eye contact while his brow furrowed with concern. "Look… I dragged you and Dale into this, and for that, I'm sorry. I need your help, Shay, but I won't force you to stay. If you need to go to him, you go."

Shay nodded, contemplating his offer.

"Thank you," she said. "You're probably right. He's safe. They're somewhere safe. Besides, I *want* to help. I'll stay."

"You're sure?"

"Yes."

"OK. Good," Brody replied, giving her that sympathetic smile again. "Now, let's move some more things against this door. We need to keep two Fae, whose capabilities I know nothing about, an entire mafia, and a wild beast out." He patted her shoulder. "No pressure."

Shay cracked a smile, and so did he. A little humor sometimes helped when all seemed hopeless.

After Brody, Chuck, and Shay moved as many pieces of furniture as they could—the settee, the coffee table, a sideboard, two end tables, and a desk—they were as satisfied as they could be with the library's barrier. While it wouldn't keep Redcap and the Bakers out, as Chuck had said, it would buy Brody and Lizzie a little time.

It was then that Brody resumed his search for the secret doorway. He removed books from all levels of the shelves, letting his fingers graze across the wood for any grooves or openings, levers, or anything that might fit a key. But Brody couldn't help but wonder if they were on the right path. Maybe the key wasn't to a doorway. Perhaps it unlocked something else entirely.

"We have to move faster," Brody urged. "There's no guarantee there even is a secret room. Maybe we're searching in the wrong place."

"No, there is. I'm sure of it," Lizzie argued.

"But we have to consider that even if we find a secret room, the pendant may not be in there," Misty offered.

"And then we've wasted the only time we had left," Brody added.

Brody's earpiece buzzed again, but he didn't hear Hemmy's call sign emanate from the other end. Instead, he heard screams as if someone was being attacked by something. The beast. He took his earpiece out and shoved it in his pocket.

"Is it bad?" Lizzie asked, reading his facial cues.

"It's bad," Brody said. "Really bad. Let's hope the answers are in here because we absolutely cannot go out *there*." Brody walked over to the library door and made sure that the items he, Chuck, and Shay had pushed against it were secure. "And we can't let anyone in."

"What about the tree?" Misty said. "The one carved into the floor. I'll check for a keyhole."

Misty searched the tree, but eventually, she lifted her head and shook it side to side.

"We really are all out of options," Lizzie said, defeated. "I really thought…"

"Wait…" Shay said.

"What?"

"You said cold iron could hurt the Fae," she said to Chuck.

"Yes," he replied.

"And there's only one thing in here with iron." Shay shifted her gaze and then hurried over to the skinny wrought-iron cabinet against the wall. "This curiously placed *iron* cabinet of journals right here."

Lizzie went to touch the bars, but Brody gently took her hand in his and pulled it away.

"Not now," he said, resting his eyes on hers. "Just in case."

"I've never had a problem before," she said.

"Maybe not," Brody replied. "But you've changed overnight." He turned to Chuck. "Chuck, assuming that there are other faeries here on Earth, why aren't they affected by the iron? Like Lizzie, for instance?"

"Those born here have some kind of immunity to it. But the closer a person gets to Elgoria…" He stopped. "Let's put it this way, I wouldn't take the chance getting anywhere near iron."

She gave him a gentle nod and pulled back, allowing Brody to examine the journal cabinet. It was narrow, much more so than a normal bookshelf. If it were a doorway, only one person could squeeze through sideways. Claustrophobia be damned.

"Do we have the key to open this?" Misty asked.

Brody produced the library key from his pocket, but it didn't work.

"No," Brody replied. "The innkeeper, Ermington, gave me some journals to look through, but he didn't get them from this cabinet."

"Do you think he has the key?" Shay asked.

"Would it matter if he did?" Brody replied. "We can't find him now… don't even know if he's still alive."

"Can we try Lizzie's key?" Shay asked.

"I don't think it'll work," Brody said.

"Let's try it anyway," Shay pressed. "We're desperate."

Lizzie handed Shay the gemstone key, and she tried to fit it into the keyhole.

"Just… please be careful with that," Lizzie warned. "It's fragile."

"It's a key," Shay said.

"Yeah, but it's easily breakable."

"How are we getting in there then?" Shay asked once she

realized the gem key didn't work either.

"The only thing we can do," Brody said.

"Break the lock," Chuck said, reading Brody's mind. Chuck ran his palm over the stubble on his chin and then reached into his black bag and pulled out a set of gloves. "Gloves normally don't protect Elven-Fae from iron, no matter how thick the gloves are. That element has a strong energy that seeps from it. Even getting too close to it can hurt us, but a friend of mine made me these. They're military grade. Faraday materials can block out EMFs and radiation, but these babies can block out all kinds of elemental energies." Chuck approached the lock and, carefully, with his gloves on, took a long, thin metal pin out of his bag. He twisted the metal pin in the lock until he heard a clicking sound.

"Where'd you learn how to do that?" Misty asked.

"You probably don't want to know," Lizzie said.

Chuck tugged on the iron bars to open them. After the door opened, Shay immediately began removing the journals from each shelf. Misty and Lizzie took turns stacking them in piles on the floor. When the cabinet was empty, it looked like a make-shift iron cage, its back identical to the wall.

"That's… odd," Misty said.

"Give me the gem key again," Shay said after she ran her fingers along the second shelf.

Lizzie handed it to her once more.

"I think I found something," Shay continued. Her voice waned as she reached far back into the cabinet with the key. "I'm not sure if it's a keyhole, but…"

Click, click, click.

Shay tugged slightly, and not just the cabinet but the wall itself began to move outward, like a door. Brody helped her pull, and soon all that was left was a narrow, dark opening where the cabinet had been.

"Well, would ya look at that? A hidden room," Brody said,

looking at Lizzie. He winked at her, and for the first time since their heated encounter the night before, she smiled. Her eyes were wide with a wistful hope, a look that tugged at his heart.

"I'm going down there to check it out," Brody announced. He would have to use his phone as a flashlight, and thankfully, he had a little battery left. Brody stepped toward the dark, narrow opening, but Chuck placed a hand on Brody's chest before he could take a step further.

"I'll go," Chuck said. "Ya'll don't know what's down there."

"Then, I'm coming with you," Brody stated, letting Chuck know he wasn't going to take no for an answer.

"You'll stay up here and protect my daughter," Chuck ordered.

"I'll protect your daughter," Shay offered. "I do this for a living, you know." She offered Chuck an impish smile.

"You can both go," Lizzie told Brody and Chuck. "Shay, Misty, and I will stay up here. You're right. It's possible the pendant isn't even down there. So the three of us can search through these new journals for clues while you two search the secret room."

chapter 43

rody watched as Chuck lit a match from a small matchbox he retrieved from his pocket. Though the flame was small, it lit up a hollow opening that seemed to stretch into a dark, endless abyss. Chuck turned his body sideways, stepped into the darkness, and grabbed a torch off the wall. He handed it to Brody and then ventured once more into the darkness, producing another torch that had been fixed onto the wall. Clearly, someone had explored the passage before.

Chuck lit Brody's torch, then his own. *All Chuck needed now*, Brody thought, *was a brown, wide-rimmed sable fedora and a map.* As Chuck headed into the dark corridor first and began his sideways descent, Brody followed closely behind. The curvature of the narrow stone walls and thin spiraling steps made it difficult for them to walk down without bracing against the wall. The torch illuminated the way, and Brody wiped his free fingers along the glistening walls.

Water. Strange.

The steps continued in spirals for much longer than Brody imagined was possible. As they continued, Brody noticed more foliage, some variation of ivy, clinging to the walls. The smell reminded him of a rainy spring day, pleasant but damp. Soft, blue, twinkling lights flitted around him like fireflies on a summer night. When Chuck reached the bottom of the stairs, he stopped. A thick branch dangled in front of him, and he pushed it aside, careful to keep the flame from touching it as he stepped forward into an earthy darkness. Brody followed behind, encountering more branches hanging in his way.

Chuck held his torch up, revealing the sight before them. In the middle of the room was a tree, but it appeared to be upside down. The trunk branched outward, the roots coiling downward from the ceiling, while the still green branches and leaves looked as though they grew upward from the ground. The blue twinkling lights darted around the tree's leaves and blossoms.

Brody stared at the lush greenness of the tree's toothy leaflets and the white flowers arranged in flat-topped clusters. This tree was underground. With no sunlight, it should be dead and certainly not growing upside-down. And it appeared to be… breathing? It moved outward and inward with slow, meditative breaths.

"How is this possible?" Brody asked, marveling at the sight before him. "What is this?"

"An Elgorian Elder tree," Chuck mused. "Ain't she beautiful?"

Brody stepped forward, extending his finger to one of the hundreds of dashing blue lights.

"Don't touch that unless you want to lose about ten years of memory," Chuck warned.

"What is it?" Brody asked.

"Pixies. As quick as hummingbirds, maybe quicker. Nasty little sprites. Gah." Chuck swiped the torch to stave off the blue pixies who flitted away at the threat of fire. "In the old days, before the war, pixies swarmed Elgorian Elder trees to keep the Fae from using them as portals."

"So, this tree is a portal to Elgoria?"

"I don't know," Chuck said, shaking his head, the flickering flames lighting one side of his weathered face. *Too weathered,* Brody thought, *for a man in his early seventies.* "Not all of them were, but the last I remember, all the Elder trees of Elgoria were destroyed."

"If you're from Elgoria, how did you get here?" Brody asked.

Chuck spoke in a low voice, keeping his eyes fixed on the tree as he reminisced.

"Elgoria is divided, always has been, in an eternal civil war between good and evil. The Elgorian Scrolls say that long before Shadow and Light, Elgoria was ruled by three great elemental powers. Together, they shaped the world. But something happened, something so devastating it shattered them completely. Out of that destruction, two forces were born: Shadow and Light."

He paused before continuing.

"Shadow contained everything dense, despicable, revolting… and Light contained everything nimble, beautiful, and kind."

He looked at Brody.

"Out of the shadows came all sorts of creatures, some so evil and ruthless that you wouldn't stand a chance in their presence. Others look as human as you. But they lack empathy. Love. Their hearts beat in darkness. That's how it's always been. For a time, they coexisted. Light and Shadow. But the creator never meant for them to live apart. Shadow and Light were supposed to merge and become one. The problem was that neither wanted to give up their power. To merge, one would have to lead. But who? Shadow? Or Light?"

"They couldn't agree," Brody said. "So…"

"The peace ended." Chuck didn't wait for him to finish.

"And the *war* began."

Another pause. Chuck's voice tightened.

"A senseless war that's raged for ages. I've seen some awful things working for the Agency on Earth. But nothing compares to what I saw in Elgoria. The stories say Shadow Fae are the worst of them all."

"You feel differently?" Brody said, noticing Chuck's solemn expression. Suddenly, he remembered Chuck's words from upstairs. "You're a Shadow."

"I am."

"But you're not... that ruthless?" *Although some would say that's debatable*, Brody wanted to joke, but now was not the time.

Chuck let out a strained laugh.

"My family experienced an awakening. It seemed to happen overnight to my parents, a light within the shadow, not unlike the transient flicker of this flame."

Brody's eyes briefly flickered to the flame before fixing back onto Chuck.

"A Seethio had badly wounded a Light Fae soldier," Chuck continued. "Seethios are heinous creatures of the shadows. Anyway, the dying soldier sought refuge in my parents' hut. A Shadow Fae would not dare help, even if a person were in peril, but my mother told me that something in that Fae's eyes... she couldn't stand to see him suffer. After that day, both of my parents changed."

"Changed how?" Brody asked.

"They still possessed the Shadow, but they felt the Light. They felt compassion and love. My mother had never shown emotion, but overnight, she was warm and kind. My mother thought the location of their hut was an influence. We lived by the border, next to the Nightshade Forest. The magic contained in that forest is so great and so evil that neither a Light nor a Shadow dares to enter if he wishes to live.

Anyway, after the awakening, we kept mostly to ourselves. My father would go to town, but he acted as his Shadow self, never letting on that he felt differently. No one knew or paid us much mind until my brother wandered into the village, and one of the Shadow soldiers found him and questioned him. Questioned my family. Despite my parents' best efforts to pretend, the King of Shadows found out the truth by sensing the Light in my parents and in us. That's when the Shadow Fae staged a witch-hunt… killed my parents, my brother, my sister, and tried to kill me, too. We were an abomination to all Shadow Fae."

Chuck let out a deep sigh before continuing.

"I escaped and ran as fast as I could. I reached the Nightshade Forest and figured what the hell did I have to lose? But I wasn't thirty seconds into the forest when I tripped, fell into a murky pond, and woke up in Rittenhouse Square in the wholesome city of Philadelphia, smack in the middle of the sixties. I was a young kid alone in a world I didn't know or understand."

Brody didn't respond. *What could he say to that?*

"I did the best I could," Chuck added.

Chuck had lost so much. *No wonder he'd made the choices he had*, Brody thought. *He did everything he could to survive.* A thought occurred to Brody then.

"Are you saying there's a portal to Elgoria in Philadelphia?" he asked.

Chuck shook his head.

"The truth is, besides this one, I've only ever seen one other Elder tree," Chuck said. "They were rare but sacred in Elgoria. Most of them burnt down at the height of the last war. Only one remained. And that's gone now, too. It was already burning when I tripped and fell into that pond. I got tangled in the tree's roots and was supposed to die in there, but the tree gave me one last gift before it succumbed to its fate. If this is indeed a gateway, it may very well be the *last* gateway to Elgoria. And if that's true, we aren't the only ones looking for it from this side of the gateway *or* from Elgoria."

chapter 44

As Chuck and Brody explored the hidden room beneath the library, Lizzie, Shay, and Misty combed the journals, looking for clues that might lead to the pendant's whereabouts. Lizzie tried to block out the sensations that screamed throughout her body. Her hands shook as the extrasensory vibrations pulsed through her veins, flooding her mind with images of death and despair. She felt the fear of innocent people dying outside those library walls and sensed their souls leaving their bodies. The SWAT agents were doing their best to keep Cedric and Redcap at bay, but Lizzie knew she was running out of time.

"All of these journals are useless," Misty said, closing one and tossing it onto the floor beside her.

"Not *this* one," Shay said. She sat on the wooden floor of the library next to Misty, her two hands gripping an old brown leather-bound journal tightly. "This journal is by Paul Watson. Listen to this. *The date is February 1928. Had I known what this inheritance would cost me, I would have given it to the Bakers and been done with it. But another issue looms on my horizon, something I found in my Aunt Greta's trunk after her death, when her belongings were passed on to me. At the bottom of a jewelry box in a secret compartment, I found a pendant with odd, colorful jewels. In the trunk, I found three scrolls, and I quickly learned the pendant and scrolls belonged together, for the design on the pendant was also on the top of the scroll. I could not decipher any of the words on the scroll, and the only man willing to help me was my old friend, Harold Newbury. He knew a man in Whitemoor, an old, odd fellow from near the equator named Zaffi, who had developed a hobby for translating texts from around the world. I learned a few, albeit powerful, pieces of information from him. The scrolls predate Sumerian. Three words are easily translatable. Prophecy, Elven-Fae, and opening. The scrolls contain important information."*

Shay stopped and thumbed through a few pages before reading again.

"Zaffi says the language is an ancient Elven-Fae tongue found in Scottish lore. We debated for long hours on the existence of supernatural beings, but I am beginning to believe Zaffi is telling something of the truth. Through Zaffi's translation, I learned that the pendant had been kept hidden for years and would one day, through unusual circumstances, be opened, an event that would set off several others in the prophecy. Zaffi believes I have a role to play, but he does not yet know what. And then further down he writes," Shay continued to read. *"Zaffi says, I am the gatekeeper in the prophecy… The man who possesses the scrolls."*

"If Paul Watson was my great-grandfather, then he passed the scrolls down to my grandfather," Lizzie said. "Does that mean my grandfather was the gatekeeper, too?"

Misty shrugged. "Would Watson hide the pendant and never reveal it to anyone, or would he entrust the information to his son? That's the question. Because if it's the latter, your grandfather might have entrusted that information to someone before he died."

"We can only hope," Lizzie said. "Because he sure didn't tell me that information."

"Okay, listen to this," Shay continued. *"The pendant is of ancient magic, those born of Elven-Fae, the oldest of the Fae people. The pendant's magic is the last of the ancient magic. It's meant for the one, but none other than the one shall touch it, or he shall die."*

"The magic is for the one," Lizzie repeated. "That's what the Elders told me in the woods."

"But," Shay read. *"If the magic does not reach the one, the King of Shadows will reign."*

"The King of Shadows?" Misty asked. "That... doesn't sound like someone I want to meet."

"Maybe it's Redcap," Shay suggested before returning to the journal to read more. *"The prophecy remains unwritten after this, suggesting the ending had yet to be written."*

"We can't let Redcap or Cedric touch that pendant," Lizzie said. "If they get the ancient magic..." She shook her head. "It's over."

"Is there anything else in that journal?" Misty asked.

"Something about a Shadow Breaker?" Shay said.

"What does it say?" Lizzie asked.

"Nothing concrete. Just speculation, but he writes that *the Shadow Breaker will unveil himself through some great sacrifice.*"

Misty picked up another leather journal and combed through it.

"You said he wrote that in February of 1928, so he likely kept notes on the journals that followed that," Misty said. She paused for a moment. "Like right here!" she exclaimed. *"I have no choice but to follow the coordinates to this place and find the Elgorian Elder,"* she read. Misty sped through the text, reading it to herself and giving Lizzie the highlights of the passages. "Watson finds the Elder tree. He swears to protect it, but something happens before he can shroud it safely. Something comes through the gateway."

"What comes through?" Lizzie asked, her eyes wide, her

heart beating unrhythmically like an out-of-beat song.

"A beast," Misty whispered, shifting her eyes from the journal to Lizzie. "An army. And… the man in red."

"Redcap," Lizzie said, the crease above her brow deepening. But what did Redcap want with her? She shuddered to imagine what.

"I hate to state the obvious, but if the gateway to Elgoria, the one they came out of is here," Misty said, "Then aren't we sitting ducks?"

Lizzie heard a bang and jumped. Someone was trying to break into the library. They weren't just sitting ducks; they'd been lured here on purpose. A thought blazed through her mind like a comet through the sky. She wasn't the bait to trap the bad guys… she was the offering to them. The Bakers would get their inheritance; Redcap, and Cedric would get the pendant; and Lizzie would be their sacrifice. If that was so, who stood to gain from all of this? *None of that matters* right now, she thought. What did matter was she had a gun, and whoever busted through that doorway was going to get a cold iron bullet straight to the heart.

chapter 45

"You were stuck here," Brody said.

"Not stuck," Chuck said. "I didn't bother trying to go back because there was nothing to go back to. I made a life here. And I thought I could protect Lizzie from this part of her ancestry. But that's only because I didn't believe the ancient saying of our people, that *Fae always seek each other out, are always fixed to each other in the end.*"

"What does that mean?" Brody asked.

"They say Elven-Fae will always find each other. Lizzie's mother never knew her family's history," Chuck continued. "Harold kept that from her. I had no idea she was Fae. Yet, we found each other. And eventually, I learned her parents had sought out one another, and her grandparents were the same."

"They never married someone who wasn't Fae?"

"No," Chuck replied. "It's an instinctual behavior to keep the Fae bloodline pure."

"But they don't realize it," Brody said.

"You can call it whatever you'd like… a soulmate, love at first sight, a *knowing.*"

That couldn't be true, Brody thought. He felt deeply for Lizzie, but he knew for sure he wasn't Fae. His heart sank as he realized that maybe he and Lizzie didn't have a chance, not if some other Fae out there was meant for her.

"Anyway," Chuck continued, "the authorities couldn't find any information on me, and since I was a minor, they decided to take pity on me, assign me a new life, and stuck me in the foster system. My last foster parents kept me on the straight and narrow, and I ended up joining the military. But by the time I met Francine, Lizzie's mother, I had already gained a reputation with the Agency. My skills were different, and they knew I could help them. I never intended to fall in love, but when I met Francine, I fell instantly."

He paused.

"Francine and her father didn't have a good relationship. When we did visit him, he would spout off about a pendant with a relic at its center and about a set of scrolls that described an ancient prophecy. I read the scrolls; I didn't tell Harold I could read them easily. Didn't tell him *anything* about me, and he hated me, probably because deep in his gut, he knew I was a Shadow, and his ancestors were Lights. But I'll tell you what, as soon as I read those scrolls, I knew what I had done could not be undone."

"What did you do?" Brody asked.

"Light Fae and Shadow Fae aren't attracted to each other."

"Ever?" Brody asked.

"Not traditionally."

"Why not?"

"They're too different," Chuck said. "Even if they tried, it wouldn't work. Something innate. My folks were an anomaly because they were awakened."

"You said Elven-Fae before. Are there different kinds of Fae people?"

"Elven-Fae, whether Light or Shadow, are taller, look a

lot like humans, really. But there are all kinds of Fae, like those pixies or evil entities like a Seethio…”

“I see,” Brody said, finally understanding. “Then, because you were Shadow Fae and had a child with Francine, who was a Light, Lizzie was…”

“An Elven-Fae that was a mix of Light and Shadow, something that has never happened before, at least not to my knowledge.”

Brody began to understand the implications of what Chuck was saying. He bit his lip as Chuck continued.

“The scrolls spoke of a prophecy, about a being that would unleash powerful magic upon Elgoria and create what is to become.”

“Which is what?”

“Either unity across Elgoria,” Chuck said. His voice became low, gravelly. “Or destruction.”

“And you think the scrolls were talking about Lizzie?”

“I prayed they weren’t and did all I could to ensure she never knew a thing. I left my family; I kept Lizzie in the dark; I tried to disassociate with her as much as I could, but no matter what I did, her fate still came to pass.”

“What part do Cedric and Redcap play in all of this?”

“We Fae aren’t all that different from humans, you know. The Bakers may be the largest mafia family on the East Coast, but Redcap and Cedric are part of the Syree clan. They run the same as the mafia, except they’re ten times more brutal, if you can believe it. And some of them hold positions of high power. In the mafia scope, Redcap is just a soldier; Cedric is below that, but Cedric is royalty, a wayward prince who rules over a bit of land near the South Shadowlands. The point is, you don’t want to meet the capos or anyone else in the clan. And even more so, you don’t want to cross paths with the don, the King of the Shadows.”

“Understood.” Brody felt his insides bubble uncomfortably.

If Chuck Degan was scared of these guys, maybe now was the time to consider exhibiting at least a healthy amount of fear.

"What do *they* want with Lizzie?"

"I have some ideas, but now isn't the time to discuss them," Chuck said. "There was more in those scrolls, but Harold hid the rest. He'd figured out what they said. I don't know how, but whatever it was, it was enough for him to hide them. They might be hidden here, at the inn."

"Why would he hide them?"

"The innkeeper promised Harold he would keep the library preserved and untouched as he had for Harold's father. He was both Watson and Harold's confidant."

"Francis Ermington?"

"No," Chuck said. "Who is that? I'm talking about Ray Moorey."

"Ray?" Brody's mind raced. "Are you sure Ray didn't retire or... pass away?"

"I spoke to Harold before he passed. Ray was set to keep things afloat and help Lizzie through all of this."

"Then we have a problem," Brody said.

"What's that?"

"Ray Moorey is gone. The only person running this inn is Francis Ermington."

"Brody!" A scream sounded from above. Shay's voice. Brody lost no time running as quickly and safely as he could back up the stairwell, Chuck at his heels. Another scream sounded as Brody continued up the narrow spiral stairs. Back in the library, he heard loud booms. The doors opened slightly, revealing a small bit of light from the other side. Someone was trying to break down the doors. Thankfully, the furniture didn't give way to the force just yet. Redcap was here, and they were no closer to finding the pendant.

At the top of the stairs, Brody lost no time and shouted,

"We need to get down to the room below us. Now!" Assessing the worried faces in the library, he continued. "There's something you all should see."

Shay looked at Brody.

"Take Lizzie and Misty," she said.

"No," Brody said. "We all go together. Stay together."

"Go, Brody. Now."

"No," Brody insisted. "It's too dangerous."

"We'll block the passage to the secret room, and we'll be loaded and ready for these bastards once they break down the door."

"Shay…" Brody warned, his eyebrows lowering to match his discord.

"Leave your guns with us," Chuck said. "We're going to need all the ammo we can get."

"I'll be fine," Shay assured Brody. "We have iron bullets. What could go wrong?"

Finally, Brody nodded, giving in to Shay's demand. Still, he pulled her in for a sisterly hug.

"Give 'em hell," he said.

"Would I do it any other way?" she asked, a coy smile crossing her lips.

Meanwhile, Chuck handed his torch to Lizzie, and then Brody, Misty, and Lizzie began their descent. But as he led Lizzie and Misty back down the spiral staircase, he couldn't help but wonder if allowing Shay to stay up there had been a mistake. Could she face such an evil as Redcap, or had he doomed his friend to die?

chapter 46

"Ray Moorey was the innkeeper," Brody said as he led the way down the winding steps of the narrow corridor. Shay had secured the door behind them.

With the bars being made of iron, Lizzie hoped it would slow down Redcap, but even if it did, the Bakers would have no issues opening that door for Redcap and his men.

"What do we do now?" Misty asked, trailing carefully behind Lizzie and Brody. "If we don't have those journal passages, we won't find the relic."

Lizzie couldn't help but notice the dampness, the water-slicked walls, the darting blue lights. What kind of room were they walking into?

"What the…" Lizzie said when they reached the bottom of the stairs. "Brody, what is this?" Lizzie whispered. She breathed in deeply, watching the magnificent tree in front of her squeeze inward, then outward as she released her breath.

"It's an Elgorian Elder tree," Brody said.

Lizzie stretched out her hand toward the little blue fireflies, who then swarmed around her finger.

"Lizzie!" Brody yelled, but she didn't hear him. "Lizzie!"

"What?" she asked. Broken from her trance, the pixies flitted away in several directions.

"You need to be careful," Brody answered. "Don't touch the tree, and especially don't touch the pixies."

Lizzie dropped her hand but examined the tree's breathing and how it matched her own. *Was it real or just imagined? She couldn't tell.*

Suddenly, an image passed through her mind as soft as a gentle whisper. An image of a man holding the pendant.

"We should start with the walls," Brody said. "The relic might be contained within them, but we need to be careful of the tree's roots. As you can see, they're…"

"I know where the pendant is," Lizzie said suddenly, a slight smile spreading across her face.

"What do you mean?" Brody asked. He was right by her side now, gazing at her out of those crystalline pools.

"We don't need Ray Moorey or the journals. The relic isn't inside the walls."

"Then where is it?" Misty asked.

Lizzie turned her gaze back to the tree. "The tree is protecting it," she answered. "It's been protecting it since Watson found the last Elgorian Elder and built the inn."

"Are you sure?" Brody asked.

"Yes," Lizzie said, nodding. "The pixies told me."

"They spoke to you?"

"Well, in their own way," she answered.

Brody heaved a sigh and then scratched his head.

Once again, the pixies began to swarm around Lizzie and flooded her with images.

"The pixies say no one has been down to visit the tree since Moorey," she continued. "So they've been caring for it. Apparently, Moorey would come almost every day. But one day, he didn't return."

"And Ermington?" Brody asked.

"They're not showing me anything about him," Lizzie replied.

"If Ermington is Fae," Brody surmised, "maybe he couldn't come down here because of the iron bars."

"If the relic is inside the tree, why are we waiting around?" Misty asked suddenly.

"Magic can be a dangerous thing," Brody warned. "At least, that's what I learned from the little I studied about it. If the pendant is in there, I would bet there's magic protecting it, and if that's the case, then that tree isn't going to hand over the relic to just anyone."

"Won't it know who Lizzie is?" Misty asked. "If the pixies recognized her connection to the Elders, wouldn't the tree?"

"Not necessarily," Brody replied. "And besides, a protection spell is a protection spell no matter who you are."

Lizzie knew Brody was right, but she didn't see what other option they had. If she didn't at least try to obtain the relic, then all of this was for nothing.

"Excuse me," Misty said, "But you said Ermington couldn't come down here because of the iron. So if Ermington wanted to get down here, he would need someone to unlock the…"

"They were using us the whole time," Lizzie interjected. "Ermington knew I needed my grandfather's clues to find the key to open the door."

"This isn't good," Brody said, his mind racing. Had Nunez known all along? Was she working with Redcap, and this was a setup, or had she been blinded to the truth as well, and in an attempt to help Harold, she uncovered something horrible?

"Brody is right, though," Lizzie said. "The tree isn't just going to hand it over. Magic is protecting this tree."

"Do you know what kind of magic it is?" Misty asked.

"Me?" Lizzie asked. "I don't know anything. I get glimpses, but the Elders said nothing about this… I don't know."

A loud boom from above made Lizzie jump.

"No time like the present to find out," Brody said.

Lizzie nodded and breathed deeply as she stepped closer to the tree.

"It isn't safe," Misty pressed.

"What other choice do we have?" Lizzie asked, passing her torch to Misty.

Lizzie knew that if she hesitated too long, she might lose the courage to take action, so she pushed her hand into the tree without a second thought. Immediately, she felt an intense pulsing, and then something repelled her hand. She flew backward with force, nearly smacking against the room wall, and landed on her bottom.

"Lizzie!" Misty shrieked, running to Lizzie's side.

Brody hurried over, too, and immediately bent down to help her.

"Are you okay?" he asked, using his free hand to help steady her.

"I'm fine," Lizzie nodded. "Looks like there is a protection spell."

"No kidding," Brody said.

Lizzie started to walk back toward the tree when Brody and Misty began to protest.

"What are you doing?" Brody asked.

"I'm trying again."

"Lizzie, the tree clearly wants to keep everyone out. Even you," Brody said.

"I agree with Brody. There has to be another way."

Lizzie ignored Brody's and Misty's pleas for her not to attempt to rechallenge the tree magic. Instead, Lizzie stood before the tree and drew a deep breath, counting in for four and out for eight. She kept repeating this, letting all the thoughts in her mind clear. All the fear, the worry, the pain, the hopelessness drained from her as she focused only on her breath. And when she was sure her mind was settled, she put her hand out again, this time just outside the tree. She let it linger there, let the tree's energy field mingle with hers, sensing her, accepting her, and then slowly moved her hand closer and closer in small increments.

She inched closer to the tree. Like the vibration of a cat's purr, a humming engulfed her body. Her bones ached, longing to return to a place she didn't yet know. A single phrase repeated in her mind. Soft and steady, like snow drifting from the sky.

She whispered it first, then again.

"I am Lizzie Degan," she said. "The heir of light and shadows."

The tree responded, each limb unraveling piece by piece. The trunk widened and stretched with each rhythmic hum, until it revealed a hollow space just large enough for a person.

And then Lizzie stepped through.

chapter 47

Miles and Dean trekked quietly through the eerie silence of the inn. Room by room, they made their way until they heard murmuring that emanated from the direction of the library. Dean led the way in the direction of the voices but stopped abruptly, pushing Miles back behind a wall that separated the stairwell from the drawing room that led to the library.

Miles carefully peered around the wall and observed burly soldiers clawing at the library doors. Redcap stood by, barking orders, his long, red cape trailing behind him. Cedric stood by his side, brooding like a truculent, privileged prick who had just learned he was getting cut from his daddy's will. All of them were completely oblivious to Miles and Dean's presence.

"I want that door *ripped* apart," Cedric growled.

"Patience, Cedric," Redcap counseled.

"She's *mine*," Cedric said. "And every minute we waste, those Light Elgorian *scum* gain more power!" His lip curled upward as he rebuked Redcap. "Where is your beast? If your brusque brutes can't do the job, then let that gnarled beast do it for Shadow's sake."

His tetchy tone unnerved Redcap.

"You would do well to watch your tongue with me, *Prince*," Redcap warned. They faced each other now, one malicious being shouting at the other.

"My father…" Cedric began.

"Your *father* answers to Barbadoa, the King of Shadows," Redcap chided, "just like all the other Shadow Kings of Elgoria. Do not assume that because you were promised the woman, you are somehow better than the rest."

"How dare you compare me to those repulsive swine? You of all Fae know that I am here because the King *favors* my father and our lineage."

"Hmm," Redcap sounded, unaffected by Cedric's words. "Is that so? Then perhaps I should summon the Druiz again, let you air your petulant whines to him."

Cedric didn't respond; he simply let out a grunt and stormed away through the only other archway that led away from the library.

Druiz, Miles thought. *Was he the shadow figure Dean had seen in the old farmhouse?* Dean's nod affirmed Miles' thought, and Miles pointed toward the stairwell. If Cedric had exited the other way, there was a chance he might come back around and expose Miles and Dean. While Dean stood alert, his gun readied, Miles continued to observe what Redcap and his men were doing to the library doors. Miles could tell something was blocking the doors to the library, which meant that Lizzie was assuredly inside. He prayed she was safe and that someone, even if it was Brody, was with her.

Redcap's brawny soldiers hurled themselves into the door once more. This time, whatever was behind it budged, leaving a tiny opening. Immediately, one of the men burst through the door. Miles heard a gunshot from inside the library and watched as the Fae soldier, who had just entered, was thrown backward out of the library, so far that he landed just feet from Miles. Miles moved further out of view, but even then, he could still see the top half of the Fae soldier who writhed in pain and clawed at his uniform. A bullet had pierced his now bare chest, and Miles watched as the Fae's veins began to turn black and spread throughout his body.

"Iron!" one of the men yelled.

At that moment, Miles realized that the Fae were affected by iron, and by the looks of it, that effect wasn't mild. But who could have known iron would take down a Fae? Surely Lizzie didn't. And Brody didn't seem like the type of guy who studied up on Fae literature… if there was any.

Another shot from inside the library made Miles peer around the wall again. He watched as several Fae soldiers stormed the library, and shots continued to be fired. If only Miles could get a glimpse inside and see who was fighting the Fae, he and Dean could devise a plan. The soldiers flew backward, and, similar to the first Fae who was shot, they were clawing at their skin.

"They're not very bright, are they?" Dean whispered over Miles' shoulder as they watched yet another soldier fly backward. But Miles knew better than to assume the soldiers were blindly going into battle.

"They're sacrificing themselves," Miles whispered back. "Once the bullets are gone, Redcap will storm the library, and he's betting that whoever is shooting those bullets will run out of ammo by then. Whoever is firing those shots doesn't have much time left." From the way the shots sounded, Miles could tell there were two shooters. He hoped Lizzie wasn't one of them.

Miles didn't see how he and Dean could get into the library unnoticed. There was only one entrance. Dean quickly pulled Miles downward, until they were completely out of view as more of Redcap's soldiers bustled inside and lined themselves up, ready for sacrifice.

"What do we do?" Miles asked his brother.

The soldier who had landed by their feet sputtered as he took his last breath, the streaks of black trailing throughout his body all the way up to his face. Finally, he lay still.

Dean was supposed to command his men to turn on Redcap and his men, but Miles didn't see how that was possible. First of all, Redcap had more soldiers than Miles previously thought. Miles had no idea where these soldiers had been when Redcap had first arrived at the Farmhouse. Secondly, Miles hadn't seen one of his own men yet, which wasn't a good sign. Were any of them even still alive? Or had Redcap sensed betrayal and slaughtered them all? Had the Director of the FBI gone back on her word and murdered them? Even if they were alive, what would be the plan? Why had Redcap even needed The Family's men, if he had so many of his own? The Family wasn't equipped to attack these soldiers. They didn't have guns loaded with iron.

"Without our men, we can't do anything," Dean replied.

"What do you mean?"

"Don't you know anything about the art of war, Miles?" Dean asked. "Right now, we're outnumbered. It would do us no good to plan any kind of attack. Now, whoever is shooting those guns in the library is our ally. Redcap is willing to sacrifice his soldiers to get inside that library. With enough of them gone, all we are fighting is Redcap and Cedric. With our allies on the inside, we might be able to surround him and Cedric. But make no mistake. We are not Redcap's equal matches. We need more allies."

"But what about *our* men?" Miles asked. "Why haven't we seen anyone yet? And what's our plan? Our weapons are useless against them."

"We have to assume they're dead, or worse, Redcap is using them for something horrible."

"That's reassuring," Miles said.

"At this point," he whispered, "We need to do everything not to get caught."

"Which is unfortunate," a voice sounded, startling both Dean and Miles. They looked up to see Cedric standing there, a snide grin painted on his face. "Because you *have* been caught."

chapter 48

A bright white light engulfed Lizzie once her body had completely submerged into the tree. She shielded her eyes with her hand, attempting to make out her surroundings. *Was she in Elgoria?* she wondered. When the light dimmed slightly, she observed that she was inside the vaulted tree. A soft melody played in the room, repeating four chords: C, D, E-flat, and F. The sound was breathy and ethereal, like a soft, comforting orchestra, and Lizzie realized the sound was the tree's breath, a harmonious congruence of beauty within the cavernous trunk. A soft light streamed through the cracks of green foliage below Lizzie's feet. She stepped on soft yet sturdy green branches. Looking upward, she saw that the striated wood continued up the trunk and into the roots. Tiny pixies flitted about, making the inside of the top of the tree look like a night sky. Suddenly, the pixies began to move. They slowly gathered into a circular swarm and lowered themselves like bees, moving as gently as a feather falling from the sky.

They swarmed a few feet from Lizzie's face, and she worried they might hurt her. But their shape gradually changed into an arm that extended into a wrist and eventually into a closed fist. And then, the palm opened, and fingers uncurled one by one to reveal the pendant. Lizzie could not help but marvel at the pendant's beauty… a black, inverted, pear-shaped object with edges that stretched out like tiny, curled vines. The intricately designed vines wove around each other to reveal the relic in the center, where a silver and iridescent mixed magic swirled around like a caged beast, just waiting to be released. It was more beautiful than Lizzie could have ever imagined.

"Take it," a voice echoed.

At first, she thought it was the pixies, but soon she realized it was the tree speaking. The shifting foliage under her feet made Lizzie steady herself. But she didn't take the pendant, didn't even try. She wasn't the one. Surely, she couldn't touch it.

"I can't touch it," Lizzie said.

"It cannot hurt you unless it breaks," the voice bounded, reading her thoughts. The vibrations of the tree's voice made Lizzie struggle to steady her balance atop the tree's foliage.

"You must fulfill the prophecy, child," the voice said.

"What am I supposed to do?" she asked, shaking her head.

"Go… willingly."

"Go… where?" When the tree did not respond, Lizzie said, "You mean with them?"

No, she thought. *How could the tree suggest she willingly go with Redcap and Cedric?*

"You must," the tree echoed, seeming to read her thoughts again. "The fate of our world depends on you."

"Me?" Lizzie said. "But what can I do to help a place I've never even been to?" Lizzie asked.

She could accept that she was part of the prophecy, but that someone's fate depended on her made the bile rise in her throat.

"You will know what to do when the time is right," the

tree's voice boomed. "Go willingly, and the answers will be shown to you."

Lizzie could not believe what she was hearing.

"You want me to go to Elgoria. How? Are you the gateway?" Lizzie said.

"You are the gateway," the tree answered. "Without you, there is no gateway for me to guide you through."

"I don't understand," Lizzie replied.

"We are one. The last Elder tree of Elgoria gave your father its last breath. You carry on the wisdom now. It is why you can hear the Elders."

Lizzie felt tears fill her eyes. She didn't know what she expected to hear, but not this. She didn't understand how it was even possible, but in her heart, she knew it was true. Some truths were like that—an inner knowing.

"Protect the pendant at all costs. You must ensure that the Shadow Breaker comes into possession of the pendant. If it finds its way to the King of Shadows, all hope for Elgoria is lost."

"And who is the Shadow Breaker?"

"The inhabited one."

"The inhabited one?" Lizzie asked. She didn't know what the tree meant. Riddles were not helpful right now. What she needed was the cold, hard truth. Who, as in a name, so she could deliver the damn thing to him. But the tree wasn't going to give it to her. The pixies placed the pendant into Lizzie's hand and then scattered away, back toward the roots of the tree.

"Go, child," the tree continued, "before it's too late."

Lizzie wanted to protest and ask more questions, but a forceful pull from the pixies dragged her through the tree's foliage. She reached out her hands in an attempt to stay, but the force pulled her backward. She felt an energy pulsate around her, and the tree showed her images then of a beautiful world with crystalline blue rivers and the greenest trees, of children playing and Fae laughing. Then the images slowly changed, and Lizzie saw death, destruction, and a horrible shadow that made her insides twist. The images came so quickly, she could not settle on just one, but as they passed, the tree gave her one last message.

"May the heir of the Light and Shadow Fae fulfill her destiny and save us all."

<h1 style="text-align: right">chapter 49</h1>

An eerie silence blanketed the room beneath the library as Brody frantically tried to communicate with Lizzie. Incredibly, she had gone inside the tree. *But would she ever come out,* he wondered? Was she safe inside there or struggling? Was the tree a gateway, or had it swallowed her whole? He attempted to follow her, but the tree's defenses threw him backward, just as they had repelled Lizzie the first time she tried to enter it.

"Lizzie?" Brody called as he circled the tree now. He heard nothing. "Lizzie, can you hear me?"

Still, he heard nothing.

Shots continued to explode from the room upstairs, and Brody knew Chuck and Shay were firing cold, iron bullets at the enemy. He hoped Shay and Chuck had won the battle. Part of him wanted to go up there and help Chuck and Shay, but he knew his place was down here, protecting Lizzie.

"Brody, look!" Misty cried. As Brody looked toward the tree, he saw Lizzie emerge, the pendant dangling from one fist.

"Lizzie," he said, running to her side. She looked weakened; some force had winded her, and she collapsed into his arms. He gently lowered her to the ground, allowing her to gradually regain her strength.

"Brody," she said, slowly coming to.

"I'm here," he said. "What happened?"

"I have to go with them," she said.

"Who?"

"Redcap and Cedric."

"No," he said, shaking his head.

"The tree said…"

He didn't care what the tree told her; she was not going with Redcap and that vile shit, Cedric.

"You told me you'd help," she said, her words barely a whisper.

"And I meant it. I'll follow you. I'll do whatever you want. But I can't let you go with them, Lizzie. They'll do horrible things to you."

"I know you're worried," she said, cupping one hand on his face. "But I need you to trust me. I need to go with them," she repeated. "But first, I need you to buy me some time."

"How?" he asked as he helped her to her feet.

"When the time is right, take the pendant and run. I'll leave the gateway open for you."

"What do you mean?" he asked.

"We can't let Redcap and Cedric get this pendant," she said, unfurling the fingers of her hand to reveal it. "It's more important than we thought. And we need to keep it away from them." Brody immediately saw the ancient magic violently swirling around inside the relic. "You'll have to fight off whoever they send after you. It'll be hell."

"I can handle it," he said, "but…"

"Meanwhile, I'm going through the gateway with them. And after we're through, only when it's safe, you come back, enter through the gateway, and find me."

"What you're talking about is insane," Misty chimed in.

"So many things could go wrong, Lizzie. Are you sure this is what you want to do?"

Lizzie had regained her strength now.

"You're right," Lizzie said, "but this is the way it has to be. We have no other options. I have to go to Elgoria. I have to save them."

"Save who?" Misty asked.

"Everyone."

"What if we went through the gateway now?" Misty asked. "The three of us? You could evade Cedric and Redcap, and you and Brody could safely get the pendant to the Shadow Breaker."

"The tree told me…"

"Did you ever consider the tree was wrong?" Misty chided.

"It's not. I'm sorry, Misty. I know this outcome isn't what any of you wanted. But I trust the Elder tree." Lizzie turned to face Brody. "Promise me you'll do this, Brody." Then, with more force, she repeated, "Promise me. You're the only one I trust to keep the pendant safe and return it to me in one piece." Lizzie looked toward Misty. "No offense."

"Please," Misty said, throwing her hands up. "None taken. I wouldn't last a minute with that thing."

"Okay, fine," Brody replied. "I promise."

Brody and Lizzie gazed into each other's eyes until the familiar pull overwhelmed him, and as he drew nearer, she didn't pull away. He gently pulled her face close to his and placed his lips on hers.

"Don't mind me," Misty said, turning away.

What began as a soft kiss quickly became more eager and intoxicating. Their warm tongues turned and pulsated over each other's with an unrelenting urgency. Each electric touch of their tongues made Brody desire Lizzie more, and he pulled her close to him so there was no more space between them. He let her feel all of him as he ran his large hands down her back, lifting her sweater just enough that his hands came to rest on her bare skin at the small of her back. Even amid the danger, Brody felt he and Lizzie were the only ones in the room. When they were together, the rest of the world faded away. He ached for her too badly now but knew he would have to stop before he went too far. Still, Brody did not want to let Lizzie go. Not yet. Because this kiss was more than an apology accepted; it was a *goodbye*, at least for now.

When Lizzie finally pulled away, she whispered, "I need to fulfill the prophecy, but I need you by my side in order to do it."

"I'll be by your side," Brody said, nodding. He kept his hands cupped around her face and didn't dare take his eyes away from hers.

"Thank you," she mouthed.

"And so will I," Misty said, turning to face them once more.

"No," Lizzie shook her head. "I'll do whatever I can to get you out of this safely."

"You're not getting rid of me that easily," Misty said. "Besides, what do I have to go back to?"

"Your family," Lizzie said.

"You *are* my family," Misty said. "You're the one person who believes in me more than even my blood. I'm not afraid, Lizzie, and wherever you go, I'll go. So, tell me what to do, and I'll do it."

"Shh," Brody said, straining his ear. He couldn't hear any more shots and realized he hadn't heard them for a while. *When had they stopped, exactly,* he wondered? Had Redcap found a way into the secret room? Suddenly, he heard the slow pad of footsteps down the narrow path, and Brody hoped Chuck had staved off the enemy. But when he heard a slow clapping and saw torches once more illuminate the hidden room, it wasn't Chuck and Shay who stood before him but Redcap and a surly-looking Cedric.

"Well, well, well…" Redcap said, his menacing smile turning upward. "I wasn't expecting it to be this easy, and yet, I have to thank you both for falling right into the plan."

Lizzie stood but stayed close to Brody, who shifted his body in front of hers, shielding her. Misty crouched behind them. *Were Shay and Chuck still alive?* he wondered. That Redcap and Cedric were down here was not a good sign. He didn't have to ask. Redcap directed his attention toward Brody.

"Hand over Lizzie and the pendant," Redcap ordered.

"Lizzie makes her own decisions," Brody said.

"Well, perhaps she'll be more influenced to make the *right* decision when she realizes lives are at stake."

Suddenly, a soldier emerged with a shackled Shay.

"Shay? Shay!" Brody called, trying to get his friend's attention. But there was no response; her eyes were glazed over as she looked lifelessly in front of her. He didn't dare run to her.

"What have you done to her?" Brody growled.

"What *should* I have done to her is the real question?" Redcap said. "If I had it my way, I would have ripped her limb from limb… but… alas, Cedric has other plans for her."

"Care to enlighten me?" Brody asked, not taking his eyes away from Redcap's menacing ones.

"Let's just say, food has been scarce, and Cedric's dragons need to eat."

Brody wanted to lunge at Redcap, strangle him with his red cape, but Lizzie squeezed his hand, the pendant clasped between his and hers, and he drew in a deep breath, forcing himself to stand down.

"What about my father?" Lizzie asked.

"He'll be coming with us. Did you know that he's famous

in Elgoria? The King plans to finish what he started…" His eyes darkened as he continued, "…when he murdered your father's family. Abominations, all of them. But I suppose he sees how your father's escape fulfilled a part of the prophecy. Still, there is little use for your father now."

Brody felt Lizzie tense next to him, and now he squeezed her hand in reassurance. He heard a growl from where Redcap stood. Cedric had observed their clasped hands, and it angered him. Good, Brody thought. *Because that fucker needed to know he was nothing to Lizzie, and he never would be.*

"I'll go with you," Lizzie suddenly announced to Redcap and Cedric.

Brody restrained himself from objecting, assuring Lizzie that he trusted her on this.

Just then, someone or some… thing slinked down the steps, a slow walk that grew heavier as it descended, and then… *Oh no*, Brody thought. The beast. *But how did it get down the narrow pathway?*

The beast stepped out of the dark archway and grew even bigger than it had been. It stood beside Redcap and Cedric, baring its sharp teeth. Brody realized he, Lizzie, and Misty were trapped, and not only were Cedric and Redcap about to take Lizzie, but they could easily seize the pendant. As Brody frantically searched his mind for another plan, he felt a sinking feeling overwhelm him. Lizzie's plan would fail; there was no escape from this room. They were doomed by a hopeless, hapless situation for which they had no way out.

chapter 50

"Good girl," Redcap said, motioning with his hands. Redcap moved closer, the beast creeping ever so slowly toward them as well. "Now, give me the pendant, and we'll be on our way."

Lizzie knew what she had to do, but she hadn't had time to think the plan through. She would pass the pendant to Brody at the last minute and pray he made it out of the room. That wasn't her best option, but it was the only one. The beast presented a problem. Brody could outrun the others, but she would need a big distraction to help him get past the beast.

"I'll give you the pendant," she said, "on one condition."

Redcap's pursed, crooked lips betrayed his boredom.

"What is it you want?"

"I want you to let my friends go—all of them. Brody included. And my father. And when we leave here, we will never return to Earth. There has to be a way to close the portal."

"So sacrificial of you," Redcap said with a smirk. "But the gateway cannot be closed. Not without some fulfillment of the prophecy."

"What fulfillment?"

"Only the one can close the gateway."

"Who is the one?"

"How should I know?" Redcap responded. "I had nothing to do with opening it, and surely, I'll have nothing to do with closing it."

No, that's not good enough, she thought. If this Elder tree was the last gateway, she needed to figure out how to close it.

"You know, I could simply *take* the pendant from you," Redcap said.

"I'll destroy it before you do," she said.

"And kill us all?" Redcap asked.

"Yes," she warned.

Lizzie held the pendant up, letting the pulsing energy inside of her wash over it, encasing it in a glistening yellow light. It glowed brightly now. Just a little more, and it would crack open.

"Do not destroy that," Cedric warned. He cast a dark gaze in Redcap's direction, signaling that he wasn't willing to gamble their lives.

Redcap seemed to back down at her demonstration, and considering her threat, he acquiesced. "It seems you leave me no choice. I'll grant you what you wish, and let your friends go."

Lizzie took Brody's hand and squeezed. He kept his hand entwined with hers, letting her know that whatever she was about to do, he would follow. That was good because what she was about to do was utterly insane. Lizzie swallowed hard and then let go of Brody's hand. She took a step forward toward Redcap.

"Let Brody go to the surface first," she said.

"Very well," Redcap said. He turned to the beast. "Atiryo, stand down."

The beast whimpered, but not out of fear. He seemed

disappointed that neither Brody nor Lizzie would be his next meal. Brody followed Lizzie's lead, as promised, and headed toward the opening of the hidden room. Meanwhile, Lizzie took another step toward Redcap, and then she closed her eyes. She asked the Elders for their help. Brody had neared the bottom of the stairs, treading slowly and carefully, waiting for her next move. Suddenly, the pixies began to swarm, gathering together like a hive of bees defending a nest. They encircled Redcap and Cedric, forcing them to swat and yell.

"Get away from me, you dastardly vermin," Redcap hissed. "Atiryo!" The beast began chomping at the swarm, and while they were distracted, Lizzie ran toward Brody. He reached his hand toward hers, and she nearly reached him when Cedric grabbed her sweater, pulling her back. Lizzie had just enough time to throw the pendant to Brody, who caught it and lost no time running up the stairs.

"He's got the pendant!" Cedric cried.

"Atiryo, the pendant!" Redcap yelled.

The beast relinquished his monstrous form into a horrid, decaying naked man and ran up the stairs after Brody.

"You fool," Redcap said, smoothing out his cape. "Now you've sentenced everyone you love to death before the commander... starting with your friend. Seize her!"

Redcap motioned to two soldiers who made their way swiftly toward Misty. Lizzie tried to escape Cedric's clutches and run to her friend, but Cedric yanked her back.

"It's okay, Lizzie," Misty said as two soldiers forcefully gripped her shoulders. "Remember...you are my family." Lizzie felt tears brim in her eyes as she swallowed a lump of guilt. Misty had only come to the inn because of Lizzie. And even though a part of Lizzie knew this situation was better than the alternative, she still didn't like to see anyone hurt her friend. The soldiers forced a liquid down Misty's throat, and soon Misty was dull-eyed and non-responsive, just like

Shay.

Misty was willing to help. She wanted to go with Lizzie. That's what Lizzie kept repeating to herself.

"If you weren't to be betrothed to Cedric," Redcap said to Lizzie, "I would slit your throat right now."

Lizzie heard a low, sinister laugh escape Cedric's lips.

Betrothed to Cedric? Lizzie closed her eyes and prayed. Prayed that Brody could outrun the beast. She prayed that her father was still alive and that all of this wasn't in vain, and she prayed that somehow, they would all make it out of this situation alive.

chapter 51

"**A**tiryo, the pendant!"

Those were the last words Brody heard Redcap utter. Brody wasted no time running up the small, winding stairwell. At the top, he turned sideways, slipped past Redcap's men, and ran through the library doors and out of the inn. On his way out of the library, he had just enough time to grab one of the Fae-killing guns and hoped there were bullets left. He'd barely noticed Chuck, chained and wearing that same blank stare Shay had. But he couldn't worry about that now. His only focus was getting the pendant as far away from the inn as possible.

The problem was the plan hadn't been thought through. Suppose he could get the pendant far away; wouldn't Redcap and Cedric wait to enter the gateway until the pendant was returned? Or did Redcap have such faith in his beast that he would leave without it? The latter wouldn't end well for Brody. And even if all worked as planned, how would Brody find Lizzie once he entered the portal? He wished they'd had more time, but here he was… yet again, acting impulsively, which seemed to be one of his habits. Then again, what else could he have done?

Brody knew the beast needed time to transform, and by the time it did, he hoped to be deep into the woods. But soon after Brody reached the entrance to the woods, he heard the panting on his trail. The beast gained on Brody now, and Brody was thankful he still had one of Chuck's guns. If this beast was part Fae, it would work, wouldn't it? But what if it wasn't Fae? Brody tried to open the long barrel as he ran, checking how many bullets were left.

Two.

That meant Brody had to make these shots count. *The beast had to be ruled by some magic*, Brody thought as he ran, holding the now-cocked gun and the pendant together. He turned and took a quick look over his shoulder. The beast was catching up to him quickly. Brody knew he had to get some advantage over the beast before he could shoot at it again. But the beast continued to gain on him, and even though adrenaline kept him going, he knew eventually, he would need to rest, if only for a few seconds.

Brody saw a trailer up ahead and wondered if he could rest there. Even if he was trapped inside with the beast clawing at him from the outside, he could ready his gun. He reached the trailer. To his surprise, the door was open. He nearly threw himself inside, dragged his weary body to the very back, and collapsed, breathing heavily. A family sat eating an early dinner, and Brody realized that in trying to save himself and the pendant, he had put them in danger. He had to make this shot count, or he'd live with the guilt if anything happened to them.

"Hide, hide," he told them, pushing them out of their seats.

They hid in the bathroom as the beast reached the trailer and immediately began clawing at it like a rabid animal. Brody readied his gun, kept it locked and loaded, and pointed it at the beast. If he could slow this mother fucker down, he'd have an advantage. He slowed his breathing, trying to gauge the beast's every move. Whatever hold Redcap had on this beast was palpable. The thing wouldn't stop until Brody was dead; he was sure of it. The beast clawed its way through the trailer, and the moment Brody saw the eye of the beast gazing at him, he took his shot.

In a situation like this, any hesitation would result in a missed opportunity.

The beast yelped, this time out of fear, and Brody mouthed, "I'm sorry" to the terrified family before he ran out of the trailer and back toward the inn. Brody had shot the beast, and it was down. It was only an eye wound, but if the beast was Fae, hopefully the iron would spread throughout its body.

Brody had already exhausted one bullet, which meant he only had one left. He ran quickly with a newfound strength after his slight recuperation in the trailer. He had the pendant, and now he needed to find Nunez. She could help. But was she still alive? He took his earpiece from his pocket and turned it on.

"Kado-1," he said.

"You're alive?" He heard a voice breathing heavily respond.

"Nunez, you okay?"

"I've been better, Brody."

Her voice was low, barely above a whisper.

"You're hurt?" he asked.

"We didn't stand a chance… but I'll live. Where are you?"

"We found it," he said. "We found the relic."

"And you have it?"

"Yes, but I'm… I'm running from Redcap's beast."

"And Lizzie?" Nunez asked.

"Redcap has her."

"Brody…run! *Keep* running!"

Those were the last words Nunez said before her earpiece clicked off.

Brody neared the inn when suddenly he saw a shadow to his left. It was the beast.

Still alive. And he was close.

He threw down his earpiece, keeping his eyes focused on his surroundings. He held up the gun, readied it, and slowly spun around to get a 360-degree view of his surroundings. The beast could be anywhere, watching him right now, hunting him.

The pendant burned in Brody's free hand as he gripped it tightly. He dared not even look to see, for any move he made would mean the beast could easily attack him. The air stilled around him, and his breathing slowed to almost nothing.

Cedric had Lizzie—he knew that. The beast had to die if Brody had any chance of getting back to her, of saving her. And what about Shay? Or Chuck? Where were they now? He hoped they were safe, and if he made it out of this alive, he would save them, too.

chapter 52

Miles didn't utter a word as he stood quietly. A thick silver, uncomfortable cuff had been fitted around his neck, and his hands were bound in chains. He and his brother were kept in one of the inn's drawing rooms, like cattle waiting for slaughter. He couldn't see a way out of this—didn't see a point in struggling. Redcap's hulking men wore strange metal headdresses that fell over their noses. They were dressed for battle, but Miles didn't understand the scope of their plan. He tried to string bits and pieces of their conversation together, but they were not forthcoming.

They were dogs, waiting for a command.

"How many more?" he heard one of the men say.

"Three," another answered.

"Six all together?"

"Plus, the girl."

The girl. Lizzie. That meant...

"What about the other one?" the first guard asked.

"Atiryo will find him. He always does."

The other one? Miles wondered.

He looked over at Dean, who gazed down at the floor,

and Miles felt guilt wash over him. His brother might've been in Mexico by now if it hadn't been for him. Why was it that whenever Miles tried to do the right thing, it backfired? Maybe life was just like that for some people, a constant string of disappointments. *If*, big if, they could make it out of this alive, Dean would blame Miles for coming back to save Lizzie. And now here they were, hostages.

The other one they spoke of had to be Brody, Miles reasoned. *But why would the beast be chasing him?*

"What will you do with us?" Miles asked. Dean, yet again, imparted one of those looks, the one he always did when he wanted Miles to stay quiet.

"Yeh're comin' wit us to Elgoria," one of the men said. "Boss doesn't like bein' disobeyed."

"If you intend on killing us, why not do it here?" Miles continued.

One of the men smirked at the other, and they shared a good laugh.

"That's not how *he* does things," he said.

"We know how Redcap does things," Dean responded. "We watched him murder Ludwig, watched the beast devour him."

"Yeh ain't in these chains cause of Redcap," the one guard said. "He would have slit yeh throat as soon as he saw yeh."

"So, why are we in chains then?" Dean asked.

"Yeh're Cedric's captures."

"Cedric," Miles responded. "I wasn't aware he even had any say working as Redcap's bitch boy."

"Yeh watch your tongue, boy," the guard said, getting so close to Miles' face that Miles could feel his hot, disgusting breath.

The thick metal cuff dug into Miles' skin now, and although he was in pain, he didn't flinch.

"So, what are Cedric's plans for us then?" Dean asked.

"Yeh?" The man shook his head. "Yeh'll be food for the dragons. But yeh…" One side of the guard's mouth crinkled upward. "Cedric has special plans for yeh."

"What… I'm not good enough to be dragon food?" Miles mocked.

"Cedric doesn't like it when people touch his things," the other guard answered. "He has a special punishment for them."

"You're talking about Lizzie?" Miles said. "Cedric *actually* believes Lizzie is his."

Miles couldn't help but scoff. He didn't give a shit that he was chained. They probably wouldn't get out of this situation alive anyway, so if he was going down, he was going to give them hell.

"I helped Cedric," Miles said. "I got Brody off his trail."

"Some fine job yeh did," the guard said. "Cedric was never goin' to let yeh live, knowin' yeh… and Lizzie, yeh know. Lizzie is his, and yeh…"

"Bring them in with the others," Miles heard a voice say, and the guard tugged on the chain, making the metal dig deeper into Miles' wrists and neck. He winced from the pain but moved. He needed a better glimpse of the situation, who else was tied up, and if there was any way to get out of these chains. He wasn't hopeful.

The guard brought Dean and Miles into the library, where Miles immediately recognized Lizzie's friend, Misty, and Lizzie's notorious father, Chuck. Next to him was a tall, beautiful woman. Their faces looked blank, as though they were in some kind of trance. A fourth person, a woman, was also chained—she'd been bruised badly and rested her back against the library shelves, drawing in deep breaths.

"Director," Miles heard Dean say.

The Director of the FBI, caught? She couldn't be working with Redcap and Cedric then, and if she was here, that didn't look good for the rest of The Family.

"Here," a sputtering voice said. Miles didn't know the old man, but it was obvious he was working with Redcap.

"Drink this," he said to the Director. When she shook her head and tried to resist, he forced a liquid between her lips. In seconds, Miles watched the Director's eyes glaze over, and she joined the others in the same silent stupor.

"Ermington," one of the soldiers barked, pointing to the old innkeeper. "Two more fer yeh."

Two soldiers dragged Miles and Dean forward in chains.

"Get the hell off me!" Miles shouted.

"Quiet, Miglio!" Dean ordered.

Miles fought against the soldiers, but it was useless. The old man gripped his mouth and poured the bitter liquid down his throat.

Right after he swallowed it, he knew the only person who could redeem him was his brother. "Tell her I didn't mean to lie," he rasped.

"Shut up, Miglio."

"Don't let Cedric win. *Please.*"

And then Miles slowly began to lose his functioning. He could walk, but he couldn't talk, could barely move. These Fae used some kind of magic to control their victims.

If he ever came back from this, he would make every one of those fuckers pay.

chapter 53

Crrrrk. A branch snapped, and Brody had just enough time to jump aside before the beast lunged. He threw his body to the right, landing into a pile of freshly fallen leaves, briefly staving off what could have been a fatal mauling. He pointed his gun toward the beast and fired the shot.

Shit, Brody thought as the beast swiped the gun out of Brody's hands and then snarled and snapped. Brody held him off with all his might, but his strength was waning.

Turned out the bullets didn't work for this beast.

That's unfortunate, Brody thought as he held the beast's open-fanged mouth inches away from him. He gave the beast a good push and might've escaped if his foot hadn't twisted on the gnarled root of a tree sticking out of the ground.

Brody felt a bite sink deep into his torso, and as Brody cried out in pain, the beast grabbed the pendant away from Brody with its mouth. Excruciating pain seared through Brody's side, but he gathered all the strength he could muster to stand. He wasn't letting that beast get away alive. Not if he could help it. The beast knocked him down again like a picky toddler chucking peas. Brody felt powerless against the massive beast, who grumbled and growled as he once more tore through Brody's flesh.

Pfft.

Brody heard a shot, soft, low.

Pfft. Pfft. Pfft.

Then he heard multiple shots, and the gnarling beast paused, removed his foam-filled mouth from Brody, and dropped the pendant. Brody struggled to snatch the pendant up as quickly as he could. Then he saw the beast stumble, and its good eye slowly glazed over. As the beast fell onto the ground with a thud and began to change, its body weight and hair diminished quickly. Soon, the beast was only a man, crumpled in a heap next to Brody. Although the beast had been minorly bruised, the man he had become was taking his last breaths.

A chortle escaped the man, who had seen better days. His teeth were missing, and only strings of hair remained on his head.

"I am… relieved of…" he spluttered. "This burden… is yours."

Brody couldn't speak and wouldn't know what to say even if he could. The man took his last breath, leaving Brody to bleed out next to him. Brody gathered all the strength he could to put pressure on his gaping wound, but he was losing blood fast, and he closed his eyes, knowing these breaths might be his last.

"Get up," a hoarse voice sounded. Brody felt a push and slowly opened his eyes to see Hemmy. The guy was a bloody fucking mess, even more than Brody. Hemmy's legs were immobile.

"How did you take him down?" Brody asked.

"I poisoned the fucker," he said. "The only thing that worked, by the way. One dose would have killed him in six hours. Figured we were desperate, and I shot him up with four. Brought some of our finest with the tranqs."

"You saved my life, man," Brody said. He didn't know how he felt about that yet, considering, but Brody would give credit where it was due.

"Yeah, figured you wouldn't hate me so much if you owed me one."

"I still hate you," Brody said, wincing in pain.

But in the back of Brody's mind, he couldn't help but think how funny it was that now that he was on the brink of death, none of the shit he cared about mattered so much. Brody took in a breath with difficulty. He assessed his wounds; they didn't look good.

"You call for help?" Brody asked.

"They… on their way," Hemmy said, his voice especially hoarse. "Don't know if I'll make it, but…"

"You're gonna make it," Brody said, clapping his old friend's shoulder. "You're too much of a dick not to."

Hemmy let out a deep, gruff laugh followed by a cough.

"I deserve that, but help is coming for both of us."

The burning in Brody's hand began to spread, and when he unfurled his trembling fingers, he realized that the beast had cracked the pendant. The magic emanating from inside the pendant was leaking onto Brody's skin, and it burned like hell, creating violent little silver streaks in his hands that were quickly traveling up his veins like the spreading roots of a tree. The magic seeped into his wounds, but this was no fairy tale. He didn't magically heal or gain power from the magic. Instead, his body burned like he'd poured bleach on his gashed arms. Because this magic wasn't meant for him. *It was meant for the one.* And he *wasn't* it.

Still, he had to keep it contained, so he clamped his fingers around the leak.

"What the hell is that shit, man?" Hemmy asked, noticing the silver trailing through Brody's veins.

"I have to get back to the inn," Brody replied, ignoring Hemmy's question.

"You'll never make it," Hemmy said with labored breath.

"I have to…"

Brody tried to sit up and groaned. He was bleeding out too much. Hemmy was right; he would never make it. Still, he had to try.

"You always were a stubborn shit," Hemmy said.

"Yeah…" Brody said.

Seconds passed as Brody considered his next words to Hemmy.

"Do me a favor, would ya?"

Brody pulled himself up again. He wasn't backing down; he had a mission to fulfill.

"No, don't give me that kind of shit, Brody."

"Would you tell my dad…" Brody felt the tears well in his eyes, and he couldn't tell if it was from the topic, the wounds, or the magic destroying his body. "Tell him I love him, and even though I was his disappointment, I hope I made him proud."

"You tell him yourself, Brody."

Brody gave Hemmy a tight-lipped smile.

"Stop," Hemmy continued. "Don't do something stupid, Brody."

"I have to save her," Brody said.

"You'll never make it."

"I have to try."

Hemmy seemed to understand Brody wasn't going to back down. Finally, he nodded.

"Yeah," he nodded again. "Yeah. Okay. You give them hell, Brody."

"I will. You better survive, Hemmy, and deliver my message," Brody said. "You owe it to me. You do that, consider us even."

With that, Brody used all his strength to stand, and then he began a slow walk through the woods toward the inn. There was no going back now because Brody knew that if he had to, he would give his last breath to save her.

chapter 54

Cedric ran his long fingers over Lizzie's jaw and gently tilted her chin upward, never taking his penetrating hazel eyes off hers. His intense gaze burned through her like dragon's breath, and his scent of bergamot, ginger, and sage kept her transfixed.

She wanted to pull away but couldn't.

Soldiers cuffed Lizzie's neck in silver and bound her hands with chains, and all the while Lizzie stayed frozen in that moment with Cedric, some intangible force tethering her to him.

"One day, you'll thank me for this," Cedric said.

"For what? Chaining me up or making me your captive?" Lizzie responded, recovering from her temporary stupor.

"Captive?" he scoffed as if Lizzie had greatly offended him. "Don't you know that you shall be my princess?"

The way his eyes flickered from hazel to amber and then back again made her heart catch in her throat. That look. She'd seen it before somewhere. As if… she was experiencing déjà vu. His brows furrowed, and she studied his polished ruggedness. He wasn't wearing a crown or royal attire, but now that he'd mentioned it, he *did* look like a prince.

"What if I don't want to be your princess?"

"You and I are bound by fate," Cedric replied. "The sooner you accept it, the easier life will be for you."

"I'll never accept it," she retorted. "I'll never be your princess. I'll never be *anything* to you or for you."

"Let suffering be your companion, then," he said, dropping her chin coldly. "As if I care."

She could only assume that something terrible had happened if Brody wasn't back, but she couldn't deal with that grief now. There would be plenty of time for grieving when it was all over. Plus, she held on to the fact that even though Brody hadn't returned, neither had the beast.

Then he began to circle the tree, groaning and grunting before chanting words in Fae that Lizzie couldn't understand.

"Apuri… gorta… apuri gorta… apuri gorta."

But the tree wouldn't budge.

"It's not working," he growled. And then he attempted to enter the tree. It threw him backward, and Lizzie stifled a laugh watching her adversary fall on his ass.

Lizzie trusted the Elder tree. Her intuition signaled to her a feeling that the tree was safe, but when she saw what it was suggesting—going with Redcap and Cedric willingly, knowing what they had planned for her—she didn't see how that would keep her safe.

Trust, she heard a voice in her mind. *Trust.*

"Get up," Redcap said to Cedric. "Try the chant again."

As Cedric chanted his words, an old man grabbed Lizzie's arm. She recognized him right away. Francis Ermington, the innkeeper.

"Drink," Ermington ordered.

"No," she said.

"I said *drink.*"

Two soldiers grabbed her and were about to force the drink down her throat when she said, "Wait, wait, wait! I can help you open the tree. It spoke to me. It speaks to me, even now."

Cedric's lip curled upward in a sly, disbelieving expression, and he laughed an obnoxious, ear-splitting guffaw.

"I'm serious," Lizzie protested.

But Ermington and the soldiers squeezed Lizzie's lips open, ready to pour.

"Wait!" Redcap ordered Ermington suddenly.

"You're not seriously considering listening to her," Cedric said. "She's lying…" His eyes lanced hers with a guileful darkness. "Delaying the inevitable. Elder trees don't speak."

Redcap slowly meandered over to her and stopped before her; his menacing dark eyes piercing hers.

"What did the tree say to you?" Redcap asked.

"It told me if I went with you, it would grant you safe passage. That only I could guide you through. And in order for me to do that, I would need to be of sound mind and body."

Even Redcap let out a snicker then.

"Let me prove it to you," Lizzie said.

Redcap shrugged and motioned for Lizzie to step forward.

"I'll need you to uncuff my hands at least," she said, lifting her wrists.

Redcap hesitated but then motioned for the soldier to uncuff Lizzie. With her hands now free, she did as she had before and held out her hands, letting the tree read her energy. But this time, she didn't walk into the tree. Instead, she closed her eyes and spoke silently to it. *I'm ready*, she said. *They're here. Please grant me safe passage. And please, if you can help it, protect me, my father, and my friends.* Lizzie opened one eye, looking for any sign from the tree. But there was nothing.

After a nod from Redcap, the soldiers grabbed her once more, shackled her again, and Ermington held her mouth, ready to pour the liquid down her throat. Suddenly, she heard a noise, a rumbling sound. Ermington backed away, and Lizzie watched as a silvery mist emanated from the tree toward her. The pixies scurried as the silver fog grew bigger and bigger, and the tree branches began to part from one another. As the gap between this world and the next began to open, a light began to shine through the cracks of the tree.

The silver mist of the tree thrust Ermington and his soldiers away from Lizzie in one swift swoop. Their bodies bounced off the walls and crumpled onto the floor, nearly unconscious. Lizzie could see a blue haze and what looked like foliage coming into view. The gateway to Elgoria was opening.

chapter 55

"Take her," Cedric said, his voice as calm as still water. He ignored the fallen soldiers and Ermington on the ground as if they were nothing to him. Passing Lizzie to one of the soldiers, Cedric said, "Bring her through."

Before they stepped through, Redcap had a soldier test the safety of the gateway. He instructed the soldier to tell him where they were, and once the Fae returned, he told Redcap what he saw.

"By the looks of the area," Redcap replied, "we're exactly where we need to be, by the edge of the Dead Graff Sea. The Elder tree has served us well."

Cedric directed his attention to the soldiers. "We'll summon the Shadow ships once we're on the other side. It'll be a day's walk to the shore. They should be there by then."

"And what of all of them?" one soldier asked.

Lizzie turned to see Shay, Misty, and her father, who were all chained just like her. There was also a woman with dark hair that Lizzie didn't recognize. Their blank faces and lack of movement signaled they'd been given the same drink as

Shay, the one Ermington had planned to give Lizzie. They stared forward, unemotional, as if they were stoned.

"You'll take them to the ship, too, of course," Redcap answered. "Cedric will take his share once we reach the South Shadowlands."

"And what of these two?" the soldier asked.

These two?

Lizzie's heart sank as two more people descended the stairwell. She prayed it was Brody, that he was safe. But to her surprise, she saw Miles and another guy who looked very much like him.

"Miles?" Lizzie called. But he didn't answer her. Instead, he wore the same blank look as her father and friends. So, he *had* been here, had helped her when she was in the woods, and had taken her back to her room.

"That one is mine," Cedric growled, pointing to Miles. And then to Dean. "This one, the betrayer, will suffer a greater fate than his men."

"Go," a soldier said, nudging Lizzie toward the opening of the tree.

"It's too late, you know," Redcap said to Lizzie, smirking. "Brody's fate is sealed. Atiryo will find his way back to us with the pendant."

"No." Lizzie shook her head. The beast hadn't returned. There was still a chance Brody was alive.

"Let's go, my sweet," Cedric said, weaving his fingers into Lizzie's hair, a simper tugging at the corners of his mouth. But he was anything but sweet.

Moving her hair aside, Cedric lowered his mouth to her neck. His lips hovered, then touched, branding her not with cruelty, but with claim. The breath that followed was hot and slow, like he wanted her to feel it.

To remember it.

She recoiled and spat at him.

"Cedric, don't play with your things," Redcap said. "Let's go."

A muscle twitched in Cedric's jaw.

"Careful," he murmured low enough for only her to hear. "When we get to the castle, you *will* obey." He let go of Lizzie and addressed Redcap now. "And what of the beast? Is it advisable to leave without him?"

"He'll find his way home," Redcap said.

"We *need* that pendant," Cedric reminded Redcap.

Redcap narrowed his eyes and spoke through gritted teeth.

"I said... he'll find his way."

Ermington and the soldiers who had been thrown from the tree slowly regained consciousness and stood up.

Redcap continued.

"Ermington, stay behind and ensure the beast has safe passage through the gateway with the pendant. Atiryo always returns, and nothing can stop him, certainly not a measly human."

With ease, Redcap stepped through the gateway. Two men in Cedric's army secured Lizzie's arms and wrists with the silver cuffs once more and pushed her along toward the opening.

Woosh.

A gush of energy rushed through her as she stepped through the gateway. The transition was quick, and soon, she found herself on a dirt path in the middle of a forest. Bright sunlight shone through vibrant green trees, not unlike earthly ones. The weather was much milder, and she felt warm in the sweater she was wearing. The soldiers brought everyone through, and then Cedric clapped his hands.

"Onward... to the ships!"

Then they began to walk, and Lizzie found herself looking behind at the gaping opening in the middle of the forest. She had entered a new and exciting world, but something inside her said her suffering was only beginning.

chapter 56

Brody hobbled back to the inn and applied pressure to his gaping wounds. Given his extensive injuries, he wasn't likely to make it, but he was going to try, no matter what his fate, to get the pendant to Lizzie and save her in time.

The cold bit through his clothes to his skin, and his teeth chattered uncontrollably. With every stagger toward the inn, he was one inch closer to Lizzie's warmth, the closest feeling to home he'd had in a while. Each labored breath deepened his resolve to get to her. But time was slipping from him, like the blood pooling at his feet.

When Brody finally reached the steps of the inn, he used his last bit of strength to crawl up them. He could stop now, quit. Call for help. Maybe survive. Determined. Steadfast. That's how people had always described him. But those people had forgotten that even the greatest of attributes contained a crippling duality. Brody was as stubborn as a damn mule, his mind resolute.

One more step, he told himself, heaving his body up. He left a trail of blood behind him as he moved. The inn's door was ajar, left open in haste from guests' attempts to flee. Some of them didn't make it, evident by the horror scene Brody crawled into. *Some fucking Halloween,* he thought, pulling his deadened weight across the inn's hardwood floors to the library.

He had to get to Lizzie. Even now, when he was so close to death, all that mattered was her.

"Hello?" he called, dragging himself across the library floor. Surely someone was still there, someone who could help him. But all he heard was the creaking floorboards beneath him. He reached the entrance to the hidden room and willed his limbs to keep moving down the dark circular stairwell, all the while aware of the burning sensation that felt like daggers piercing through his flesh. He winced, not just from the magic that raked across his skin but from the severe wounds the beast had inflicted on his torso.

At the bottom of the stairs, he saw a body half-breathing. Punk.

Brody crawled to him, his old friend.

"You're alive," Punk croaked, and Brody knew if Punk didn't receive medical attention soon, he wouldn't make it.

"Not for long," Brody said, turning his head toward the Elder tree. He could see Elgoria's sunlight through the weeping branches. But other than the tree and Punk, everyone was gone.

"They took her," Punk said. "Took them all. Nunez, too."

Brody gritted his teeth. He was too late. They would be long gone by now.

As if reading Brody's mind, Punk said, "You can still catch them."

But Brody didn't think he would make it—not like this. The magic burned greater now, and Brody realized its connection to this tree. Then he heard a stream of voices, disembodied and ominous, whispering to him.

Elgoria's fate is in your hands. You must close the gateway.

"How?" he cried, aware that he was speaking to no one.

If Punk cared, he didn't say, couldn't say, was too injured.

Stand under the tree's protection.

Brody didn't have time to grapple with whether or not the voice was authentic. He was losing so much blood that it was possible he was hallucinating. But if the voices were true, then time was of the essence, and he figured he could make one last contribution to the people he cared about if he could sever the tie between this world and Elgoria.

So he crawled over to the tree, grabbed its branches, and hoisted himself up into its opening. The voices spoke again, and he realized it was something old and ancient speaking to him.

They spoke to him at the same time the magic scalded his flesh, and they showed him glimpses of what might happen to Earth if he *didn't* close the gateway for good. If he closed the gateway with the magic entrusted to him, no one else would get hurt. But he had to carry the pendant through, make sure all the magic was drawn back to Elgoria, and absorb it into himself. In doing so, he would likely die. He was caught between Earth and Elgoria, between life and death.

The choice to die on Earth or in Elgoria was difficult. If he stayed on Earth and somehow survived, would he always wonder if he could have saved Lizzie? Would he spend his life wishing he'd gone through that gateway? If he went to Elgoria, there was a high probability he would die soon after entry, even if he survived absorbing the magic. His wounds were too great, and no one could save him, unless by some miracle.

Consciousness waned, and Brody felt life slipping away from him like the tide pulling back the sea. He closed his eyes, no longer resisting his inevitable fate.

Death.

"Brody," a voice called, but Brody didn't register it right away. "Brody, take my hand."

Brody's eyes fluttered open and focused on the blurry figure before him.

Dale. Dale was still alive. He was well. And he was there with Agent James. They'd arrived just in time to tend to Punk. Several other agents and police officers entered then, attempting to get to Brody.

But Brody didn't budge. Instead, he held out his free hand toward Dale.

"Don't," Brody warned. "You'll die. I…" He winced in pain again. "I have a chance… to stop this for good. They took Shay, but I'll bring her home."

"We'll find her together," Dale said. "Let me help you. Come out here, we'll get you cleaned up, and then we'll enter whatever this is together."

Brody knew there was no time. He had to close the portal now. And once he closed it, there would be no turning back. But he needed Dale to know Shay was alive, at least for now. He needed to leave someone with some peace.

Suddenly, someone pushed Dale out of the way.

"You killed the beast!" Ermington yelled. "Give me the pendant. Now!"

"No," Brody said. "You're too late…it's bleeding into me."

"Give it to me!" Ermington yelled, and then he lunged toward Brody, prying open Brody's weakened fist to touch the pendant. But as soon as the magic touched Ermington's hand, he burned into flames, his body evaporating into tiny embers. Just like that, he disappeared from existence.

With Ermington gone and Dale and the agents exhibiting a healthy distance now, seeing what the pendant could do, Brody knew it was time. Brody used his strength to pull himself through the gateway, into Elgoria. The pendant burned in his hand, and he watched as the ancient magic began to flow toward him. Subsequently, the portal diminished in size, smaller and smaller, until he couldn't see the hidden room any longer.

Eventually, the gateway disappeared altogether, and Brody was left alone in a fog-filled wood, screaming in desperate agony as primeval magic set his body ablaze with agonizing suffering that felt like birth and death, euphoria and desolation all at the same time.

After the magic had surged through Brody, it transformed into iridescent wisps and took off to the skies, leaving Brody bleeding out in the forest, unable to move or speak. A labored breath escaped his lips; the last vision he saw was fire blanketing an unknown land, and the last sound he heard was an ancient lament of not the Elders, but the Ancients, singing about the woman who would either bring peace to, or completely destroy, Elgoria.

And her name… was Lizzie.

They thought the gateway was sealed.
They thought Brody was gone.
But fate had other plans…

Brody and Lizzie return in *A Bond of Blood, Stone, and Fire,*
the seductive sequel to *The Heir of Light and Shadows.*

Get a taste of what's next with a sneak peek of Book Two
at the end of this book where...

Ancient magic awakens.
Alliances will shatter.
And the real war is just beginning…

A Bond

of *Blood,*

Stone,

and *Fire*

STELLA JADE

The tamer of the wicked ones
A savior in the night.
The inhabited one lives
Who sacrificed his life.

The Shadow Breaker lives
To fight an endless fight
And save us from the evil lies
That threaten all fae life.

-Ancient Faerie Song from The Scrolls of Elgoria

one

Brody lumbered through the woods, dragging the heavy paws that used to be his hands and feet. He could feel his body weakening with every step, his mind fuzzy with details of how he went from near death to the transformation into *this*…this *thing*. He didn't remember anything from that moment to this one, the last memory being the tiny embers of ancient magic dissipating into the trees.

Water.

A voice came from inside him, yet it was not his.

Find water. Find food.

I know, he replied silently to the voice as he trudged onward.

Move faster, or we both die.

Brody tried to pick up his paws, as they scraped over twigs, moss, and other foliage, but he was too weak. His legs buckled under him, sending his weighty body to the ground. He stayed there, drawing in deep breaths as the world in front of him blurred.

Then he heard voices ahead—female voices. He could smell them, a sweet, peachy scent trickling up his nose. They were…splashing. He mustered all his strength to stand, to continue on. He felt his body move just a little faster now. Water was close by.

And food… the voice reminded him.

If he could only get a sip of water, he could regain some strength. He would worry about food later.

Water nymphs… the voice said.

Water nymphs, Brody thought. He had almost forgotten he was in the fae world. He'd read about water nymphs when he was trying to help Lizzie. That moment in the library felt so long ago now, when he thought faeries were nothing but a myth. But now he was in the fae world, and real faeries were here, just a few hundred feet away. He saw the water nymphs through the clearing, their naked bodies playfully swimming in a crystalline blue spring. They laughed innocently, unaware that a vicious beast lurked nearby.

Slowly, stealthily, Brody crept closer and closer until he was at the edge of the spring. Through a dangling, green-leafed branch of a tree, Brody saw sunlight luminating crystal blue waters where the nymphs splashed innocently about.

One of the water nymphs exited the spring, her naked body dripping wet with water. Focusing on the nymph, Brody imagined seducing her, and images of he and the nymph caught in an erotic clench filled his mind.

Then, slowly, his thoughts turned... to devouring her.

Seduce her, the voice said. *Let us both be satisfied.*

No, Brody replied, pushing the heinous thoughts away.

I'll grant you your human form again, the voice said. *You lure her into the woods, kiss her soft lips, let her pleasure you. And when you have her body entangled in yours, when you've both reached ecstasy, I will devour her.*

No, Brody repeated.

Yes, the voice replied, more irritably. *Do it. Now. Do it, or we'll starve. Do you want us to die?*

Brody was not a cannibal; he didn't care how beast he was. He wouldn't lure an innocent woman or faerie, whatever she was, into his arms and then let some beast inside him kill her and eat her. Wasn't happening. He'd sacrifice himself before he would let that happen.

Do it now, the voice said. *Feel her warm, succulent flesh against yours, and have your way with her.*

As Brody's strength continued to wane, he felt the beast inside taking over. He crept closer and closer to the spring. His human needs, carnal sensations, were taking hold. He watched as the light shone on the nymphs' glistening bare skin and wondered what it would feel like to be inside her, to taste her lips…to eat her.

No! He shouted again.

He would fight whatever demon was inside of him with all he had. But Brody's defiance had made the voice inside him furious. It wanted its way and was fighting for dominance.

Do it, now! the voice yelled.

He tried to fight the beast, but his animalistic part took hold. Brody gently put his snout into the water to sip a drink, never taking his eyes off the nymph that stood just a few feet away now. Her back was to him, her backside just within reach. If he consented to the creature within, he'd turn back into a man, and she would succumb to him easily.

Now is the time. Say yes, and you'll turn.

Brody hesitated.

Say yes!

Still, Brody didn't dare move, didn't dare take his eyes off the nymph.

Say it now! the voice shouted, and Brody let out a growl. He couldn't help it; it simply escaped him. But as soon as the nymph heard it, she screamed.
"Seethio!" the nymph screamed. "There's a Seethio in the Shiremoon Forest!"
The nymphs scattered, and a louder roar erupted from Brody as he fought the voice inside his head.

You fool! You stupid, stupid fool! the voice seethed.

Brody felt himself weakening, but he thought perhaps it was better this way. If he couldn't control the beast inside of him, then the beast would do things that made Brody wish he was dead. How had he gotten here and turned into this *thing*?

Memories of Brody fleeing from a relentless beast flooded his mind. The beast damaged the pendant he and Lizzie were trying to protect, and then the ancient magic engulfed Brody. In a moment of heroism, he sacrificed himself to close the gateway from Earth to Elgoria. Brody thought he would die, but shortly after the gateway closed, he awoke as this...beast.

Had the ancient magic transformed him? he wondered.

Maybe this was a consequence of consuming the magic when he wasn't the *one*, the Shadow Breaker.

Brody lay down by the edge of the water to rest his weary body for just a moment. He would welcome death if it came for him, if only to stop hearing the scathing screams of the demon inside of him.

two

Lizzie trudged quietly through the woods, the thick silver chains still secured around her neck and wrists. They'd been traveling an entire day, and she was hungry and tired. The day never seemed to end, and she'd been staring at the same foliage for hours, although it was more beautiful than she could describe. Beams of sunlight shined through the trees, which glistened with a near-white energy. It was a subtle glow but noticeable to Lizzie.

Beside the slight murmurs of Redcap to his men or Cedric, no one spoke to her. Not even Cedric seemed to have anything to say to her, and Lizzie was just fine with that. Everyone she wanted to talk to was still in a trance from the liquid they drank back in the library, back when they were on Earth. When Lizzie felt a slight breeze, she knew they were nearing the shoreline. That, and when one of the soldiers called out in a gruff accented voice, "Shadow Ships are ready to board, sirs."

They came to a clearing in the woods which opened to a lengthy beach. Not dissimilar to Earth, the waters were crystal blue, the beaches white and grainy. The skies, too, were similar, with pillowy white clouds traveling across a cobalt sky. Lizzie found herself wondering how Elgoria could exist and where it was in comparison to Earth. The only explanations she could drum up were that it was some parallel dimension or another plane. She didn't think anyone in this camp knew the answer to that question, but still she wondered.

Anchored at the water's edge were the massive "Shadow" ships. All black and long in length, the ships were incredibly majestic, but Lizzie knew they were much more ominous. They were undoubtedly the ships of a king, flying a black banner with a symbol, a gold circle with a fire-breathing dragon in the center. The bow of the ship protruded out into a golden dragon's head with emeralds for eyes and a long fire opal tongue. Lizzie felt her gut pull at the sight, knowing that some of her friends were meant to be dragon food. The idea hadn't seemed real until this moment, but neither had dragons.

"Board," she heard a soldier demand, and he pushed her along to a ramp that opened from the belly of the ship. Redcap boarded the second ship, and Lizzie strained to see where her father and the others had gone—they'd seemingly disappeared. She prayed they would all be together—safe, at least for now. She never worried about her father, especially when she imagined he was all those dangerous occupations. But in this world, what would he be? *Would he be okay? Would she ever see him again? What about Misty?* The pit in her stomach tugged even deeper as her mind drifted to Brody, and she wondered, *had he survived? Had he brought the pendant back through the portal?* Perhaps he was on his way to her now. Or… had the beast torn him apart, and he'd died there. His death would be on her hands; the beast's return would be her answer. She still held on to the notion that Brody was alive, and that he would come for her.

The guard hurried her up a long ramp, and she complied. There was no way to break free now—she'd have to wait until she was no longer chained. As she entered the ship, she saw many Elven-Fae (that looked no different than herself) scuttling about. Men and women, many dressed in mere rags followed different orders by hulking derisive soldiers. There were several compartments in the ship, rooms upon rooms, and she wondered where Cedric planned on storing her. When the guard led her to the deck of the ship and tied her to one of the tall gold spars that carried the massive black sails, she was surprised.

"The prince wants you right where he can see you," the guard said, seemingly reading her mind.

The guard walked away, and Lizzie closed her eyes tightly. *Please, tell me what to do*, she called silently to the Elders. When Lizzie entered Elgoria, she hoped she might connect with the Elders, that they would guide her out of this unpromising situation. But any powers that she possessed on Earth were seemingly gone in Elgoria, as if she was nothing but an ordinary mortal once more. She received no wisdom, not even a whisper.

"Deep in thought, are we?"

Lizzie jumped slightly when she saw Cedric standing in front of her. He ran his long fingers through his brown curls. His crooked smile was especially unnerving. He moved his face close to her ear, and gently moved her hair away from it.

She flinched, which made him smile more.

"Soon, you'll be begging me to touch you," Cedric whispered.

"*Never*," Lizzie replied confidently. She wasn't sure of much in this world, but of that, she was certain.

DISCUSSION QUESTIONS

Hi readers! I've put together two sets of discussion questions: one for casual book clubs and one for readers who want to dive a little deeper. I'd love to hear your thoughts! Feel free to email your answers or reflections to me at stellajadeauthor@gmail.com.

Light Book Club Discussion Questions

1. Which character surprised you the most, and why?
2. Would you rather have Brody watching your back, Miles on your side, or Cedric in your dreams?
3. What was your favorite scene in the book, and what made it stand out?
4. Did your opinion of any character change over the course of the story?
5. If you could give Lizzie one piece of advice, what would it be?
6. What tropes or story elements did you enjoy most (e.g., love triangle, hidden powers, mafia danger, portal fantasy)?
7. Which moment made you most curious to keep reading?
8. Who was your favorite character, and what made them stand out?
9. Do you think Lizzie made the right choice by trusting Brody? Why or why not?

In-Depth Questions (For Deeper Reflection and Analysis)

1. The Heir of Light and Shadows explores identity, trauma, and fate. How does Lizzie's personal history shape her choices throughout the story?

2. Discuss the motif of control: both magical and emotional. Which characters use control as power, and which seek freedom from it?

3. How does Brody's emotional repression and grief contrast with Miles's compartmentalized violence? What makes each man dangerous in different ways?

4. Cedric is portrayed as both a threat and something more complex. What clues foreshadow his deeper role in Lizzie's destiny?

5. How do magical elements (like the pendant, the forest, and the beast) reflect Lizzie's internal transformation?

6. What commentary does the book offer on loyalty versus self-preservation, particularly through Brody, Misty, and Nina?

7. How does the dual-world structure (real-world Philadelphia/South Jersey vs. Elgoria) deepen the story's stakes or symbolism?

8. What role does prophecy play in Lizzie's agency? Do you believe she's truly free, or always being watched/manipulated?

Interested in a free virtual author visit? I'd be thrilled to join your book club discussion. Just reach out to schedule!

www.ingramcontent.com/pod-product-compliance
Lightning Source LLC
Chambersburg PA
CBHW070610300726
48975CB00006B/1774